THE TWIN SERPENTS

RONALD SCOTT THORN

The Twin Serpents

A NOVEL OF SUSPENSE

The Macmillan Company
NEW YORK

To
AMANDA & VANESSA
with love.

'Sow arrogance and reap
a tasselled field of doom.'

AESCHYLUS.

Contents

Part One

OBITUARY

Chapter One

ABRUPTLY, LIGHT RAIN on mid-morning London traffic, ponderous, sluggish, progressing in measured lengths between traffic-lights, a block a time. Water streaming off bus-red cellulose, changing to a thin steam-haze over heated radiator chromium, spraying out from under kerb-close tyres, muddying shoes, spattering nylons. As capriciously as it had begun, the shower ended. A wary pause, and then, like anti-flowers to the sudden spring sunlight, the black blossoms of the umbrellas wilted in unison.

The order 'Cross now' from the automatic signal unloosed the knot of pedestrians. Heads bobbing, they streamed away towards the other side of the road.

From behind, broad back, raincoat-collar up, grey hatbrim down, hands thrust in pockets, except perhaps that he was taller than most, there was nothing to single him out. Reaching the opposite pavement, he turned along it to the grimy neo-classical portico of the public library and mounted the flight of shallow-treaded steps into the building, two at a time.

The swing-doors of the reading-room flapped to, with a discreet exclamation. The librarian looked up over his half-lenses. Broad back, raincoat, grey hat passing along between the upright reading-desks, each titled boldly on seasoned oak. First the tabloids and national dailies, all places taken, necessary to peer over shoulders; then the local editions, marked hopefully here and there against items in the situations columns; a gap in the readers where the foreign papers were lumped together; on, further down the stuffy hushed room to the weeklies and illustrateds until finally a deserted table littered with technical journals, mostly unread, week in, week out.

The one he sought was easily identifiable by the grey paper cover bearing the serpent emblem of Aesculapius, sandwiched between the title *British Medical Journal* and the date, Saturday, 5 May 1962. He ran his gloved finger down the obituary index and turned to the page. It was there in full, more enlightening than the news reporters' sensational paragraphs when the story had first hit the headlines. This was the final homage by his peers to someone who had wielded a wand which, when it touched, transformed. He sat down and began to read.

A. J. CRANFORD, F.R.C.S.

On April 20 all reasonable hope for the life of Mr A. J. Cranford, consultant surgeon to St Bede's Hospital in the City of Westminster, was abandoned. He was forty years old.

His unexpected death in tragic circumstances at such an early age will come as a shock to those sections of the medical profession which knew him. The loss will perhaps be more readily felt by members—notably the female members—of fashionable international society who were his patients, and countless others who, had he lived, undoubtedly would have been.

Conventional prophecy, false assumption, life in straight lines and gentle curves instead of loops and zigzags, denoting false starts, retraced steps, leaps in the dark. Like dying. Like being born.

Born in the village of Woodhouse Magna in Leicestershire, Alexander John Cranford was the only son of the late Maxwell Cranford, the artist and writer. While a medical student at the Mountview Hospital, Alexander Cranford won the Harrison-Hardy Anatomy Prize, and qualified as a doctor just after the end of World War II. Thus, unhampered in his chosen career by military service, he immediately aimed at higher qualifications, easily obtaining his Fellowship of the Royal College of Surgeons eighteen months later. Over the next four years he held a number of resident hospital posts, both in this country and in the United States, following the award of a Potts Travelling Scholarship. On his return to England, his undoubted ability and his persuasive and engaging personality resulted in his early appointment as consultant to no less than four London Hospitals.

With most men, this remarkable achievement would have sustained them for life, but Alexander Cranford's unbounded drive and ingenuity could not be contained either by the wide scope of general surgery or its more usual subdivisions. Almost overnight his interest switched to a highly specialized field which he could justly claim he made exclusively his own.

Exclude the jabbing, hacking cough of the reader at the adjacent lectern. Disregard the smell of stale sweat and rain-sodden cloth wafting across the creaking, rustling, semi-devotional atmosphere of the cream-and-brown-painted room. Concentrate and relinquish distraction.

In 1960 he relinquished all his appointments, save the one at St Bede's, to devote his skill and time to the controversial, if not actually unorthodox, practice of cosmetic surgery. In this sphere he soon achieved worldwide repute, and his techniques have been universally emulated. He was the first surgeon to perform the operation of acroplasty of the lower limbs. This inevitably attracted publicity in the lay Press and, in spite of his privately aired protests, its results became known as the Cranford leg.

A half-stumble against his chair leg, mumbled apology, the cough again, and the reader shuffled past, grey complexion, pathetic, ill, somebody's patient.

Among his patients were numbered the illustrious, the famous, the wealthy. It has been perhaps unkindly said that the barely discernible scars left by Alexander Cranford's scalpel are the most exclusive of status symbols.
Whatever valid grounds for criticism of his work his professional detractors had, they were undoubtedly tinged with a somewhat begrudging admiration. No one can dispute that Alexander Cranford was a brilliant innovator and an incomparable technician. However, at this moment in time, it is perhaps salutary, as it is inevitably interesting, to ponder the question of down what unique paths Alexander Cranford's genius might have led him, had he lived to tread them.

'Excuse me, is that this week's *B.M.J.?*' a conspiratorial reading-room whisper from behind. Ignore it. Feign deafness, indifference, obtuseness, what you will.

H.L.G. writes: Alex Cranford and I were close friends as boys for several years; it was a happy time, when friendship meant competition at sports, sharing the excitement of escapades, and an unswerving mutual loyalty when retribution was meted out, as it frequently was. Since then my work as a lawyer and his as a surgeon kept us apart except for brief infrequent meetings, usually in the company of others, at dinner-parties or semi-official gatherings. Yet our boyhood bond allowed me to take periodic readings, so to speak, of the temperature of his personality as it developed, with a certain insight not possessed by later acquaintances. Sides of his character and facets of his behaviour were explicable to me which were either not perceived by others or, if perceived, were misinterpreted.

Alex had an exceedingly agile brain which appeared to jump to conclusions simply because he could never spare the time to explain the intermediate steps to lesser mortals. He thus often seemed oblique, obscure, or even discourteous.

'Excuse me, is that . . . ?' less of a whisper this time.
'Yes.'
He shot the word out, investing it with the snap of a deterrent.
'After you with it, old man,' cheerful, chummy, undeterred.

I remember well how, at a children's party when he was five and the youngest present, on being asked by our host's mother what game little Alex would like to play, he replied 'Let's play at walking on the ceiling.' This was naturally met by derisive laughter. When it had died down, the hostess, condescendingly trying to humour him, suggested that it was a very clever idea, but would Alex first show us all how to play it? Whereupon Alex Cranford got up and without comment, solemnly left the room. A few moments later, to our hostess's dismay, deafening thuds above our heads proclaimed the solution to his enigmatical proposition.

Had the enigma developed new proportions later, the proposition a final solution?

From those early days Alex Cranford continued to exhibit a single-ness of purpose which to some had the stamp of egotistical ruthless-ness barely hidden by a surface veneer of off-hand charm. But I was often able to see revealed in his actions an unselfishness and a humility which belied such condemnation. Alex Cranford succeeded at whatever he set out to do; it was not his success which engen-dered envy, but that he made success look easy. Talking to Alex Cranford was at the same time an irritating and compelling experi-ence. He always stimulated, he invariably provoked, but he was never dull.

It may come as a surprise to record that such a personality as his was essentially a lonely one. Even after his marriage to the Hon. Eve Binfield, former fashion model and sister of Lord Binfield, which pitched him further into the affluent vortex of social life, his isolation was more real than apparent.

The fellow was still there, thick-skinned, insensitive, breathing over his shoulder, impatiently waiting for him to finish. He turned the page angrily, taking in the last two paragraphs.

Perfectionist that he was, he drove himself unsparingly onwards in his work at meteoric speed, at what cost to himself few people realized. His was a restless searching spirit, and when I last saw him, by chance a day before his death, it was clear to me that he had reached a turning point, a crisis of intention, towards what we shall unhappily never know. He leaves behind him no children, but I am sure that there are many people all over the world who mourn his loss with a grief which comes from love and admiration.

Love is a kind of grief.

Leaving aside, in the widest sense, the value of his achievements —which the dry dust of posterity will cover with a mantle of just proportion—he is unlikely to be forgotten for a long time to come by all those who, when they look at themselves in the mirror each morning, will see something of the art and skill of Alexander Cranford.

'I'm sorry to bother you again . . . but I'm a bit pushed for time. I wonder if I could just look at something . . .'

Impulsively, heedless of regulations and petty consequences, he ripped out the two pages carrying the obituary and stuffed them into his pocket. He stood up and turning round, thrust the *Journal* at the owner of the voice.

'It's all yours,' he said, loud and clear, and strode off down the room. Startled, like animals caught grazing, the faces looked up from the desk at the back of the raincoat and the hat as they moved away, shoes wood-slapping out of sight, towards the door. The librarian stepped from his glass partition to intercept the disturber of the peace, but his prepared practised admonition stopped short as he noticed, for the first time, the expanse of expressionless bandage beneath the hat, and the dark glasses. A moment of indecision and the doors had flapped to, and he was gone.

The impetus of his desire to read without interruption, to think without distraction on what had been done, on what still had to be done, took him hurriedly down the steps of the building, back along the drying pavement, and round the corner into the next street, before it allowed his pace to slacken. Hunching his shoulders against another brief scud of rain he crossed Bryanston Square, fresh-stuccoed, elegant, into George Street, busy, traffic-laden, to the Edgware Road, and beyond it through a criss-cross of mean streets, nearer to the cheap

15

fourth-floor room which backed on to the clamorous main-line where it curved out of sight into the dark cave of Paddington Station. A room, shabby, yet with the uncompromising privacy essential to his recent and still immediate purpose.

The football came over the high wall from the screaming playground and bounced gaily, irresistibly. He stepped off the pavement, and ran towards it, timing the interception with rusty but still accurate skill. He kicked, and a long-forgotten satisfaction absorbed him, as he watched the ball soar away, slowly twisting, glistening against the watery sky, like some primitive satellite. As it dropped out of sight again, the young-voiced welcome at its seemingly magical return floated back, and the joyous sound was reward enough for his impulsive, irrelevant action.

The taxi came down the street hooting at the back of the raincoated figure obstructing the centre of the road. The driver muttered an obscenity and swerved past. His fare rapped on the glass partition behind him.

'Stop, stop.'

The cab braked to a halt.

'What's the matter?'

'Turn round.'

'What for? This is the way to . . .'

'Never mind about that. Do as I say.'

'Now, just a minute, Guv . . .'

'That person in the road. He's walking away. I want to speak to him.'

'Look 'ere, I'm not . . .'

'Quickly, do you hear? You'll lose him.'

The driver hesitated at the excitable urgency in the cultured voice, but gave way to its authority. Muttering again, he turned the cab round on full lock. Gathering speed, it returned in the direction from which it had come, and drew up at the kerb, a dozen yards past its quarry.

In the mirror the driver saw the reduced image of the man grow larger as he shambled nearer along the pavement. He heard the rear door of the cab open. The image halted. Then decisively it came on again. He glimpsed briefly the bandages under the dark glasses, as the raincoat and the hat passed by the cab.

The door behind slammed to again, and the order came, this time flat and disappointed.

'All right, you can drive on now.'

'Which way?'

'Where I told you before.'
Once more the cab made a U-turn.

The encounter had momentarily paralysed him, and the thought of the one-in-a-million chance of it was still unnerving. Only when he heard the taxi drive away, and had turned to watch it disappear round the corner, did his confidence begin to return. The catastrophe which, had the recognition been mutual, was averted; reduced to a harmless case of mistaken identity.

His landlady stood gossiping to a neighbour at the open door of the dingy, paint-peeling terraced house as he came up to it. They moved aside to let him pass, half-smiles, nods, curiosity in the eyes, wordless until his footsteps sounded on the linoleum-covered stairs, then heads together.

'Is that 'im?'

'That's 'im. Goes every day to the hospital.'

'What's been the matter?'

'Bad burns, he said. He's had an operation to remove the scars.'

'It's wonderful what they can do now.'

'Yes. They say you can 'ave a completely new face if you want one.'

'When are you going to have yours done then?'

'What about you?'

He closed the door of the low-ceilinged room behind him and slid the bolt across. He removed his hat and glasses, and hung up his raincoat before taking from the pocket the torn-out pages carrying the obituary. He sat on the bed and read it through unhurriedly. Then he put a match to the sheets of paper, and watched them burn to ash in the empty fire-grate.

He reached down a suitcase from the top of the wardrobe and checked the contents, as he had done each day whenever the room was left unguarded while he went out for food or for exercise. Especially he let his fingers probe into an old pair of shoes, after he had removed the newspaper packing, to confirm the hard edges of the stones nestling in the toes. Satisfied, he closed the case, re-locked it and returned it to the wardrobe.

He looked down through the grimy window-panes at the dull blackened ground between the bright steel lines where the electric trains moaned into the early hours; across to the gaudy hoardings with their giant-size glamorous faces urging the easy purchase of an affluent life; above them to the jumble of rear windows, washing-decked between sooty walls, where pipes, crazy-plumbed, climbed like the lumpy stems

17

of some iron-clad creeper; up over the wet roofs and haphazard chimneys aerial-spiked against a sky top-dressed with fluffy cumulus.

A few more days and the pain, and the memory and the hell of it all would fade, and he would find another window somewhere with a different view, sea-blue, sky-blue, earth-brown, small, uncomplicated, with perhaps a fluted column to cast the only shadow in the brilliant sunlight.

He went to the mirror and carefully, deliberately, began to unwind the bandages from his head. The sentence in the obituary came to life in front of him.

'. . . something of the art and skill of Alexander Cranford.'

Part Two

THE REAPER

Chapter Two

'Is GOOD, MISTER WILSON?'

The question was a mixture of pride and conviction, rather than a request for approval.

Obscured in the hot fly-ridden shade of his first-floor room, Fowler observed below him the island's part-time barber as he held up the hand-mirror for his seated customer. A chair had been brought out from the white two-roomed cubic house opposite for the operation. The street, in fact the only one on Kronos wide enough to merit the name, served as a rough, al fresco, but practical hair-dressing saloon. It also served, on occasion, as a convenient place to milk a goat, peel a vegetable, make a rug, hang out the washing, mend a fishing-net, beat a mat or a wife, spy on a neighbour, tell a joke, start a fight or, after a few glasses of ouzo, experience the undeniable pleasure of emptying a full bladder.

Keeping well back, Fowler took four more rapid shots with his Leica —a three-quarter view, two full face, and a profile—of the barber's bearded client, as he turned his head from side to side, inspecting in the mirror, it would seem with amusement, the results of the previous twenty minutes' impassioned clipping and snipping.

'Is good, Nico. Couldn't do better in Athens.'

'Then is good. You like I cut some more?'

'No. It's O.K.'

'O.K., Mister Wilson.'

'Thanks a lot, Nico.'

With a flourish, the little Greek whipped away the piece of coloured cloth, generously covered in hair, from around Wilson's shoulders. Wilson stood up, and handed over ten drachmas. The barber, who was also the carpenter and undertaker of Kronos, put the money away carefully in a small leather pocket in his belt. Business having been done to the satisfaction of both parties, smiles and handshakes were exchanged. Then Wilson, carrying his jacket over his arm, ambled away down the sloping street to where it opened out into the town's tiny harbour-square.

Six foot one, six foot two, lean, say a hundred and sixty pounds, mid-thirties, Fowler estimated. American? English? The accent was indeterminate. But then deductions based on accents could be misleading. Fowler had a dozen at his own command, invaluable assets in the chameleon-like existence, which was part of his job. Mid-thirties? The age was wrong. Or right; if you looked at it another way. He was working with intangibles. With luck and speculation too. Speculation had brought him to the island. Luck had brought Wilson for a haircut opposite the very room he had rented. The pictures had been luck too. But there were others he had to get.

He closed the catch of his camera-case and, leaving it slung round his neck, clacked his way down the short flight of stairs, and went out into the clear Aegean sunlight. He put on a pair of large-framed sunglasses, and carried a guide-book and a folding map ostentatiously. Not that Kronos was mentioned in the book, and on the map of the Cyclades it was a mere speck amongst dozens of islands, but the props filled out the role of innocent tourist which he had established late the night before, on his arrival by caique from Piraeus. Fowler followed Wilson to the square. He sat down outside the Gerofinikas, ordered a glass of ouzo and lit a cigarette.

There were two *taverna* in the square. Each had three or four tables outside. Each served the same sour wine, sold the same local latakia tobacco, could be persuaded to prepare the same indigestible food. The respective proprietors were half-brothers and for most of the time not on speaking terms. Doubts about their parentage was the reason for this breakdown of communication, which was repaired intermittently, by common consent, on days of religious feasts, weddings or funerals.

From the Gerofinikas, Fowler looked across the square to the rival O Byron where his target sat talking to two men. The black soutane of the taller labelled him as the priest. The other, dumpy, fat, a typical pyknic, and who spoke with an exuberance of gesture, was more difficult to place. The black eyebrows and sallow skin made him, if not a native of the island, a Greek or Cypriot or Turk. Anywhere else the peaked cap pushed back on his head would have suggested to Fowler a shabby taxi-driver, but as Kronos did not boast more than three powered vehicles, an old jeep converted into a primitive fire-wagon, and two tractors, clearly the cap was some badge of office. Mayor, policeman, head-man? Probably all three rolled into one creased, seam-bursting tropical suit.

The conversation appeared intimate, the mood of the group jovial, and this became more so on the arrival of a fourth character, thin, about sixty, bald-headed, who refused a proffered drink with elaborate solemnity, and then suddenly downed it to the accompaniment of laughter and a slap on the back from peak-cap. Another round was called for, and during the pause the heads bent in silent attention round the newcomer, whose voice became inaudible. Abruptly the heads jerked back and guffaws burst out. Obviously bald-head was also funnyman, the purveyor of the latest joke which appeared to run as much to form in Greek as in any other language. But Fowler hadn't come for jokes. He wanted information. Delicate information bearing the seeds of explosion. Humorists were always a good source. The funniest stories were always indiscreet. Never tell a secret to a joker. Bald-head would have to be cultivated. He whisked a fly off the rim of his glass, and gazed round the sun-dappled square, and waited for his opportunity.

What a dump, thought Fowler. Include the blue sea, the blue sky, the silver sand, the little lemon groves, the scent of verbena, the ox-carts, the cute little school-house with its flight of worn steps outside, the white-belfried twin-belled church, the picturesque fishing-boats, and it was still a dump because you had to include also the negligible plumbing, the well water-supply, the one mail a week by boat from the mainland, the absence of a telephone line, the unreliability of the lighting generator, and the unpleasantness of the ubiquitous earth-closet.

Kronos was off the route of the round-the-island cruises because the ancient half-rotten tree-trunk in the centre of the square where Hippocrates very doubtfully once lectured to his students, and two ionic columns a mile away on the other side of the island, were not enough to bring the eager-beaver culture hounds and the amateur archaeologists pouring in; nor were its assets sufficient to offset its awkward contours, expensive for road-making, and the obstinate haggling and involved property claims of its three hundred and fifty inhabitants. And so the real-estate speculators came and sniffed and went away to look at more easily developable, quicker-profit chunks of classical rock. A chance handful of tourists in summer and odd visitors with their own special reasons like Fowler were the only intruders of the peace and isolation of this dot in the Homeric sea.

Fowler's gaze came back to Wilson, amiably passing the time of day in contentment. It had to have an explanation, and yet he had no proof that the right explanation was the one he suspected. What a dump to want to put down your roots in, cut yourself off in. Unless of course you had a compulsive reason for wanting to do just that; a reason such as fear or guilt or masochism or religious conviction. He took a sip of his

23

'ouzo, lit another cigarette, and pretended he was absorbed in his guide-book.

A whirring and creaking above and behind him reached a grating climax and then the ancient mechanism of the church clock sprinkled a surprisingly light and musical midday chime over the quiet square. The magical signal set off a dozen voices and stomachs clamouring for release and the first real meal of the day. The school door opened and the children burst upon the scene, vaulting and leaping down the steps and scattering in different directions. Dogs barked and women appeared in doorways ready to greet or scold or pet or kiss. The priest hurried off on some private errand. An eight-year-old girl flung her arms round peak-cap, and then sat on his knee. Bald-head ordered another drink. Wilson stood up and walked across the square.

Fowler saw her then, at the top of the school steps. The breeze fluttered her skirt, binding it momentarily round her hips, accentuating the narrow waist, and the generous breasts above. She locked the school door and turned and waved to Wilson. Lifting up her head, her hands swept the black, shining hair away from her neck in a gesture of habit and then she was running down the steps with scarcely less abandon than the children she had obviously spent the morning teaching. As they met, Wilson swung her round, an arm circling her waist, there was a brief peal of laughter, and then she stood on tip-toe in her thonged sandals to kiss him. The laughter was repeated and, arm in arm, they walked away totally absorbed, and disappeared along the quay beyond the gently swaying masts of the fishing-boats.

Fowler finished his drink. It tasted sour and he wondered if the sourness was part of himself which he carried about with him everywhere. The idyllic little scene he had just witnessed depressed him. Life wasn't like that, and to pretend it was made the harsh reality harder to bear for the rest of humanity. Unrestrained demonstration of happiness should be a punishable offence. Except in children. They, poor little sods, had to be educated to know better. All of which merely added up to the fact that he was one who had learnt his lessons well. Fowler had enough insight to know that if he were a believer in reincarnation, he'd fit snugly inside the skin of a dog-in-the-manger, which was probably why he was what he was: iconoclast, dream-cracker, turner-over of stones, lock-picker, drawer-opener, mirror-gazer, diary-reader, the observer who made notes later and welded them into a coherent pattern. He paid for his drink, and sauntered over to the O Byron.

The little girl on peak-cap's knee was whimpering, her father rocking her to and fro, and muttering words of comfort, his fat expressive

24

features running through a repertoire of encouragement, worry, sympathy, affection, promise, indulgence. Bald-head was talking to her too and, as Fowler approached, he saw him press a hand on her brow, and request her to put out her tongue. Sage noddings followed and, as some decision appeared to have been reached, peak-cap stood the child down and, taking her hand, led her away. Bald-head said:

'Put her to bed, man. I'll bring her a bottle of medicine. Not to worry now.'

If not the words, the accent surprised Fowler. There was something incongruous in the sing-song lilt of Caernarvonshire, here in the hot-blue day, pitched against the rasping of the cicadas and the scent of lemon-flower. It was as if he had come across a shouted admonition in modern Greek in a pub in Portmadoc where the windows of the Private looked out across the grey estuary which stretched away to the dull greens and browns of Cnicht and Moelwyn Fawr.

'*Efcharisto*. God bless you, Doc,' the heavily-built man called over his shoulder.

'Good morning.' Fowler smiled and sat unbidden at the other man's table. 'My name's Green. Time for another one?'

Two small Celtic eyes blearily surveyed his own. Fowler felt the other's hesitation was all that remained of a battle lost, years ago. Stained teeth exposed themselves in an accommodating grin.

'You know that's a bloody silly question to go asking anyone.'

He banged his empty glass on the table sharply twice and the proprietor of the O Byron appeared from the gloom inside the café.

'*To dio, Petro.*' He turned to Fowler: 'What's yours?'

'No. This is on me.'

'Next time, Mister Green. It is important to observe the formalities, you understand.' He spoke again to the proprietor, '*Karme ta deo. Megala.*'

'A *mesos.*'

The man disappeared and Fowler took out a packet of cigarettes. His companion thrust them aside and shook one of an ill-packed local brand on to the table for Fowler to pick up.

'Hospitality to strangers is a kind of religion in this part of the world. I'm no longer a stranger, you see. By adoption, I'm part of the home community you might say. A *"nisitos"*. Terrible language, isn't it? They have good swear-words though. But I can match them at that. Welsh is liberally supplied with obscene expletives. You'll be an English bastard, of course.' He shot out his hand. Fowler shook it. 'Evans.'

'Doctor Evans?'

'You can forget the handle.'

'I couldn't but overhear what you said to the father of the little girl. You're the island's General Practitioner?'

'Don't be daft, man. You couldn't seriously practise medicine in this insanitary hole, let alone make a living at it.'

'But you live here.'

'I die here. That's what retirement is, isn't it?'

'I thought doctors never retired. The "call" and all that?'

'They retire if they're bloody struck off at fifty, man. Just for boozing. Nothing else. Not relevant you'd think, would you?'

'Not really,' agreed Fowler.

'No,' said Evans emphatically.

The proprietor brought the glasses and put them on the table. Evans picked up his glass and downed the strong ouzo without any sign either of pleasure or distaste.

'I'll have that drink with you now, Mister Green, if you like,' he said.

Fowler nodded to the proprietor, who shrugged and took the empty glass away to replenish it. Evans smiled toothily at him. God help anyone, thought Fowler, if they broke a leg or perforated an ulcer in this sun-soaked little paradise. God, of course, might or might not help, but it was terrifying to think that Doc Evans, in a moment of sobriety, might try.

'The habit dies hard, of course. Habits do. Good ones and bad ones. Can't help yourself, you know. That's why I still sometimes dish out a few simple remedies. For nothing you understand?' He went on as if he had lost interest in Fowler. 'That child's bellyache will be gone tomorrow. The bottle I promised will be cochineal and sugar. Sweet and red. It'll please her parents and it won't do little Melina any harm. The art of medicine is to know when to do nothing. Most things get better if you don't meddle with them.'

Another full glass appeared on the table in front of him. Evans appeared not to notice it, but his hand found it and his fingers twisted it round and round.

'Nature doesn't like being meddled with, Mister Green. That's where medicine's going wrong. It's getting too bloody fancy. Too many bloody fancy drugs like thalidomide.'

The words were beginning to slur, and as Evans now took a drink he spilt a little of it, adding another unheeded stain to the collection on the lapels of his suit.

'Doctors used to have some respect for the individual,' he went on, 'but they've lost sight of him in their new fantasy world. Medicine gone mad. Madmen who shove electric shocks through the brains of

26

other madmen. Madmen who transplant tissues and organs from one gullible fool to another.'

Here was the opportunity, Fowler decided. And the best lever to draw Evans out might be the indirect one through Cranford. He applied it.

'You don't approve, then, Doc, of modern techniques?' asked Fowler. 'Like cosmetic surgery, for instance?'

'Cosmetic surgery? Just a fancy name for face-lifting.'

'Hasn't it gone a bit beyond that stage? I mean with people . . . say, like . . . Alexander Cranford?'

As he dropped the name, Fowler watched Evans carefully for any reaction, a significant hint in his expression, or better for some reply such as, 'You mean the surgeon who operated on Wilson? The man you just saw walk away across the square with the dark pretty young schoolmistress?' But there was no reaction, no hint in the expression.

'Alexander Cranford's dead,' said Evans. Something in the befuddled tone made Fowler chance another random shot.

'You knew him?'

'I met him once or twice many years ago,' he said quietly. 'He operated on my wife when he was still a young registrar. Did a magnificent job. She had carcinoma of the colon, you see. Died two years later from secondaries. But it was a wonderful piece of surgery.'

Evans looked away into the sunlight where the huge gnarled split tree-trunk of Hippocrates made a blot of inky shadow against the dazzle of the dust on the ground. He swung round suddenly and drank some more of his ouzo as if it were a bitter-tasting elixir.

'What you don't seem to grasp is that people like Cranford are all part of the madness.' Evans spoke with his earlier vehemence and then shook his head. 'Fancy a man like that turning into a fashion-plate practitioner.' He drained his glass. 'No, Mister Green, I don't approve of all this ruddy meddling about with people.'

'You mean disguising people to look like other people?'

'I mean turning them into other people. If it goes on like this, man, pretty soon when we're asked by a woman who we are, we'll say, "I was born Daffyd Evans, but I got one of Dai Jones's kidneys, Hugh Griffiths lent me his spleen, my liver used to belong to a man who lived in Moscow—I never did discover his name—my face has been made to look like the President of the United States, but my penis is my own, would you like to try it for size? If it doesn't suit you, I can get a new one next week. Bigger and better, you see?"'

'I like the idea of that,' Fowler chuckled.

27

'Do you, now? You wouldn't mind someone else doing your dirty work for you then?'

'Better than doing it for someone else.'

Fowler made the remark for his own benefit. It gave him a taste of the sick self-pitying pleasure of the cynic.

Evans banged again with his glass and shouted over his shoulder. *'Psia onema tou theou, Petro, fere mou tin botilia.'*

The unintelligible words were translated into action by the owner of the O Byron, who appeared once more and put a bottle on the table. Smiling, he muttered something in Evans's ear. Evans wafted him away and poured himself another drink. Fowler covered his own glass with his hand. Evans nearly tipped the bottle over as he endeavoured to replace the cork. Fowler steadied the bottle for him. At this rate Evans would soon be useless as a source of information. No time to lose. As he began framing a direct question about Wilson, the doctor forestalled him. In the inquisitive game it was always a mistake to underestimate the curiosity of others.

'Miss'r Green,' slurred Evans. 'What exactly did you say you did?'

'I didn't,' said Fowler.

'Ah.'

'But I'm a writer.' Glib, easy.

'And what are you writing just now?' More difficult, but still easy. He hesitated, not because he couldn't have produced a dozen plausible extempore replies, but because he liked to let his imagination take exercise when it could. It made the work seem more agreeable.

'I'm doing a travel-book on the lesser-known Greek islands. A commissioned job. That's the bread-and-butter reason for my coming to Kronos,' Fowler answered easily. 'But as always, I'm on the look-out too, for a story I might use for a novel.'

'You won't find one here, man.'

'My experience is you never know where you might find a story. After all, I found you here.'

'What good am I? Don't be daft with me, Mister Green, or I'll 'ave to knock you down.'

Fowler was unmoved by the empty threat.

'You're a character. That's all I meant. Good stories begin with characters. Perhaps there are others on this island. Interesting ones.'

'What's interesting about a bunch of Greek peasants, a drunken old Welsh medico, and a painter who's married a local girl?'

'Was that the tall fellow who was with you?'

'That's right,' said Evans.

'Two men and one girl,' mused Fowler. 'Attractive too from what I saw, in a burnt-earth kind of way. Primitive surroundings. The situation has all the basic ingredients. Of course, the real interest would have to centre in the other man. What's his name?'

'Wilson. Johnny Wilson. I told you, didn't I?'

'Yes, of course,' agreed Fowler quickly. 'A painter you say?'

'Yes, he does a bit of painting, but he doesn't thrust it down your throat like some of these clever artists.'

'You mean he's not a professional painter? He's not always been one?'

Evans pondered this a moment.

'He sold a picture last summer to an inquisitive visitor like you, Mister Green. That would make him a professional, wouldn't it?'

'Is he any good?'

'I don't know a ruddy thing about art, but I know he's a lovely man, is Johnny.'

'Where does he live?'

'Up beyond the quay.'

'How long has he lived here?'

'Turned up one morning about two years ago.'

'Where from?'

'Across the water.' Evans made an uncontrolled sweep with his hand. 'Across the lovely blue water. Deceptive like a woman. You should see it sometimes when we have a storm.'

'But where exactly across the water?'

'I never asked him,' said Evans, and began chuckling into his drink. 'On the island, you either come from across the water, or you're born here.' He suddenly turned on Fowler and shouted at him. 'You're from across the water, Mister Green, and you're asking too many bloody questions. Why don't you go away again? You sound like a bloody policeman.'

'I'm sorry,' said Fowler, undeterred. 'Bad habits. I'm just interested in people. An author in search of a character, that's all. And Wilson sounds interesting.'

'He's a lovely man, is Johnny.'

'So you said.'

'You don't believe me?'

'Shouldn't I?'

Evans looked at him belligerently. Fowler observed the now drooping lids and the swaying movement of the head. And then, as quickly as it had kindled, the drunken resentment died down, and Evans embarked on the stage of alcoholic conspiracy, the emphatic confidences dispensed as profound truths, muddled with sentiment and the desire to impress.

'You know something, Mister Green? Johnny Wilson's the only man I ever come across I could honestly say was a good man. I don't mean good in a religious meaning, or any of that chapel-going, Sunday-suited nonsense. I mean good as one human being to another. If you understood the language, Mister Green, and went round asking your questions to every single person on the island, you wouldn't find anyone who didn't think Johnny Wilson was a lovely man.' Evans drained his glass. 'Happiness. That's what it is. Happiness comes out of Johnny like steam from a kettle. Although you're smiling, Mister Green, you look as though you could do with a whiff or two of happiness.'

Fowler ignored the observation, but it pricked a sensitive spot and he jerked his head aside with irritation as a bumble-bee zoomed past him and out again across the square in erratic exuberant flight.

'This happiness,' he said. 'Is it the girl, do you think?'

'Girls don't make men happy; it's the other way round, man.'

'Then how do you account for it?'

Evans stood up.

'You'd better ask God about that, Mister Green.'

'Do you think it would be quicker to ask Johnny Wilson?'

'It might,' said Evans. 'But privacy on this island is a highly respected commodity. Don't stick your nose out too far. You never know, someone might flatten it for you.'

Evans lurched away into the sun, and Fowler watched him slip out of sight down a narrow alley to the side of the church.

Fowler paid for the bottle of ouzo and, after an hour's delay, managed to fight his way through a mountainous plate of moussaka. Then, in the heat of the afternoon, carrying his camera, and the first stabs of acid dyspepsia with him, he walked unhurriedly in the direction of the quay.

Chapter Three

'MY NAME IS Green,' said Fowler, formally. 'Is Mr Wilson at home?'

The child, the younger sister, he guessed, of the girl in the square,

stood inside the open doorway and stared at him with the unselfcon-
sciousness of eleven-year-old curiosity. He made the ridiculous inef-
fectual gestures commonly believed by the English to overcome any
language barrier.

'Wilson. At home? Here? Want to see. Talk.'

A smile half-formed itself around the full young lips, but quickly became lost again in the impassive disconcerting scrutiny of Fowler's
face, which he now wiped with his handkerchief. The climb up the
precipitous path from the curving beach had brought out a generous
covering of sweat, already garlic-tainted from the moussaka. A word
occurred to him which might establish communication. He tried it.

'Johnny?'

The dusky little features responded immediately with an expression
of pleasure and affection.

'Perasse messa, tha tou po.'

'Thank you,' said Fowler, correctly interpreting the gesture of invitation, and followed her into the house. She left him immediately
and pattered bare-footed across the stone floor, through an open doorway and up some steps beyond it.

The interior was light and cool. Clearly the adjacent walls of three
small houses had been pierced to make a long, low room, pleasantly
divided by open rough-stone archways into three recesses. There was
nothing extraneous; table and chairs at the far end—four, he noted;
cushions strewn over divans against the wall; an open fireplace filled
with Judas-tree branches bearing soft-scented purple blossoms,
guarded on each side by sentinel vases patterned with the leaping
fawn of Rhodes. No dirt, no squalor: clean, cared-for. On the grey
scrubbed flags of the floor were three Persian rugs, worn, a little thread-
bare, but still bearing deep intricate patterns which answered the ar-
ray of colour on the white-washed walls.

It was more, much more, than Fowler needed. There were dozens of
canvases, some framed, others hung simply on their stretchers. There
were at least twenty of the girl, nudes, portraits, some of the younger
sister; others of an old woman, seated, head covered in a black lace
shawl. She was big and rotund, fierce. The pose was that of the ema-
ciated sadness of Whistler's mother, but the mood was Madame Suggia
deprived of her 'cello. There were a few self-portraits of Wilson, which
was a bonus he could not have hoped for. As well as the figures and
faces, in almost every picture there was something else, subtle and
vaguely disquieting, but precisely the feature he was interested in.
The style was discursive, intuitive; but what worried Fowler was the

feeling of maturity, the impression that these were pictures by an artist who had worked all his life to reach this stage of development.

He could hear voices at the back of the house. Seizing his opportunity he opened his camera-case and clicked away rapidly, moving down the rows of paintings. He was well past the arch of the second recess when the sudden realization that his antics were observed made him start. He recognized immediately the black lace shawl and the fearsome features. The old woman in the picture rocked gently in her chair behind the arch and nodded at him. It was probably a greeting, but, still surprised as he was by her presence, it seemed to Fowler that it was a movement of accusation, a secret she would hold, as if to say, 'I've caught you red-handed young man. I won't do anything about it now. But remember I know what you're about. So watch your step.'

Fowler closed his camera-case and grinned back at her awkwardly. Idiotically, he said:

'Good afternoon.'

'Good afternoon.'

He swung round at the voice behind him.

'Maria say you wish to see Johnny, my husband?'

The girl spoke the words slowly with the careful practised pronunciation of a student but the intonation owed nothing to English. The effect was at once amusing and charming, so that the meaning of the simple sentence became strangely altered by the accenting of the last word, as though she were surprised beyond belief that she was fortunate enough to have a husband such as Johnny. Her head was tilted to one side, her cheek gently pressed against the delicately rounded head of the baby in her arms. She rocked the child to and fro and regarded Fowler with a curious composure. He had the impression that, depending not so much on what he said, but how he said it, would she make her own feminine assessment of him, which in turn would decide whether she let him see Wilson, or offered him some excuse. The latter, he guessed, from the fathomless almost black eyes, he would only circumvent at the risk of a passionate and fiery protest.

'Yes,' said Fowler. 'Is your husband at home?'

'Do you know him?'

'No, I . . .'

'Then you are not a friend of his?'

Once again the unusual stressing of the words gave an oblique meaning, and the sentence read, 'You are an enemy', and Fowler wondered if that was what she indeed meant and, if so, what she knew, and if it was what he also wanted to know.

He smiled at her, wishing that it was a smile some men had, a combination of candour, and humour, and a gently ruthless determination which opened for them, more often than not, the door to the bedroom. But he knew it wasn't. Somehow on his face it turned into a vaguely lecherous grimace. He checked it quickly.

'I'm interested in pictures, and I was told in the town he lived here . . .'

'Who tell you?' Sing-song this time, not aggressive, but still demanding a satisfactory answer.

'Someone called Evans. I happened to be having a drink . . .'

'Doc Evans. Yes, I like. A friend of Johnny,' she said, and it appeared to Fowler that he had given the correct password, for she smiled now and, cooing to the baby, took the child over to the old woman in the rocking-chair, and returned to him.

'My grandmother. Very deaf. But she sees everything.'

Fowler nodded. 'You bet,' he nearly said. The girl offered her hand in an old-fashioned gesture, and he had the ridiculous notion of kissing it, but didn't do that either.

'How do you do, Mr . . . ?'

'Green, Bill Green.'

Her fingers were cool and the skin felt lubricated, not with oil, but with the dry slipperiness of graphite.

'I am Thalia, Mr Green. And Johnny is my husband. My baby is called Paul, and you meet already my sister Maria. It is the whole family.'

She laughed then, and this time Fowler was caught up in the emotional translation which said that this was life and love, and the whole world, and what a wonder of joy to live in it.

'I hope I'm not disturbing you,' he said lamely.

'Oh no, we are just touching up. Johnny will not mind. Follow please, Mr Green.'

She led him back through the archway and up the steps where the child had disappeared. The rear of the house, where normally he would have expected waste ground or a yard, had been simply converted into a wide patio with a sloping lean-to roof made of criss-cross laths supporting a well-trimmed vine which filtered the light evenly. At the end of the patio, Wilson was at his easel. The sister stood by him with intense concentration, watching him work.

'Who is it, Lally?' Wilson called without looking up.

'It is Bill Green.'

'Who?'

'A friend of Doc Evans.'

Wilson spared him a brief, not unfriendly glance.

'What can I do for you?'

'I was told you were a painter, Mr Wilson, and being interested . . .' he let the sentence trail off casually as sufficient explanation of his presence.

'In painters or paintings?' Wilson smiled.

'Can you separate the two?' asked Fowler.

'Not without raising philosophical difficulties, I agree.' Wilson stood back a little from the canvas, squinting at it. 'Singer without a song, worker without a job, lover without a loved one? Is that the sort of thing you had in mind?'

'More or less. Surgeon without a patient, murderer without a victim . . .'

Wilson laughed. 'The examples are infinite. What are you, Mr Green? A hook without a bait?'

It could be an idle, innocent remark without significance. Fowler tucked it away for later consideration.

'Sit please, Mr Green,' the girl interrupted his thought. 'You like a drink?'

'No, thank you. I've had quite a few with Doc Evans, and in this climate . . .'

'Fetch some glasses, Lally,' said Wilson. 'Custom of the island. There's no escape.'

'Well, I . . .'

'You must,' smiled the girl, and spoke to her sister, who followed obediently into the house.

Fowler stood rather awkwardly. Wilson continued painting, apparently willing to let the silence lengthen. Now that he was able to look at Wilson for the first time from a few feet, he found it hard to match up the hooked nose and the slanting mischievous eyes, the prominent ears, the dimpled cheek, with the memorized image of the photograph he had carried for so long, and which was in the wallet inside his breast-pocket. Of course, when the shots he had taken across the street that morning were developed and blown up to size, it would be easier to make a point by point comparison. But the unconcern of the spare lean man in front of him, the utter contentment of the expression, the dubious misfiring of his own first salvo, and the warm insect-hum of the afternoon, made him suspect he was on an expensive, whimsical, kinky, wild goose-chase of an idea which would end abortively in his bringing home a dead duck of a story.

'May I look?' he asked.

'That's what pictures are for,' replied Wilson.

The painting was of the girl again, but in a new role. Mother and

34

baby, Madonna and child, the infant absorbed by the full pear-shaped breasts. It could have been trite, stylized, sentimental, but it was glowing with life and feeling and colour, the background, as in all the others, endowing the composition with a startling vitality. Here was no subconscious scrabbling, no sterile, abstract pattern-making, no schizoid action-daubs; here was passion and love and, yes, the effervescence of happiness the old man in the square had spoken of. Fowler felt his throat tighten as the waves of heartburn rose into it. This sort of thing didn't exist, didn't happen any more. The only thought which made any sense of his own life was the conviction that such expositions were make-believe, ending in disillusionment and self-destruction. Yet here it was, and as he watched the olive-shaped end of the paintbrush stab a new patch of cerulean somewhere amongst the folds of the skirt, he immediately wondered why he had not seen that the blue mark at precisely that point was absolutely necessary. He began to feel an admiration for this man whom he had never met before. Up to now he hadn't felt any personal involvement. Now he did, and the idea of destruction was distasteful to him. But he had to go on.

'What will you get for that?' he asked.

'I've got it,' said Wilson. 'Satisfaction.'

'I meant in terms of reality.'

'Ah, the great illusion. Money?'

'I'm making you an offer.'

'You like the picture?'

'It's very beautiful. I think I know someone who might be interested in it. In all your work, in fact. Who handles it at the moment?'

'I do.'

'You haven't an agent?'

'I don't need one.'

'You do, to sell at the right price.'

'I don't sell. Not yet, anyway.'

'You paint just for yourself?'

'And for my wife and son. A capital investment for them, if you like.'

'But you sold a picture last summer, or so I'm told.'

Wilson laughed.

'Poor Mrs Iverson. A sad rich American. She fell in love with a small portrait of Lally. Said it reminded her of her daughter who was killed in a road accident. She offered me a mint for it.'

'So you *do* sell if the price is right?'

'I gave it to her,' said Wilson.

'But why?'

35

'I liked her.'

The dark-haired subject returned and placed a tray of drinks on the wooden bench beside them. Wilson put his palette and brushes away, wiped his hands on a rag, and smiled amiably at Fowler.

'Now I'll make *you* an offer. Of a drink,' he said.

Fowler sat down, and was surprised to find that the glass he was given contained a good liqueur brandy, and that a box of Havana cigars was being held open for him by the girl.

'My only remaining extravagances,' said Wilson. He sat down, his wife kissed him and then, with a graceful, almost Eastern gesture of hospitality, walked away again, leaving them alone.

'That sounds as though you've known another kind of life,' Fowler observed.

'Several kinds. Haven't we all?'

'What used you to do?'

'Make money.'

'How?'

'I was an engineer.'

'What made you stop?'

'The same reason which makes you go on, Green. Because basically I wanted to, I suppose.'

'And now you don't need to?'

'I've saved enough to live here. It's very cheap.' He made an expansive gesture. 'What more could I want?' Wilson rolled his glass in his hands. 'How do you make a living, Mr Green? Or more important, do you enjoy making it? You're obviously not an art-dealer.'

'Why are you so sure?'

'You said the picture was very beautiful. No dealer would make a remark like that. It's not only bad business, but there's no criticism in it, no interpretation. Dealers can't resist pretending to themselves they have made a discovery; that they have such heightened sensibility that they see values of which even the artist himself is unaware. They haven't, of course. As their name implies, they don't love pictures, they love deals. What sort of deal have you in mind with me?'

The quizzical amused stare disconcerted Fowler. He smirked defensively.

'You're quite right,' he said. 'I'm not an art-dealer. I'm a writer.'

'Green? Bill Green? I don't think I've ever . . .'

'I use a pseudonym: Frank Fowler,' said Fowler. Deception on deception. Names disguising people. People living up to names. The confusion of truth.

'Do you write fact or fiction?'

'Both. They're often difficult to separate. I'm doing a biography at the moment. Actually, that's why I'm wandering about in this part of the world.' He watched Wilson carefully. This was the hunch, the lever, the intelligent guess. 'It's a book on Alexander Cranford.'

Wilson frowned and then said:

'Cranford? The plastic surgeon?'

'You knew him?'

'I believe Doc Evans did. You've talked to him of course.'

'Yes.'

'Was he much help?'

'No, not much.'

'Poor old Doc. He might have been a good physician, but for one or two things. Then many people might have been this or that but for one or two things.' He drew on his cigar. Fowler noticed that his own had gone out. Wilson passed him the matches. There was no reaction, nothing.

'I remember very well reading about Cranford's death in the papers, a couple of years back.'

'Out here?'

'No. I was in England then. Rather tragic the whole thing. His wife, too. Very beautiful in the photographs. I'd like to have painted her. Cranford of course had quite a reputation one way and another, I believe.'

It was off-hand, mildly interested, polite. It could mean nothing or it could mean exactly the opposite. With reluctance, Fowler pushed the probe further.

'I've been following up a lot of his patients,' he said. 'There are quite a few round here. Kcamaris, the shipowner; Melissa Kyriacou, the film-star. Getting their reactions. You know the sort of thing. "Since you changed the shape of your nose, madam, has it changed the shape of your life?"'

Wilson laughed and said:

'Or "Did you find life more exciting, sir, after Mr Cranford changed the shape of your wife?" Must be a fascinating piece of research.'

'Some are pretty cagey of course. Deny all knowledge of the man.'

'Oh? Why is that?'

'His patients were drawn from an astonishingly wide cross-section. Society right down to the criminal strata; people who wanted to change their appearance completely, change their name, escape into a new existence as a perpetual safeguard against discovery.' He looked straight at Wilson. 'Those are the ones I'm most interested in,' he ended.

'And the most difficult to track down, I should imagine.'

'All the more rewarding when one does,' smiled Fowler.

Wilson finished his brandy but continued to hold his glass. Fowler could not decide if the oscillating reflection of sunlight from it was due to a slight tremor of the artist's hand, or was caused by the fluttering of the vine-leaves above them in the afternoon breeze. Well, it was as far as he could go, and hell, how far was it? He drained his own glass.

'It's very pleasant here,' he said. 'Kind of you to let me trespass on your hospitality, but I must be going.'

'Glad you came,' said Wilson.

'That friend of mine would still be interested in your work, I'm sure, if you ever change your mind about a sale.'

'Get him to come along sometime.'

'I might do that,' said Fowler.

They walked along the patio, and through the house to the other side where the ground tumbled away to the sea below.

'Send me a copy of your book when it comes out,' said Wilson. 'What are you calling it, by the way?'

Fowler hesitated. A title came to him.

'The Twin Serpents,' he said. 'You know: the snakes on the doctor's badge.'

They shook hands, and although he didn't look round as he picked his way down the steep winding path to the level of the beach, Fowler sensed that Wilson was watching him all the way.

He walked back to the harbour and spoke to the owner of the caique who had brought him to Kronos the day before. The man tried to make him believe there was a storm on the way, but a few more drachmas seemed to dispel the threat. Having settled the fare, he collected his bag from the island's equivalent of a bed and breakfast establishment in the street behind the square and returned to the boat with it. As the motor chugged the craft ponderously out of the harbour, he caught a glimpse of Wilson and the girl running along the little beach. Laughing, they plunged into the shining, dazzling water. If Wilson had anything on his mind, he could apparently shake it off without much difficulty.

Fowler turned his gaze towards the horizon. It was flimsy, all very flimsy. He had strongly suspected for some time the whole thing was pure fantasy. But then again there were certain points too sharp for coincidence. What was certain, however, was that he'd have to make what he could of it. It would take a few days to dictate it all in the comfort of his expense-account room in the King's Palace Hotel in Athens.

It would take a few days too to get the films developed and printed. After that, the next move, if any, was not his.

Perhaps the best place to start would be in Cranford's consulting-room two years back. He must somehow project himself there, observe the scene, hear the dialogue, get inside Wilson's skin, so to speak. Yes, that's how he would present it. That was the place to start.

Part Three

THE SOWER

Chapter Four

'THESE DRESSINGS MUST not be disturbed for ten days. No Peeping-Tom nonsense to see how things are getting on, you understand?'

'I understand, Mr Cranford.'

'Unless you feel any pain. Then get in touch with me at once.'

'O.K.'

'After a complete facial reconstruction, Mr er . . .'

'Smith. John Smith. . . .'

It was always Smith or Jones, or Black or White. He never pried or probed. People had their reasons. It was not for him to question motives.

'. . . Mr Smith, it's necessary to give complete rest to all the muscles of expression. The only way to do that is to cover up your face completely. Splint it, in fact. Irksome, I know, but when we take all this off you'll look a new man, I promise you.'

'That's why I came to you. Thanks for doing the job.'

'Thanks for the cheque, Mr Smith.'

Cranford put his finger on the concealed bell-push, and went with his patient to the door. As he opened it, his receptionist came down the hall to meet them. He shook hands, and the nylon-coated girl took over, sprinkling bright cliché-spangled chatter as she helped Smith or Jones or Black or White into his raincoat and handed him his hat. With swathed face and dark glasses, almost the Cranford trade-mark, the man went out into Harley Street. The girl closed the door.

'That the lot, Celia?'

'Yes, Mr Cranford.'

'Off you go, then. It's late. Good night.'

'Good night, sir.'

Cranford went back into his room. He wrote a shorthand note on the file card and returned it to its proper place. He checked his appointment book, neatly written up in his secretary's clear hand. '8.15. Major Wharton. Rhinoplasty. Bulstrode Clinic.' Nothing after that. He should be home by 9.30. From habit he picked up the 'phone to ring Eve, to offer his almost daily excuse for being too late for dinner, to tell her to

43

apologize to any guests she might have asked, to opt out of any social function she might have arranged. Then, as he remembered she was still in Paris, he put his receiver down again. Her excursions were becoming more frequent. But it was no more than he could justly expect. What time, what part of his waking life did he really give to her? A broken weary hour or two at the tail-end of the day. He decided, for the hundredth time in the last six months, he would have to do something about it.

Outside in the street his chauffeur opened the door of the Bentley.

'Are you still here, Bateman? Isn't it your night off?' he asked.

'Yes, sir, but Mrs Cranford rang through from Paris this afternoon and asked to be met at the airport at ten-fifteen. It was hardly worth taking a couple of hours off. I mean there's nothing much you can do in a couple of hours, is there?'

'No,' Cranford agreed.

'I expect she forgot it was Wednesday. I don't mind, sir. It's all right.'

'No, it isn't, Bateman. You run along. I'll collect Mrs Cranford myself. Ten-fifteen, you say?'

'Yes, but it's O.K. sir. . . .'

'Nonsense. Enjoy yourself. Good night.'

'Good night, sir. Thank you.'

The middle-aged man saluted and walked briskly away down the street. Cranford got in the front seat and drove round the two blocks which separated his consulting-rooms from the private clinic where he carried out most of his operations. How like Eve, not to let him know personally she was returning today. How like her not to consider the private lives of lesser mortals, such as employees. In her world, the world she had been brought up in, such people were expendable, replaceable, like a hat or a fur coat. Or a husband?

The thought worried him, but instantly it became confused with another. She was coming back, and he had missed her.

'Beauty lies skin deep, but ugliness penetrates to the soul. Ever think about the soul, Sister?'

'Not when I'm on duty, Mr Cranford.'

The accented reply came through the mask, prim and muffled with Presbyterian disapproval. He knew his constant stream of comment and badinage while operating ruffled her professional dignity, puncturing the solemnity and tarnishing the glamour of her calling. But it was a habit, developed over the years, which paradoxically helped him to concentrate and exercise to the full the skill of his hands.

The water permeated the thicknesses of plaster of Paris gauze, cut

44

and fashioned to fit the new nose. The displaced air rose in bubbles, making a milky champagne in the stainless-steel bowl. Cranford removed the gauze, squeezed out the surplus water, and moulded the plaster on the patient's face with expert care, like a chef wrapping soft pastry round a meaty morsel.

'Why is it one can dissect away the body layer by layer, tissue by tissue, and yet never discover that elusive organ?'

'I'm sure I don't know, Mr Cranford,' compressed, bitten-off.

'Perhaps God always gets to the soul first, eh, Sister? Operating a few scalpel-lengths ahead, bringing off the immaculate excision. "*Anima*", the soul. If diseased, cut it out. Perform the divine animectomy. You think that's a possibility?'

'I have no idea.'

Smiling, he heard her sigh of exasperation and made sure the pressure of the plaster was evenly distributed, so that there was no distortion of the carefully assessed angle between the columella and the upper lip. Satisfied, he nodded approval.

'Well, that should look better than the Bergerac he came in with.'

Berenger swivelled round on his stool and turned off the oxygen and carbon dioxide. The conical metal floats settled down in their glass tubes.

'Let's hope the major's wife recognizes him,' he sniggered.

Cranford moved back from the table. 'Thanks, Douglas. Thank you, Sister,' he said and walked briskly out of the theatre into the scrubbing-up room.

The irritation was so intense it demanded imperative attention. He ripped off the rubber gloves violently, and flung them into the wiremesh tray. Hopelessly, for a second, he tried to resist the temptation, keeping his hands apart. Then compulsively, unreservedly, he gave way to it, scratching first one palm, then the other, with ecstatic vigour. Gradually the initial, irresistible torment became more bearable. In order to avoid excoriating the skin, he abandoned his nails as instruments of relief in favour of the blunter contour of his knuckles. At length he was in control again.

He went over to the wash-bowl and thrust his hands under the jet of cold water until its slaking balm extinguished their tingling fire. He held them in the stream for some time longer, savouring the feeling of normality as if it were a new-found positive pleasure.

The nurse banged through the swing-doors from the theatre, making him start. She untied his gown, and while he took off his mask and cap she picked his gloves out of the tray. With a practised movement she flipped the wrists over and squeezed the air into the fingers, so that they popped out noisily like inflated cocktail sausages. Cranford dried his hands gently, patting them with the towel. She took the gloves and his other soiled articles into the sterilizing room and heard him call almost immediately.

'Nurse! Where have you hidden my little jar?'

She ran back to find him poking about on the instrument trolley.

'There's a fresh one on the lower shelf.'

She unscrewed the lid and held the jar for him. He dug his fingers into the jelly and smeared it liberally over his hands before rubbing it in.

'That's the second one this week,' she ventured.

'Is it?' He hadn't realized he was using so much of the stuff. 'Mustn't let aids to beauty get out of control, must we, Nurse?'

Involuntarily her hand went up to her mouth to hide the forbidden-on-duty trace of lipstick.

'I'm sorry, sir. . . . I hadn't time to take it all off before . . .'

'I didn't mean that,' smiling. 'Quite a pretty colour.'

She blushed and put the jar back.

'Ridiculous rule devised by frustrated matrons, but don't quote me on that.'

'I won't, Mr Cranford,' she laughed. 'Good night, sir.'

'Good night, Nurse.'

She disappeared again into the theatre. He picked up the container and checked to see if the dispenser had labelled it as directed: 'Mr Cranford's Special Hand Cream.' It was a proprietary cortisone preparation, but the legend concealed, purposely, its composition. Rumours could grow from suspicions first voiced in nurses' common-rooms. The trouble with success was that you could never afford to be off-guard, never really let up. There were always twenty men breathing down your neck, waiting to snatch your coat, step into your shoes, speculate with your money, sleep with your wife.

He wiped his hands off on the towel. A faint prickling sensation was all that remained.

In the surgeons' dressing-room Douglas Berenger stirred his coffee. The movement of the spoon was delicate and uncertain, like the voice, like Douglas.

'Are you through for tonight, Alex?'

Cranford nodded as he fixed his tie in the mirror. The face above it was handsome, the eyes wide and well-set, nose a shade too broad, perhaps, the cheeks definitely too well-fed, he observed. Must get some weight off.

46

'One of the advantages of cosmetic surgery is that only occasionally can improvement on nature be regarded as an emergency.'

Berenger laughed with sycophantic deference. Irritated, Cranford offered his case.

'Cigarette?'

Berenger waved it aside.

'I've given up.'

'Coward,' said Cranford.

He put a cigarette in his mouth and lit it. Berenger laughed again. The raillery in the accusation was reassuring. It promised admission on equal terms to the robust successful world of Cranford, like a slap on the back from the Captain of Football. Cultivating Cranford wasn't easy. But important for someone like himself, still in the outer circle. Cranford put on his jacket and poured out some coffee.

'Look, don't drink that muck, Alex,' Berenger tried the direct approach. 'Why not come round to my place now, for a brandy, on your way home?'

And ruin it with shop and eager nervous platitudes from Berenger's ex-nurse of a wife, thought Cranford.

With one or two notable exceptions, he found the company of his medical colleagues dull and wearisome. Nine-tenths of their time was occupied with disease, abnormality, death. And when their work released them for the other tenth they floundered, at a loss in the unfamiliar medium of normal life, like priests who preached virtue without experience of sin. He was glad he had an excuse to refuse the invitation.

'Can't, Douglas. I'm meeting my wife at the airport.'

'Well, why not bring her back with you? Joan would love to meet her. She's very good at making dresses. They should have a lot in common,' Berenger persisted hopefully.

The idea of Eve, back from Paris, with at least one new Dior and God knew what else in her luggage, settling down to a homey late-night chat about patterns and materials, would have been faintly amusing, were it not in some way disturbing. Suddenly, Cranford felt envious of Berenger, with his unsophisticated existence and the pride he took in his uncomplicated wife, who would in due course bear him uncomplicated children.

'Some other time, Douglas. . . .'

Berenger hesitated, assessing the tone of the voice, balancing weariness against boredom.

'It would make it pretty late, I suppose.'

47

He got up and stood awkwardly a moment, but Cranford didn't help him.

'I'll say good night, then.'

The laugh was added briefly like a defence, which it was.

'Good night, Douglas.'

Accepting defeat, Berenger closed the door behind him uncertainly. Cranford drank some of the now lukewarm coffee and pushed the cup away in disgust. Berenger was right about that, anyway. Perhaps he had been rather rough with him. He'd been rough with a number of people over the last few weeks. It was neither a profitable nor a usual mood. He must remember to tell Eve to ask the Berengers round to one of her parties, where they would be suitably diluted.

At the end of the corridor Sister Garland stopped him.

'I'm glad I've caught you, Mr Cranford.'

'What can I do for you, Sister?'

She proffered him a drug-sheet.

'Would you write up something for Major Wharton, please, in case I need it?'

'Is he round yet?'

'Barely.'

He took the board and scribbled a prescription.

'Everyone else behaving themselves?'

'Yours always do, Mr Cranford.'

He smiled and handed the notes back to her. She must have been pretty, ten years ago.

'I'll be in late tomorrow afternoon. But call me whenever you like if you're worried.'

'Yes, Mr Cranford.'

'Good night, Sister.'

He walked down the sound-damped spacious corridor of the Bulstrode Clinic to the lift. Stacked at the end were the vases and bowls of flowers, tributes of affection and anxiety, but mostly of ostentation or emotionless convention. Early tomorrow they would be put back into the privacy of their separate wards, to provide the visitors with safe talking-points at uneasy moments. The colours and the scent vaguely depressed him, throwing up a recently recurring desire for a simple unfettered job which carried no responsibility. He buttoned it up brusquely with his overcoat and let the lift carry him to the ground floor.

Outside under the street-lamps a sprinkling of April snow dressed the roofs of the parked vehicles crouched at the kerb, black slugs with salt on their backs. He went over to his car and unlocked the door. As he opened it, something cold and wet struck him on the back of the neck. He swung round and two boys cat-called from the opposite pavement. He scooped up some snow, moulded it into a ball and flung it at them. The shot was well wide but the surprise of his retaliation made the children run away, shouting, down the street.

He stood a moment watching them, remembering the lawn at home years ago and a battle in the snow with his father.

He took out his handkerchief and wiped his neck and hands. Then he got in the car and switched on the ignition. Contact with the snow had started up the itching again but, if he feigned unconcern, it would grow less in a few minutes. He placed his hands resolutely on the steering-wheel.

The tyres of the Bentley made frosty crackling sounds as they eased out from the kerb.

Chapter Five

THE JET SCREECHED along the runway, the impact of rubber on bitumen transferring cushioned shocks through the undercarriage, discreetly pressing well-lined stomachs against the restraining loops of safety-belts. Now that the trip was over, the filaments of tension inside Eve's body retracted, sealing themselves off, factually ending the episode, but still leaving its memory. As the plane taxied to a standstill in front of the main airport building, she unhurriedly loosened the buckle on her lap-strap. Allowing the other passengers their head in the scuffle towards the exit she waited for her mink to be brought from its hanger behind the curtain rail, and then gathered up her gloves and handbag.

Cranford scanned the group from the aircraft, marching like obedient pupils behind the uniformed hostess across the lighted tarmac. Failing to pick her out, he was about to enquire resignedly the time of the next arrival, when he saw her immaculate figure emerge at the top of the steps. She paused briefly for chance flash-photographs before making a glamorous, graceful descent.

Eve carried the whole thing off with perfection, her studied progress towards the reception lounge below him appearing natural, spontaneous, and oblivious of female stares, whispered surmises, or frank masculine leers which tended to develop wherever she went. The performance produced in Cranford a mixed sentiment of longing, admiration and annoyance. There was a total self-sufficiency about his wife which neither familiarity, nor tenderness, nor his possession of her had succeeded in disturbing. He thrust his hands into his overcoat pockets, and went down to meet her.

As she came through the Customs baggage-check, Eve noticed her husband a few seconds before his eye could catch hers. Quickly she dropped her gaze to her handbag, making an imaginary search. She had wanted to drive home from the airport alone to allow time to resolve her guilt, or at least salt it away for later contemplation. Had she known, she would have asked Willy to be there. Willy was always a morale-raiser; a witty facetious protector against Alex's sometimes formidable catechisms. She felt uneasy because she had not completed her defence in depth. She snapped-to the gilded clasp on her handbag and waved to him gaily.

'Darling, what a wonderful surprise. Where's Bateman?'

'It's his night off.'

Cranford kissed her on the cheek.

'Good trip?'

'A bit bumpy.'

She took his arm and the porter followed them towards the car-park.

'How was Paris?'

'Full of spring.'

'Any money left?'

'One and sixpence.'

'Lucky for you I came,' he smiled.

Lucky for me I went, she thought, and watched the porter put the three white suit-cases and the hat-box in the boot. Cranford gave him ten shillings and got in beside her.

The sudden privacy of the car accentuated the strange shyness of the very familiar after a brief separation. They did not speak again until they were speeding down the Great West Road towards the rose nightglow in the frosty sky which was London.

'Any news while I've been away?'

'No, except that you've been away.'

'Haven't you been up to anything?'

'Only my neck in work.'

'And besides work?'

'Work.'

Eve laughed, and a little of her tension began to leave her. Perhaps it wasn't going to be so difficult.

'Then I'm very pleased with you,' she murmured.

'Why?'

'For making lots and lots of lovely money.'

She settled down into the deep seat and a yawn overtook her. Cranford drove on in silence. Replies to Eve's hedonistic extravagances were superfluous. Like compliments about her beauty. He accepted both; and the need to pay for them.

Her face seemed thinner than when she went away. As the amber of the traffic lights joined the red, and he let the car slide forward, he noticed that even her superb skill with make-up couldn't hide a certain duskiness below the eyes, which were now closed, demonstrating their long mascaraed lashes.

'You look tired, Eve.'

'It was very nice of you to meet me. You shouldn't have bothered. What did you say, darling?'

'I said you look very tired.'

'I'm exhausted,' she nodded.

Cranford turned left past the Gillette factory, making for Ealing and the North Circular Road.

'You've lost weight, too.'

She opened her eyes, sat up, and scrutinized her reflection in the mirror on the sun-visor. It was useless to deny it. High cheek-bones were one thing, hollow cheeks another. She should have known his professional eye wouldn't miss anything.

'Six pounds if you want a figure,' she said.

'It's madness, Eve. I've told you before, that rapid dieting . . .'

'This wasn't intentional,' she said with feeling, and then cursed herself for the admission, wondering where it would lead.

'What do you mean?'

'I . . . I had food poisoning. Moules marinières. I thought I was going to die.' Part truth, anyway.

'Good God, why didn't you let me know?'

'Darling, what could you have done—from here?'

'At least have ensured you had a good doctor. You did see a doctor?'

'Yes.'

'What was his name?'

'I don't think you'd know him.'

'I know several in Paris. Was it Leoville?'

'No . . . I don't remember. He was German or Austrian. His name was quite unpronounceable.'

'How did you get hold of him? The hotel?'

'No. Not the hotel.' She wriggled imperceptibly in her seat, believing the near-truth safer than the outright lie. 'Actually Norah Britt produced him. By the way, she sends her love.'

The name meant nothing to him, but he was used to the common currency of verbal affection bandied about by Eve's friends.

'I wish you'd rung me,' he said. 'Some of these continental boys can be rather unorthodox. . . .'

'Oh, he was very efficient.' She hurried on, trying to emphasize the triviality of the matter. 'Quite up to Harley Street standards.'

'I'd better drop him a line.'

'What on earth for? I'm fine now. Just tired. Like you said.'

'It would only be courtesy. . . .'

'He's had his fee.'

'He charged you?'

'No, but it's so much easier in the end. I insisted on paying him. Next time, come with me. Then I shan't eat the wrong things.' She put her hand gently on his arm, reassuring him, deceiving him. 'You don't get away nearly enough, Alex.'

Two, three weeks a year at the most, snatched in odd parcels and those scarcely a relaxation. Somehow, with Eve, things always turned into a social round; joining someone else, having someone else join them; for the shooting, for the sailing, for the racing, for the gambling. No wonder they hadn't got children. There was no place for them in Eve's endless race for living.

'We ought to take a long weekend,' he said.

'Heavenly.'

'I mean alone, without the crowd.'

She laughed, hiding the uneasiness in the sound.

'Are you sure you wouldn't get bored with just me?'

'Would you?'

She settled back in her seat again.

'It's worth thinking about, Alex.'

There were always ways of postponement. She closed her eyes shutting off the conversation, hoping she'd killed it.

Cranford left the North Circular Road for Highgate, and once over the top of the hill, it was less than a minute before he was running up the drive between the well-kept lawns and into the garage, which the somewhat sedate Bentley shared with the white sports Mercedes. Like husband and wife, he thought.

When Eve had shed her things and returned to the living-room, Mrs Bateman had unobtrusively produced a tray of tea, with a choice of sandwiches and light fluffy little cakes. They wished her good night but, after she had gone, Cranford declined the tea and poured himself a brandy and soda.

'It's lovely to be home.'

She could have said, 'It's lovely to be home with you, Alex.' But the familiar surroundings were the greater comfort, the greater sense of security. People changed, had their own feelings and needs, which disturbed serenity. A painting, a beautiful rug, the fragmented light from a chandelier were immutable, without argument, making no awkward demands.

'I think I know just the place,' said Cranford.

'Place? For what?'

'Our long weekend.'

Since her casual suggestion in the car, the idea had taken root. Perhaps the problem below the surface up to now, put off or casually shelved, might be solved against a fresh, unfamiliar backdrop.

'Oh, that,' she laughed. 'Yes, we'll have to talk about it seriously, sometime.'

'That's what I'm doing, Eve.'

His tone precluded dismissal of the subject. She'd have to go along with it for the time being.

'Well, why don't we go to that fabulous hotel at Eze? You know, where Monica always stays. Or we could fly to Rome. The Wendells have a gorgeous villa, fully staffed, and Muriel's forever begging me to make use of it. Or we might . . .'

'Make a complete break from all the Monicas and Muriels, don't you think?'

Cranford drained his glass. It was frightening how in less than two years they had each scored their own grooves; concentric, revolving faster, the space ever widening between them.

'Where is this mysterious place you want to go to so much, darling?'

She spoke in the maddening way she could at times, pouting her lips and mouthing the words so that her voice became deeper and took on a glutinous toffee-like quality, as if she were indulging a favourite poodle, fretting to go for a walk.

'It's called The Admiral Benbow.'

'I've never heard of it.'

'No more will Monica or Muriel.'

'What is it? A pub?'

'Yes, at Shinglestrand, in Suffolk. I stayed the night there a couple of years ago when I went to read a paper at Ipswich.'

'It doesn't sound very gay.'

'It isn't. On the contrary, it's real, and solid and unpretentious. A shingle beach, an old martello tower, sea-gulls and, at night, wood fires, strong beer and the undisputed homeliness of a friendly dialect.'

The blue eyes opened wide. He sought a flicker of excitement, anticipation. He would even have welcomed a magazine-like sentimental mistiness, but all he saw was incomprehension.

'It must be quite primitive,' she exclaimed.

'Isn't it about time we were?' he said roughly, and turned away, annoyed with his sudden resentment, afraid that it could slide into anger. He noticed he was scratching his hands, and with determination he gave them something to do. He poured another brandy, and heard her laughter behind him.

'Darling, you really have missed me, haven't you?'

He turned round slowly, and the provocation of her beauty took hold of him.

'Yes, I have missed you, Eve.'

She stood up, yawning and stretching purposefully, before his movement towards her could become an embrace. Not now, not tonight, the parrying, the subterfuge, the ingenious excuses.

'Alex, do you mind, I must get to bed. I'm terribly tired.'

The hint of desperation in her plea checked him. Rarely had he seen her face so drained and pale. If she didn't look any better in a day or two he'd have to get old Dinsley to give her a check-up. He made a sudden decision.

'Why not let's go this weekend? The day after tomorrow, in fact?'

He rapidly assessed what arrangements he'd need to make. Khouri was perfectly reliable. The best registrar he'd ever had.

'We can't, darling,' she said quickly. 'It's . . . Willy's party on Saturday.'

He wanted to say, 'To hell with Willy'; but instead he replied, 'All right: the weekend after.'

She hesitated, measuring the persistence in his request, deciding on the tactical withdrawal.

'Could be,' she said.

'That's a deal, then?'

'It's a deal.'

She walked across the room, gracefully, languorously, the perfection he had married, but capricious like the thoroughbred she was, needing delicate handling: an art he had never quite mastered.

After she had gone, he finished his drink thoughtfully. His hands were starting up again. He allowed himself a brief moment of relief and then, before he could be tempted further, he switched off the lights and went along to his own bedroom.

When he was undressed he searched amongst the sweaters and shorts in the bottom drawer of his tallboy until he found what he was looking for. It was years since he'd used them, and then for the purpose for which they were made. Now they were to be a protection from himself during the semi-conscious restlessness of the night.

He slipped his hands into the padded fives-gloves and knotted the tapes firmly round his wrists with the assistance of his teeth.

Chapter Six

HE HAD BEEN half awake for some time before the deferential tapping announced the official beginning of the day. He gave no acknowledgement save to make sure his hands were out of sight under the embroidered sheets.

After a respectful pause, an ordered succession of familiar sounds: double plosive of well-hung door, open, shut; near-silence of measured tread between door and table; closer, fricative statement of baize-backed tray on inlaid satinwood; brief ceramic chatter between china-cup and saucer; second longer deeply-Wiltoned silence at seventy shillings a yard for the ten yards to the window; finally the maracca-like exclamation of brocade-curtained runners. Then sunlight and the hired pseudo-personal greeting.

'It's seven-thirty, Doctor.'

'Thank you, Annie,' reflexly mumbled.

'Not Annie, sir. Rose.'

'Then thank you, Rose.'

Of no importance. They came and went, leaving faint elusive ripples on the mirror-surface of the household domestic pool, created by Eve in her own image, flawless, efficient, elegant, exorbitant.

'It's going to be a beautiful day, Doctor.'

'Yes.' Witness as to fact, not opinion.

A flurry of overalled nylon, pink legs, white shoes, blue carpet, the door again, click, click. Then distantly, in Eve's room, the maraccas, the

55

repeated phrases, her voice inaudible, her body unseen, stretching, supple, unmarked.

A few seconds longer to hold off the beautiful day, to postpone in mock-sleep the moment of secret observation, the assessment of anxiety.

Cranford brought his hands out from under the clothes, untied the tapes and then removed the padded gloves with deliberation. He got out of bed and, taking a reading-glass from the desk, went across to the window. In the sunlight the magnification threw up the ridges and furrows of the skin, and the natural creases of the palms like a personal desert criss-crossed with dried-up watercourses, seen from twenty-thousand feet.

Surely there was improvement, slight but definite improvement? The heightened colour, the generalized erythema, was less marked, and the itchy, faint, pigmented patches were still dry and only minutely flecked with fine silvery scales. There were no rounded vesicles, no sign of the feared development. No weeping exudate.

He put the framed lens down and pressed each palm with the opposite thumb, testing for any subcutaneous induration, the forerunner of contracture. Reassured, he extended his fingers wide-spread like a palmist's advertisement, so that the skin was stretched, blanching the lesions, making it look normal. He remembered a drunken visit to a fair-ground between the end of his finals examination and the announcement of the results, and heard the gypsy's forecast.

'Headline very strong.' Knowing laugh. 'Not much gets by you, does it, sir?' Indulgent smile. 'Heartline . . .' Significant pause, head-shaking and pursed-lipped grimace. 'Naughty heartline, isn't it? There will be many loves in your life, sir, many loves.' Brush-back of wisp of greasy hair. 'Lifeline.' Theatrical drawing-in of peppermint-odoured breath. 'Never seen a longer one, no, really, sir. Oh! And children. Lots of children . . .'

He clenched his hands irritably on the crass credulity which paid heed to such superstitious clap-trap. Examine the victims of a disaster, regard the wax-like extremities in any mortuary, and the absurdity of the linear octogenarian promises was too obvious, too sad for comment.

From outside he heard a car-door slam, and through the gnarled tracery of the cherry-tree branches, sugar-pink dusted with the first spurts of blossom, he could see Bateman vigorously buffing the chromium expanse of the Bentley radiator. Beyond, and hazily, the distant sky-line of Whittington's City offered the spring morning its smoke-tinted salute.

He turned back into the room. Wherever he looked the soft velvety surfaces, the patina of old veneers, the gleam of ormolu, all implied, like the landscape, an ordered, successful affluence which, though he had created it, was even an emblem of it, filled him with unexplained mistrust.

He poured out a cup of tea, and sat on the edge of his bed to drink it. Of late he had taken longer over the procedure; spent lengthy minutes in random reflection, which a year, six months ago, would have been compressed into seconds, or discarded as irrelevancies in the eager forcing pace of the day with its hundred and one tasks, and confident decisions.

He gazed round the room. Its elegant opulence depressed him. Things, possessions, money, the complementary projections of achievement, yet unsatisfactory, unsatisfying. Just as the sprawl of London could be obliterated in one time-blink leaving a meaningless neutronic memory, he had a capricious senseless whim to sweep his own personal world into oblivion; a child's desire to knock down the laboriously erected tower of wooden bricks; the illogical, but satisfying end to the game.

He put his cup back on the tray, and carried it for collection to the marble top of the *bombe* chest near the door. His eye caught the picture above it, one painted by his father and rescued from the bailiffs by his mother. It was a portrait of her against a background of abstract shapes and colours and lines conveying a mood, a feeling, a moment of heightened perception, but to Cranford's boyish imagination it was a dark blue-green forest where the fiery eyes of unimaginable wild animals flung their challenge from between the trunks of the trees. And even now the shapes still looked like trees and eyes, and he supposed for him the picture would forever have just that meaning. 'Your father was a failure, Alex. You're old enough now to see that for yourself.' His mother, smiling, soft-voiced, gathering, as it seemed to him then, an inexplicable pleasure from her genteel resignation. 'Oh, he was a good artist, an important one, so they say—I've never really known how to tell—but still a failure. In the really important things.' 'What things, Mother?' 'You're not old enough to understand.' 'But you said . . .' 'Come along, Alex.' Outside, three suitcases, his and his mother's, his school playbox, a cricket-bat, and father's picture, all piled on the handcart for the porter to trundle to the station, because it saved two shillings on a hired car. 'You mustn't be a failure, Alex. You're going to be a doctor. Doctors aren't failures. And I know you'll go right to the top.' And the laughing echo of his father's voice, the same words, pouring the whisky. 'Right to the top. Good stuff, Alex. Want to try some, boy?' 'Bed-time, Alex. Mummy doesn't wish to have to call you again.'

Time for bed. Time to get up. Early to bed early to rise, makes little Alex healthy, wealthy and wise. And the eyes of the wild animals still glinted greedily from the Prussian blue between the trees.

Cranford opened the door into his bathroom. Time to get up, time to bath and shave, and go down to breakfast and come up again, and knock on Eve's door, and cross the empty bedroom, and find her lying there in the sunken blue-tiled bath, a splendour of pink soap-flecked bath-salted skin, blue silk tying up her hair, red-nailed hand holding a Prussian-blue telephone to her ear.

'. . . heavenly idea . . . Yes, we'd adore to.' Slender bubble-coated fingers covering mouthpiece. 'Fiona wants us down at Redlands for a weekend housewarming.' Explanatory, thrown away, certain of compliance. Back into phone. 'Yes, of course, darling. . . .' Fashionable enthusiasm. 'My best love to Roger, too. . . .' Empty affection. 'Bye now.' Phone away, slither into water, the bright smile and the proffered cheek, 'Morning, darling. It's heavenly to be home again.'

The same words, the contracting vocabulary, the never-ending repetition of triviality, the same people, the same wonderful crowd, different names, different times, but interminably the same entrenched viewpoint, the overfed faces, the clichés, the same rich smothering annihilation. He touched the soft contour with his lips and turned away, blocking the desire to hold her vigorously, roughly.

'Sleep well?'

'Perfectly.'

Needless anxiety. She looked completely refreshed.

'Which weekend were you signing away for us?'

'The one after next.'

'But that's . . .'

'I know, Alex, but we can easily go to your little pub another time. I'm looking forward to it, really I am. A little postponement won't hurt, will it? Besides, I've just accepted Fiona's invitation. I can't just tell her . . .'

'Why not? You're telling me.'

'That's hardly the same thing, is it?'

'It's more important.'

'Really, Alex, you're making a terrible fuss. . . .'

'No, Eve. Just trying to hold you to a promise. You'd better ring her back.'

Drops from the faucet punctuating the seconds, the day ahead, and outside the spring morning. He reached for the instrument.

'Or if you prefer, I'll . . .'

'No, I'll do it.' She grasped the receiver, holding it down on the connexion bar. 'You're very professional this morning, Alex,' the blown kiss costing nothing. 'Don't work too hard.'

He accepted the velvet dismissal without reaction, because in the small victory as in the great, it was in his nature to be generous.

When he had closed the door, she lifted the 'phone and dialled a number. While she listened to the ringing tone, she cupped a breast with her free hand, caressing the nipple with her fingers, sending snaking reflections down the perfumed water. The mirrored surround threw back at her its indulgent admiration.

'Hello . . . ? Willy? . . . I've got to see you. . . .'

Chapter Seven

'ARE YOU READY now, Lady Wesdon?'

'Yes . . . yes, I'm . . . I'm quite ready.'

Her voice was pitched up, doubting, like the uncertain clutching of her ring-encrusted fingers, as she drew the blanket up to her chin, lowered it a few inches, and instantly raised it again on Cranford's entry into the examination room. Fixing his expression impersonally, he peeled down the woollen covering from her body in one gentle revealing movement.

The great breasts slopped out in their white flaccid enormity, two cream cheeses slung in muslin-bags from the rafter of the breast-bone. Fine silvery striae radiated from the brown areolae of the nipples; extinct volcanoes with age-cold streams of lava; huge fatty organs long past their usefulness, their youthful contours, long since abandoned.

Cranford palpated each breast thoroughly to exclude any suspicious nodules of induration, following with care the axillary tails into the armpits. He asked her to sit up, and evaluated the pendulous sagging, estimating the amount of unnecessary tissue he'd have to remove. The nipples would need careful re-siting.

'Thank you. You can dress up now.'

The interest was over, the operation already done.

'Can you do anything for me, Mr Cranford?'

The confident, professional smile.

59

'Of course. I can reduce the size to nearly half. You should feel much more comfortable.'

'I'm not worried about the comfort—though Heaven knows the harness I have to wear is murderous at times. . . .'

He kicked the carpeted stool to support her foot as she climbed off the couch and snatched her voluminous brassière from the chair.

'It's the embarrassment . . . I've suffered bravely for years, Mr Cranford . . . people make fun you know; headwaiters, dressmakers, tradesmen—not that they matter—but when one's own family openly make jokes . . . do you know what my grandchildren call me?'

Cranford shook his head in feigned interest.

'B.B.! And that does not stand for Brigitte Bardot, though they'd have me think so. No, it's "B.B." for "Busty Bags".'

She flipped the shoulder-straps of her slip into their accustomed fleshy grooves on top of her shoulders and then glanced slyly at Cranford.

'I suppose you think I'm a silly, vain old woman?'

Cranford zipped up her dress. It was all part of the service, as much a detail of success as the hair-line scar of the near invisible incision.

'Silly? Certainly not. Vain? A woman's privilege. Old . . .'

'Don't go on, Mr Cranford, or I shall think you're insincere,' she broke in, but the laugh which cradled the interruption registered acceptance of the flattery.

Cranford followed her back into the consulting-room and turned up his operation appointment book. Rhinoplasties, mammaplasties, removal of naevi, rhytidoplasties, meloplasties, facial rejuvenations; the constant battle against the years, the desperate yearning for more time, more security, more love.

He looked across the desk at the ageing, not unattractive woman whose ample bosom, in a different decade, another century, would have caused no comment. She invoked no pity, and he felt no compassion. The only meaning she had for him was a financial one. Money. More money for borrowed time, lent security, bought love. Suddenly, inexplicably, he had an overwhelming desire not to operate on this woman.

'Are you sure you want this operation, Lady Wesdon?'

'I . . . I wouldn't be here if I didn't, Mr Cranford.'

'Nor would I,' she thought she heard him say.

'I beg your pardon . . . ?'

'I'm afraid you'll have to wait quite a time.'

'I don't mind that. . . .'

He flipped over the pages of the diary until the entries thinned out and eventually ceased, but he continued through weeks of blank, featureless days before he stopped at random.

'Three months on Thursday?'

'Three months . . . That'll be after Ascot. What a bore. Three months really is a time. . . .'

'Time to change your mind.'

'I don't want to change my mind.'

'Does your husband know about this?'

'Yes.'

'And he approves?'

'If I want anything, he agrees.'

'I wonder if he'll agree to my fee?'

'I expect so. What . . . what is your fee?'

He watched her, wondering if by grossly inflating it he could put her off, and wondering why he wanted to. He took the fee, doubled it, and added fifty. Then he pushed it forward between them, like a stake at poker.

'Seven hundred and fifty guineas.'

Her hand came up nervously and fingered her necklace, as if of its own accord gambling two rows of pearls against two up-tilted caress-seeking age-deceiving breasts. To his surprise the hesitation dissolved and the hand dropped on to the desk.

'That'll be quite satisfactory, Mr Cranford.'

Her cards were down: he had won the hand, but he had lost the game, and anger welled up because he couldn't understand why he was always playing it.

'After all, you have a reputation.'

'For overcharging?'

She looked at him levelly.

'For being the best. One always has to pay for that.'

The smile was superior, unforced, but the tone had edged away into the assured key of breeding and condescension. She felt quite at ease for the first time since she had entered the room. It was simply a question of a grasping tradesman who had added an extra sixpence to a bill.

'Lady Wesdon . . . that fee . . .' he began, but she got up and he could only follow her mutely towards the door.

'How is your beautiful wife, Mr Cranford?'

'Very well,' he replied automatically.

'I've never met her, but I do know her brother, Lord Binfield. As a matter of fact it was poor Willy who recommended you to me.'

Recommended like the butcher, the baker, the little dressmaker round the corner, the hand-made shoemaker, the hand-made surgeon who'll fit you like a glove, my dear, costs the earth, darling, but worth every penny. Willy told me, dear little Willy, 'The trouble is, Alex, unless you're born to money, you never know how to spend it.' 'Your father never knew the value of money, Alex. He spent it all, just let it soak away.'

'Goodbye, Mr Cranford. I shall look forward to seeing you in three months' time.'

Dismissal, with no avenue left to re-open negotiations. He walked along the hall with her and saw her down the steps to the pavement. Outside, the morning had lived up to its earlier promise, and the spring sunlight mellowed the fresh paint on the Georgian stucco, making Harley Street seem as if it could live up to its reputation.

Chapter Eight

'REPUTATION? BUT EVIE, my pet, people like us are the only kind who have a reputation. The rest simply don't count.'

Willy double-folded the wafer-thin slice of brown bread and butter until it achieved the dimensions of a thick postage-stamp, then placed it on his tongue and twitched it into his mouth chameleon-fashion. Chewing, he sucked the last Whitstable off its shell, and chased it down noisily with a gulp of champagne.

'You are a disgusting eater, Willy.'

'So was Henry the Eighth.'

The empty circle of shells was removed deftly from in front of him. 'Another dozen, sir?'

'No.'

'Half a dozen?'

'Go away,' snapped Willy, and then belched.

The waiter withdrew imperturbably. Eve sighed. Willy was showing off. It was a destructive process, involving others, but ultimately directed at himself. Memory of Willy spending laborious weeks making a doll's house for her, and her thoughtless exclamation. 'What a funny chimney. It's all crooked.' Savagely he had torn it off the roof, leaving an irreparable ragged hole, and then stumped away across the nursery on his child-size crutches. She drank some wine and made her protest gently, without conviction.

'It's been unfashionable for some time now to be rude to waiters.'

'Was I?' Willy pretended amazement, and patted her hand. 'Never mind, you can increase the wretch's tip.'

He poured some salt on to the table-cloth, dipped a moistened finger in it, and licked off the adherent grains appreciatively, as if he had hit upon some new and strange delicacy.

'From which remarks you will gather, my only darling wonderful sister, that funds are again running low.'

'Willy, you are tiresome. What have you been doing?'

'Special pleasures, debts of honour, an unreasonably importunate tailor, an exquisite piece of majolica, and one or two other items.'

He gave a wave of acquiescence to the hammered sheet of red meat proffered for his approval, before it became a Steak Diane. Eve shook her head.

'I can't let you have a penny till the first of the month.'

'Why not?'

'You know perfectly well why not.'

'What about the joint account?'

'I daren't. Alex isn't a fool.'

'No, but he's a good worker. Quite a little gold-miner in his way, thank God. And after all, I do cultivate the uglies and push them in his direction, so I don't see why . . .'

'Stop it, Willy. You're here to help me. . . .'

'Darling Evie, we're here to help each other.'

The ignited alcohol from the Steak Diane exploded upwards, the lick of flame giving way to a curl of blue smoke an inch from the ornamented ceiling.

'I don't want a repetition of last week.'

Eve noticed she was breaking a piece of Melba toast into unmanageably small fragments.

'There never could be repetition, if you'll do as I say and . . .'

'I . . . I don't want to do that, Willy. Not yet, anyway.'

'The alternative is worse, my pet.'

She didn't answer and he looked at her quickly, trying to keep the anxiety out of his voice.

'You still feel the same about everything, don't you? We've discussed, decided, you and I, Evie, we two . . .'

'Of course, Willy. I feel just the same. I always shall.' Emphatic, sealing off revulsion, fear.

He looked away, and drank some champagne, and said:

63

'I couldn't bear to see you . . . to see it happen to you, darling.'

He put out his hand towards hers again and touched it, reassuring himself by the light physical contact, of the deep, painful bond between them, the scoffed-at unity of twins, the aching jealousy of part of himself torn away, as he had once watched her from an upstairs window, chased into the shrubbery by some beefy boy playmate.

'You're a very special person, Evie.'

Her rognons came and some crisp strips of chicory, and with a repentant reversion to manners, Willy waited till she had taken her first mouthful before he let his knife sink effortlessly through the pepper-flavoured steak.

'You must understand that you married Alex for various reasons,' he began.

'I'm fond of him, Willy.'

'We both are, darling, but you don't sacrifice yourself for fondness. He has no right to expect it.'

'Alex doesn't see it as a sacrifice, and certainly regards it as a right.'

'Has he said that?'

'Not yet. But he will.'

'Put him off, prevaricate, side-step.'

'I can't for ever.'

'You've done it up to now.'

'Now it's more difficult, don't you see? Pretty soon there'll be a terrible explosion. Lately Alex has been so moody and unsettled, and oddly determined. He wanted me to go away this weekend with him to some dreary little pub somewhere . . . just the two of us.'

'God, how awful.' Willy stabbed at his steak distastefully. 'Inglenooks, mutton stews, pewter mugs, bonhomie and all that jazz, I suppose. Really, the sickly respectability of the middle classes makes me puke.' The words came through the food in jerky saliva-wrapped parcels of sound. 'You're not going, are you?'

Eve shook her head. 'I told him you had a party on Saturday; so please, Willy dear, rake everyone in as quickly as you can.'

'But darling, the cost . . .' Willy signalled the waiter irritably to replenish his glass. 'I thought I'd explained. I'm flat. And the lower orders no longer understand the meaning of the term credit. They look at you as if you'd uttered a dirty word.'

Eve reached for her handbag resignedly.

'All right: we'll have to pop something.' She took out the emergency pack she had brought with her, a small blue jeweller's box and pushed it across the table to Willy. 'See what you can do with that.'

She watched him open it and lift up the ring, a square-cut sapphire with hunched diamond shoulders in a continental setting. 'Oh, Alex, what a wonderful present. How very sweet of you, darling. Thank you.' 'You should thank Mrs Sanderson for the bags under her eyes.' And the touch of his hand on her neck, the faultless profile in the mirror, and the adding of another trophy to the collection, rows of sparkling power, to touch and admire, translating the caress into a totally satisfying perpetual tribute, giving all and demanding nothing.

'We'd get much more if we sold it.'

'No! I want it back.'

'But you have so many, Eve. The little doctor would never notice.'

'Willy, do as I ask. I'll redeem it next month.'

Her brother put the ring away, snapped-to the lid of the box, and slipped it into his pocket.

'Christ, why the hell couldn't father realize what a pittance the death duties would leave us with? The truth is, of course, he was a mingy bastard, couldn't bear to lose control of a single shekel.'

'Daddy could be an angel, sometimes.'

'To you. Not to me. I made him feel guilty. Somehow he blamed himself for my affliction. It degraded the family. A blot on the escutcheon and all that. Which is all the more reason why he shouldn't have left us dependent on whoever you married. I know he makes a packet; but Alex is so . . . so nondescript.'

'He's quite an outstanding surgeon, darling.'

'That's not the same thing. He hasn't even a second cousin or a distant aunt who's remotely related to a border-line entry in Debrett. How we endure it all, I sometimes don't know.'

Willy's voice trailed off petulantly. When she didn't reply he began again, trying, but failing, to keep the whine out of the sound.

'Evie, why did you choose Alex? You could have done . . . well, he's not one of us, is he?'

'It doesn't make any difference,' she said. 'To you and me. Nothing ever will. That's the important thing to remember, Willy darling.'

She closed her fingers over his and a waiter removed the plates as another approached the table. His foot touched one of the ivory-handled walking sticks leaning up against the wall. He caught it before it fell and mumbled an apology before addressing Willy with a sheepish grin.

'Coffee, m'lord?'

'What do you bloody well think, you clumsy oaf?' snapped Willy.

Chapter Nine

IN THE ST BEDE'S HOSPITAL dining-room the coffee was dispensed to the resident housemen by a coloured maid from an old wooden ward-trolley. It came ready-mixed with milk, in thick, white graceless cups. At the consultants' smaller table it was given a status tag by way of a Cona, a cream-jug and brown sugar.

Cranford lit his after-lunch cigarette, inhaled, and found pleasure in the action. He observed that he was almost alone now in the habit. There was Dinsley's pipe, and Keble's diminutive apology for a cigar, but otherwise the empty-lipped faces wore the self-righteous, holier-than-thou expressions of the recently converted. Addicts on parole, their relapse rate would be high, and idly he wondered in what order these men of will would fall from grace. He gave Creech two months, Keble six. Berenger was probably cheating already and smoking in the lavatory. Munro would make out, though, through sheer force of native highland stubbornness. As a veteran pipe-smoker Dinsley didn't count. Cranford inhaled again, weighing his own perversity of habit, letting the talk of shop billow round him.

Keble was saying, 'Mortonson claims he gets only a two per cent recurrence rate with his hernia repairs.'

'Just possible, I suppose, with specially selected cases.'

'His aren't. They're all-comers. Every age-group.'

'How big's his series?'

'Over five hundred.'

'Then it's a damn lie.'

Creech, fifty, balding, shovelling the sugar into his cup, making the coffee overflow into the saucer, fearless in an emergency, invaluable at the advanced clearing-station, unbeatable at the 230 yards drive, but irascibly heavy-handed with the five-foot putt or the intricate resection.

'Not a lie, Creech,' laughed Dinsley. 'Just statistical exaggeration.'

The senior physician, bland, wise, sceptical, the doctor in the round, allowing for human failings, never missing the patient for the disease.

'I've read the article. It's quite impressive. The figures speak for themselves.' Berenger, with the safe dependable cliché.

'They speak a damn sight more for the fellow who's compiled them,' Creech assented with begrudging admiration.

'Quite a character, Mortonson,' went on Keble. 'I was his "gyne" H.S. just before the War. He used to get his nurses spread round the theatre, and shell out uterine fibroids at them like a fast bowler with three slips and a silly point.'

Cranford waited for the amusement to subside and then threw in his own anecdote.

'Gynaecological cricket can be fun, but surgical rugger requires greater skill. I remember assisting old Tubby Harworth to remove a huge slippery abdominal cyst. He was fiddling around for ten minutes trying to get a clamp on the pedicle. Just before he succeeded he said in that fruity gargle of his "If I don't get rid of this ball soon, Cranford, someone's going to tackle me".'

Laughter, responsive, immediate, rippling round the table and back to Cranford again, leap-frogging a dead patch centred on Munro, from which he stared across the ruckled table-cloth. Irritated, Cranford asked:

'What's the matter, Munro? Heard it before?'

'No, I'm happy to say.' Plain statement, evenly accented, dry and spiky as summer gorse. 'I realize I'm in a minority, but at the risk of sounding priggish, I don't find it particularly amusing to pretend that medicine's a game, or that suffering can be made an occasion for a cheap joke.'

After-eddy of silence rivetting them momentarily, then dissolving variously into embarrassment, incomprehension, resentment.

Creech recovered first.

'There was no risk about sounding priggish, old boy.'

Keble exhaled noisily.

'Well, unless I'd heard it . . .'

'You should've told him one about a Scotsman,' Creech winked at Cranford.

'Funny thing, sense of humour. I remember . . .' began Berenger.

'I wouldn't, old man, if I were you,' Keble shook his head sadly. 'How high-minded can you get?'

'Wrong word, Keble,' smiled Dinsley. 'Don't you mean single-minded?'

'I think you've put your finger on it,' said Cranford. 'The doctor wasn't so much accusing us of bad taste as issuing a mild rebuke at our lack of dedication, deploring a certain deficiency of honesty in us as professional men. Isn't that right, Munro?'

Munro's colour had risen perceptibly during the derisive barrage following his remark, but he rode Cranford's sarcasm with a determined smile.

'Ay, you could say that.'

'There are worse things in medicine than dishonesty.'

'Such as?' asked Dinsley.

'Carelessness, incompetence, ignorance. They can kill. Dishonesty at worst only makes a profit.'

Munro's cup came down audibly in its saucer, and his voice took on a new animation.

'I'm quite sure, Cranford, in your case, profit is the guiding principle,' he said.

The unexpectedness of the accusation made Cranford laugh.

'It's one of them.'

'If I had my way, money would not be paid for operations whose sole justification is vanity.'

Cranford's hand paused in the movement of putting out his cigarette, visually punctuating the silence which this time was of a different kind. No longer occasioned by one man off-key with his fellows, now it was the silence of an audience watching two men in conflict, anticipating the blows of battle.

Cranford was suddenly shaken by the realization that Munro was looking at him with an unmistakable emotion. This humourless mediocre little pathologist actually despised him. A casual conversation had unwittingly uncovered a deep antagonism. Abruptly laid bare were the bones of censure, of personal attack, unsubtle, offensive. He looked round the table at the other faces turned expectantly in his direction, and the suspicion took shape that in some measure his colleagues were a party to it, watching him, measuring his reaction, waiting for his answer.

He stubbed out the cigarette firmly, compressing his mounting rage into manageable proportions.

'I have an operating list at this hospital this afternoon,' he said evenly. 'Two fenestrations, a sub-mucous resection, and a tonsillectomy. If you think relieving deafness, restoring obstructed breathing, and removing a seat of infection which has already led to chronic ill-health, is vanity, then that's all right. We're talking the same language.'

'I'm not questioning your skill, Cranford. Only your motives for exercising it.'

'Good God, my salary for this appointment is hardly a motive.'

'I don't doubt that.'

'Then why do you think I come here? For the food?'

Munro hesitated. He couldn't withdraw now. He licked his lips and ploughed doggedly on.

'I think you come here as a kind of penance for your fashionable and lucrative practice; it's your lip-service to socialized medicine, in which of course there is no place for cosmetic surgery.'

Cranford could see the venomous self-satisfaction in the pursed lips, and abruptly he lost his temper.

'What the hell do you know about cosmetic surgery or any other for that matter? And what in Heaven makes you think you have a right to criticize what I do, or why I do it?'

As his words tumbled out, Cranford sensed that his raised voice had stopped the conversation at the junior table. Whatever he'd said now in anger would be heard by every houseman in the room, to be repeated to the nurses, enlarged upon, thrown out of context, talked about at the Royal College, and soon dropped inconsequentially in the ears of prospective patients at cocktail parties, another titbit about the notorious Cranford; all of it, in the end, doing him no good. Better to laugh it off, leave it where it was. But he didn't want to leave it where it was, inconclusive, undefended. Damned if he would.

'Listen, Munro,' he went on. 'If I needed to justify what I do, it's simple. People with big ugly noses, with ears that stick out like elephants', people without chins, and overslung lips, go through hell all their lives. Quite often that hell makes them sick people. Most of them have been sick anyway since the first time another child pointed at them and jeered. But unlike other illnesses theirs can't be suffered in privacy. They have to carry their affliction around like a bad advertisement. Well, I try and do something for them. There are others who just wish to look less ugly, less old, because it will make them feel less unhappy. An understandable longing. I try and help them satisfy it. No other justification is needed.'

Cranford paused, his glance defying comment.

'But that isn't the reason I go on with it all. At times it amuses me; at times I get a huge technical satisfaction out of it. But even that isn't enough. I go on doing it because I don't know of any other way to make such a good living.'

He saw the smirk creeping back across Munro's features.

'Where I differ Munro, from people like you, is that I'm not a bloody hypocrite. There is perhaps a moment early on in our careers when we all feel the call of a way of life, full of romanticized self-denial and sacrifice. Precious few doctors retain the ideal, though, except in the sort of bunkum you see on T.V.' Dinsley was an exception; Dinsley still had it. Cranford scanned round the table again. 'Unfortunately too many of us wallow in a fictional aura of spurious single-mindedness. Every time we go into a ward we're absurdly treated either like little tin gods or geniuses. That in itself is reward enough for some.' Berenger preening himself, 'Good morning, Sister.' 'Good morning, Dr Berenger.' 'But in reality, for a hundred reasons the true spark gets swamped, pushed aside, worn down. Other things replace it, other motives sustain us. Ordinary, everyday human things. Drink, gold, the stockmarket, wives, mistresses, children.' Above all, children, he thought. 'You're a fool if you think doctors are special dedicated people. Like lawyers or jockeys, or estate agents or plumbers, they're ordinary, everyday human beings, doing a job.' His gaze swung sharply again to Munro, now playing sardonically with a spoon in the sugar-basin. 'Doing a job, Munro. For money. Like me, like you. To pretend otherwise is to be conceited, muddle-headed, dishonest, vain. Which, as a quite ordinary doctor, Munro, you should try not to be.'

The silence extended expectantly, but when it was clear that Cranford had finished, an embarrassed shuffling developed as chairs were pushed back from the other table with soft muttered references to the time and work to be done. The housemen began to leave the room, and the coloured maid wearing her perpetual grin came in to clear the remains of the baked jam roll and the execrable coffee.

Munro stood up and buttoned the jacket of his suit laboriously, as if wishing to display its off-the-peg misshapenness and the reagent stains on the cuffs.

'You should have been a politician, Cranford,' he said. 'That can pay off handsomely too.' He turned abruptly to Berenger, who was next to him. 'If you're interested in that *post mortem*, laddie, I'm about to do it now.'

Berenger hesitated. He wanted to say something, make some gesture to show Cranford whose side he was on, but he couldn't think of a suitable remark. It would have to be witty, pungent, and bear the earmark of success, sealing their common ground, but it was beyond him, so he laughed and made a feeble awkward gesture with his hand, and then followed Munro out of the door.

'Christ,' exclaimed Keble. 'Of all the bloody nerve. But why?'

'Chip on the shoulder,' said Creech. 'He's always had it. Tried for years to get on a hospital staff as an orthopod. No go, so he switched to pathology. I must say, Cranford, you took it pretty well, considering.'

Cranford felt weary suddenly of the whole episode.

'Munro's all right,' he shrugged. 'He does his job. He's entitled to his opinion.'

'Interesting what you said,' Keble couldn't drop it. He looked at

Creech. 'Tell me, Bob, honestly now, why did you go in for medicine?'

'My father was a G.P. My grandfather, too. He was a student with Lister.'

Keble laughed. 'Proves your point, Alex. If his old man had been a tailor, he'd probably be sewing on buttons instead of sewing up ruptures.'

'Is there much difference?' enquired Dinsley, with an innocent smile. 'What about you, Keble?'

Keble chuckled and got up.

'I just wanted to play rugger. I couldn't get into the varsity, so the best way seemed to be to sign on at St Mary's.'

Creech joined him round the other side of the table, and put a hand on his shoulder. 'I suppose rugger's as good a way as any of learning the rudiments of orthopaedics. Bags of bruises, fractures, and ligamentous strains.' The voices trailed off. Old boys together, the students' songs, the security of a bawdy élite.

When they had gone, Dinsley knocked out his pipe. The maid had disappeared again and he and Cranford were alone in the room. He walked along the side of the table to where Cranford was still sitting.

'Quite a speech, Alex,' he remarked. 'How long has that been boiling up?'

Cranford looked up at the older physician. The eyes had the grey-blue serenity of a man who has resolved his personal conflicts; peaceful, but still wary and objective, like a sailor's after a storm.

'I don't know,' he replied. 'A lot of nonsense signifying nothing.'

'I wouldn't be too sure of that.' He took hold of Cranford's fingers and turned the hands so that the palms faced upwards. 'While you were talking, you were going at these like Lady Macbeth.'

Cranford snatched his hands away instinctively, clenching them, hiding them from the professional scrutiny. Then, recovering, he opened them slowly. He noticed immediately the criss-cross excoriations where, unaware at the time, his nails had broken the surface of the skin.

'Did everyone see what I was doing?'

'I doubt it. They were too absorbed by your eloquence.' Dinsley smiled reassuringly. 'Don't worry. It's safe with me. Let me have a look.'

Dinsley sat down in an empty chair, and this time Cranford let him take his hands without resistance, feeling a certain relief that the secret was sprung. He'd put off seeking a colleague's advice, because to have done so was to admit that the condition was not a passing triviality. Dinsley had saved him the trouble, and Dinsley's opinion should be worth hearing.

'Any lesions elsewhere?'

'No.'

'How long have you had it?'

'Six months. On and off.' Cranford watched the other's expression, but it told him little. 'What do you think?'

'There's nothing specific about it. Could be a contact dermatitis, or an allergy.'

'That's my bet, too,' he said, vaguely disappointed. 'I've tried different soaps. I thought it might be the rubber gloves, or the talc. I've rung the changes on everything. Doesn't make any difference.'

'Ef-cortelan. Things like that any good?'

'Not much. As you can see.'

'Tried something old-fashioned, such as zinc?'

'How can I? I'm scrubbing up practically every day.'

'Is it better at weekends?'

'Yes, I think so. Difficult to tell.'

Dinsley took out his pipe again, and sucked on the empty bowl.

'What are you going to do about it?'

Cranford flexed his fingers a few times, then picked up his cigarette packet. It was empty, and irritably he screwed it up and tossed it on to the table-cloth. He was annoyed now he'd let himself enter into a discussion of the problem. Dinsley hadn't produced much in the way of concrete suggestions.

'Ignore it,' he said. 'And I'd be glad if you'd do the same. I don't want anyone to . . .'

'You shouldn't operate with those hands, Alex,' Dinsley interrupted quietly.

Cranford looked at his watch, pushed his chair back, and got up.

'They happen to be the only ones I've got.'

'I meant don't scrub up for a week or two. See how the skin reacts to a rest. These things can flare up pretty badly. I should . . .'

'Thanks, Dinsley,' he broke in. 'I'll think about it.'

'But, Cranford, it's important not to . . .'

The door closed behind him, cutting off Dinsley's sentence in mid-flight. The old man sat a few moments in thought, then shook his head, put away his empty pipe once more and went out of the room.

The maid came in again from the kitchen. Humming, she began to clear the consultants' table, brushing the crumbs and the crumpled packet lightly into her dustpan.

Chapter Ten

BORN IN THAT arid part of the world where heat and drought, and the pitiful inadequacy of the soil imposes a proud, defiant passivity on the features, Khouri had learnt from boyhood to divine the mood behind the mask, to seek in eyes and hands, in gesture and movement, and in the colour of the voice, the meaning between words, the truth beneath the lie.

While they were changing before the list, donning their cotton singlets, their shapeless linen trousers, and overlarge rubber boots, he had detected a short measure in his chief's usual affability. There was a preoccupation which ignored the casual remark and allowed only the disinterested nod in response to his own observations. During the first fenestration, Cranford's habitual patter while operating was strangely absent, creating in the white-walled, sound-proofed theatre an atmosphere of emergency, of danger, where no danger existed.

The second operation, a sub-mucous resection, was easy, straightforward, the routine removal of a damaged nasal cartilage; but it was carried out with the forcing speed of a life-and-death procedure. Twice Khouri had the retractor he was holding, unnecessarily it seemed to him, adjusted by Cranford. A strained Spencer-Wells forceps was discarded dramatically by a toss on to the floor. A scalpel was rejected with a brusque shake of the head, which flustered the theatre-sister. The instrument handed back as replacement was acknowledged by a grunt of acceptance which intimidated the probationer nurse doing her first week on theatre.

To Khouri's surprise, before the second fenestration Cranford said, 'You do this one on your own. I'll watch.'

Intensely concentrating as he was on the intricate procedure, Khouri was yet aware from time to time of the older man's bulky presence behind him, hands thrust in his trouser-pockets, bunching up the green un-sterile gown below his waist, rocking on his heels, withdrawn yet deceptively observant of every move.

They broke for tea before the tonsillectomy, last because it was the only 'dirty' case. Khouri was pleased with the way the fenestration had gone, but he didn't seek any approving comment or venture any remark to the back of the man who had been his boss and mentor for over a year, and who stood now, staring moodily out of the partly misted panes of the dressing-room window. Khouri poured out a cup of tea and sat at the scrubbed wooden table.

'When does your job end here, Khouri?'

'Another three months, sir.'

'What are your plans after that?'

'I shall go home. To Azadan.'

There was a warm enthusiasm in the reply, eager, anticipatory. His chief turned from the window with an impatient movement.

'Bury yourself, in fact. What a bloody waste.'

Khouri's Arab pride struggled with pleasure at the implied compliment. After a brief contest it came uppermost. What did this rich, successful man understand of waste, of poverty, of the bitter acceptance of disease, widespread, universal, eating away the soul as well as the body?

'We have just built a new hospital,' he said. 'It is not much by your standards, but it is a start. We are a very small country and a very poor one. Later on . . .'

'Later on you could be a top consultant over here, or in the States, anywhere you like.' Cranford sugared his tea and stirred vigorously. 'I wouldn't say this unless I meant it, but in operative ability you're quite outstanding. That fenestration was a text-book classic.'

The remark produced in Khouri a tingling excitement, a delicious glow of achievement, the more so because he believed in the sincerity of the surgeon who had hitherto praised him little, but taught him much. A hard man to please because of his own exacting standards. Khouri repressed with difficulty a smile of pleasure and satisfaction.

'Thank you, sir,' he said formally. 'I am honoured by the compliment.'

'I'm not trying to compliment you,' Cranford snorted. 'I'm making a factual observation. You'll get bogged down in a place like Azadan, doing hack work anyone could do.'

Khouri shrugged.

'Someone has to do it.'

'But you won't have the same opportunities there. . . .'

'Opportunities for what, sir?'

'For . . .'

The other broke off, hesitating, changing his mind, seeking words, rejecting them, discarding others. He drank some tea, and Khouri met

74

Cranford's eyes over the top of the cup. He read appraisal, doubt and, for some reason, hostility. He saw them look away to the plate between them. Cranford picked up a biscuit.

'What do you get out of surgery, Khouri? Why do you do it?'

The question sprang out harshly, aggressively.

'That would take a long while to answer, sir. There are many reasons. I'm not sure which is the most important.'

'Well, you'd better find out, believe me. The discovery can be as important as the reason itself.'

Khouri was troubled by the odd intensity of Cranford's interrogation.

'Excuse me, sir, but I am not understanding you completely. . . .'

'If you suddenly had to give up surgery. Couldn't go on. What then?' Cranford interrupted.

'You mean because of illness . . . ?' He was trying to keep pace with the switches in the trend of the conversation.

'Possibly. Not necessarily. For any reason. What would you do?'

'In this situation you are suggesting, I would still have my hands?'

'Yes. You'd still have your hands.'

Khouri thought hard, noticing Cranford's clenched fingers resting on the table, but he could find no suitable reply. These things could not be considered in the abstract. How could a man tell what he would or would not do in this or that situation?

'I would be very unhappy,' he replied truthfully.

Cranford got up abruptly as if the words had caused offence.

'That's no answer.'

The sister knocked and came through the door to tell them the next case had been brought down and the anaesthetic induction begun. Khouri nodded thanks, and when she had gone he said:

'I am in some difficulty, sir, in deciding the exact point we are discussing.'

'You'd better get on and do that tonsillectomy,' said Cranford brusquely, and began stripping off his singlet. Khouri watched him, puzzled. He stood up.

'You are not finishing the list?'

Cranford disappeared behind the shower-curtain.

'No. It's all yours. You can do it as well as I can. That's what I've got a registrar for, isn't it?'

The hiss of water blocked any reply Khouri could make. There was something wrong, but he couldn't think what it was. Probably in the way he had expressed himself. Often he found himself misunderstood because of some idiom incorrectly used, some word which turned out to have an unsuspected second meaning. Yet he sensed that the unease in the room had no part in him. For which he could be thankful. Operating on his own, he would enjoy the next half-hour without distraction.

He went across the corridor into the scrubbing-up room, his rubber boots making slapping sounds on the washed tiles of the floor.

Chapter Eleven

CRANFORD STOPPED IN the front hall and spoke to the porter.

'My chauffeur will be here at five. Tell him I've gone on. He can pick me up in Harley Street at six-fifteen.'

'Very good, sir.'

At the top of the steps, he put on his hat and gloves. The spring of the morning had lost itself somewhere in the damp grime of the London afternoon. Not yet giving way to fog, the light had a flat uniformity about it, blurring detail and reducing perspective to two dimensions. He felt a plucking at his elbow.

'Can I get a taxi, Mr Cranford?'

The porter had followed him to the entrance and was looking up in deferential enquiry.

'What? No, thank you.'

'Are you walking, sir?'

The surprise in the question, bordering on amazement, irritated Cranford unreasonably. Anything unexpected, anything which deviated a millimetre from the accepted routine, threw these people into consternation.

'I'm going to try,' he said curtly. 'Unusual, isn't it?'

He strode down into the courtyard, leaving the old man gaping after him, but by the time he had reached the main gates he had regretted his rudeness. As he crossed the road and turned up the narrow littered alley which led to Oxford Street, his regret had extended to include his bad humour in the operating theatre, his rough demeanour with Khouri, right back to his outburst against Munro at the lunch table.

Yet in honesty the regret was not for what had been said or done, nor for the feelings of those at the receiving end. It was for the unfavourable distortion of the Cranford image. Little cracks had appeared in the charm-polished surface, the sheen dulled in places, the bloom rubbed away. He felt deeply disturbed by the revelation, but he shied away from delving for its origin. He was loath to peel the fruit for fear it was rotten. Sternly he reminded himself that the purpose of his walk was to do just that.

When he reached the great thoroughfare, the noise of the traffic assaulted his ears and the diesel fumes of the heavy vehicles settled round him like an oppressive pall. The packed pavements made progress a series of stops and starts, sidesteps, and unmannered buffetings. It was so long since he had moved without the screening protection of chauffeur-driven comfort that he had forgotten the energy-sapping struggle of travel by cheaper, less exclusive means.

The teeming rush-hour anthill bustled round him. Animation everywhere, movement, action, lights, noise. Humanity articulate, unafraid, yet strangely satiated, without enthusiasm, joyless. He sought in the expressions some complement to his own uneasiness and thought he glimpsed it here and there. But try as he might he felt no kinship, no common identity. He thought he saw in the faces the same look which he suspected was on his own. A kind of determined evasion. Questions too difficult, answers too complicated, the effort to find them too exhausting, too disturbing, even dangerous. Evasion was easier. Evasion was safer. And evasion paid off. It was visible in the bus-queues of overfed, plump, suburban wives, satisfied, parcel-clutching, forward-looking to the evening's routine with easily-prepared food from the well-stocked 'fridge, and afterwards the universal domestic balm of the 'telly', putting off arguments, softening doubts, and removing the need for conversation, escaping the effort of long-since distasteful and more intimate activity.

Cranford squared his shoulders and thrust his way forcefully across the road in front of the protective traffic-lights. He must cast out evasion for the cunning swindler that it was. The age had been reached when fundamentals had to be reassessed. The world had to do it or else disintegrate. By the same token he, Alexander Cranford, F.R.C.S., had to do it. He couldn't directly help the world, but he could help himself. His responsibility to the one was the extent of his responsibility to the other. The thought was encouraging, but the emotion was short-lived. He felt his resolution, grand and high-sounding though it was, squirming away, refusing his command to bear down on the conundrum of existence.

He noticed he was sweating with the effort of his progress. There was a problem in itself. He was overweight, out of condition, getting flabby. There was never enough time for regular exercise, never time for a whole catalogue of activity, mental, physical, emotional, because of the murderous pressure of work, and more work, leading ever on up the spiral of ambition to what? The Birthday Honours List, the chance, if lucky, of two coronaries, and finally the glowing obituary notice.

He turned up Rathbone Place, grateful for the fewer pedestrians on the pavement. The lessening of impediment encouraged him to shake off his mood of cynicism. No impartial observer would say that the path he had chosen, and had followed with unswerving application, did not lead to rewards which were both great and enviable. In any event, it was too late now to have doubts, nor was it a time to falter and throw away the hard punishing years of effort.

He stopped in the blaze of coloured light from a shopwindow, and took out a cigarette. He lit it and flipped away the match, and then paused before he put on his glove again, his gaze compulsively drawn to the palm of his hand. Dinsley could be right. A break from the end-less stimulus of operating might be the answer. Tissues grew tired, complained if over-used. Yet it was the remedy he least wanted to entertain. He was prepared to make certain concessions, as when he hadn't scrubbed-up for the second fenestration, and had left Khouri to finish the list on his own. Such half-measures had the merit of staying comment, preserving the well-kept secret, but as the cold air whipped up the familiar prickling irritation, he knew his own particular eva-sion, the postponement of decision about his hands, could not be put off much longer.

'Hello, what on earth is the busy, brilliant Mr Cranford doing win-dow-gazing in the middle of the afternoon?'

The unexpected greeting spun him round, making him drop his glove. Quickly, awkwardly he stooped and snatched it up as if it were some guilty clue he had to hide. He raised his hat to the brightly ver-milioned smile, the tweed suit, and the guardee-projected voice, but the action brought no name to mind. She could be one of a thousand women who looked alike, talked alike, wore the same expensive well-made unexciting clothes, the class-symbol of a bogus élite. The surprise was to find one on foot in this unfashionable damp side-street, rather than in her natural habitat thronging the lifts in Harrods.

'No, Alex, you don't remember. It's no use pretending.'

He peered at her intently, wondering if she were a patient, a face he had set in the mould desired, demanded, and paid for.

'I'm sorry . . .'

'Norah Britt. At the Wendells'. New Year's Eve.'

The name flipped up an association, but he couldn't pin it down.

'Yes, of course,' he lied. 'How are you?'

'Exhausted.' She brandished a bulky parcel dolefully. 'I've had to traipse all over here to get this particular set of paints and what have you, for a nephew of mine. Really one has so many birthdays to remember it becomes a full-time occupation.'

Over her shoulder he looked through the window of the shop and noticed for the first time the displays of brushes and tubes of pigment, the cedar-wood palettes, an easel with its white inviting canvas; and he smelt momentarily, vividly, the turpentine as his father thrust a brush into his small podgy hand. 'Now, Alex. There are the paints. There's a spanking blank canvas all to yourself. All you have to do, boy, is paint a picture on it.' Hesitation and, 'But what shall I paint, Daddy?' 'Whatever you like. A green cat with three tails, a gory red sunset, a misty blue mountain, a herd of elephants or just a whole splodge of lovely colour.' 'What would you like me to paint?' 'Never mind about me or anybody else. It's your picture. It's you that matters. Just paint something you really want to paint. Only do what you really want to do. Remember that, Alex. Now then. Off you go.'

'. . . Still, it's much less trouble than having brats of your own, don't you think?'

'No, I don't,' reflexly, coming back to the complaining emptiness of the woman's voice.

'Oh . . . ?' She drawled the word out, inflecting it, inflating it with meaning and pleasurable surmise, letting it modulate without break into an arch chuckle. 'Well, rather Eve than me. By the way, how is she?' She augmented the question with raised pencilled eyebrows. 'Back from Paris safely?'

He nodded, trying again to fit her name to a recollection.

'I'm so glad. And do give her my fondest love. But I'll be seeing her on Saturday, won't I? And you too.'

'Saturday?'

'Your brother-in-law's party,' she gasped.

'Oh, yes. Eve told me about it yesterday.'

'I thought as much. The naughty boy tried to pretend he'd only decided on it this afternoon. He rang just before I came out and implored me to go. Very awkward, but I wouldn't miss one of Willy's orgies for almost *any* prior engagement. You will be there, won't you? I shan't enjoy a minute unless you are.' The lips pouted in mock despair. 'Or will you be stuck in that gruesome operating theatre of yours?'

'I don't know. I'm not sure.'

The words repeated themselves, mocking, distorted, making an echo-chamber of his skull. 'I don't know. I'm not sure,' the distillation of indecision which this importunate woman's frivolous chatter had wrung from him. Indecision about Willy's extravagant parties, about Willy himself, with his pathetic arrogant dependence; about his own hands which at the moment were clamouring for attentive relief; indecision about Eve, his wife, and the unfulfilment of his love for her, lacking the benison of children. 'I don't know. I'm not sure.' Angrily, he trampled on the sentences, blotting them out, and then resolutely set them in reverse, following up his attack until their retreat was a total rout, for indecision was not a basic element of his nature.

'No, I shan't be at Willy's party. Nor will Eve.'

The sudden belligerence, like the aggressive bark of a dog, made her start. But she quickly recovered. She had been used to dogs all her life. Dogs and the worship of them were the nearest her family and friends, and those who might be elevated to friendship, got to the faith of a religion. The deeper the faith, the more elevated the friendship. She smiled and put out her hand fearlessly. The unspoken words were 'Down Rover! Down boy!' but she said 'What a shame. I do hope you'll change your mind, Alex. And if you do, remember next time the name's Norah. Norah Britt.'

She patted his sleeve, turned away, and screamed 'Taxi!' at a passing cab.

Norah Britt. Paris. The unpronounceable doctor. The connexion slotted into place. He hurried after her to where the cab had pulled up. He reached the door before she had closed it. She greeted him with renewed enthusiasm.

'Are we going the same way?'

'No. I've just remembered something. Your doctor in Paris. What's his name? Eve's forgotten it.'

The eyes opened wide under their twin arches.

'She told you about him, did she?'

'Not very much. But I gather he's quite efficient at dealing with dietary indiscretions.'

'Oh, yes,' she said. 'Yes, he is.' Amusement spread across her face. 'Just a minute. I think I have him down in my address book.'

She opened her bag and began searching about inside. The cab-driver made an impatient movement at the delay.

'Damn. It must be in my other croc. I'll look it up when I get home and 'phone it through to Eve.'

'It's not very important. I simply wanted to send him a courtesy note of thanks for looking after her.'

'Ah. Professional etiquette.'

'Something like that.'

'It must be an awful bore at times.' She put her gloved hand over his, which was resting on the window-facing, leaving it there fractionally longer than a casual gesture merited. A fresh gurgle escaped from the vermilion. 'For patients as well as doctors, Doctor.'

Cranford shut the door and stepped back from the kerb as the cab moved on. He turned distastefully away, ignoring her wave of gaiety. Over the years he had been boringly subjected to the coquettish antics of her kind. In the consulting-room they undressed brazenly, removing every stitch when no such total exposure was needed, hoping at best for some familiarity, at worst, some compliment. But it was a spurious bravado. They were fully aware that no doctor, except a complete fool, would risk his livelihood for the doubtful pleasure of a momentary indiscretion. They were as safe as with a priest; but the baring of the flesh had a more tangible excitement than the uncovering of the soul.

Cranford looked at his watch and lengthened his stride, going northwards through the dingier streets of Soho until he reached Mortimer Street, where he turned left, making for Portland Place. He was a big man and he walked with the vaguely shambling, slightly pin-toed gait of the once-trained athlete. He had the muscular physique needed for rowing bow, coupled with the speed required for an opening fast-bowler. Whereas earlier in his walk the effect of the unaccustomed exercise had dismayed him, he found now the tentative complaints of half-forgotten muscles invigorating. He recognized in the sensation its mental counterpart, a feeling of release, which had begun outside the artists' colourman's, and had now developed into a plan of action. Not a complete plan, but one which would take care of the next few days.

At the Bulstrode Clinic he led the sister briskly round his cases, cutting to a minimum, but not eliminating the sociable bedside banter expected of him. There were no serious complaints, no annoying complications. Major Wharton, the previous night's rhinoplasty, was faintly truculent. He had a headache, and disliked the weight of the plaster on his nose. Swift reassurance and a prescription for codeine disposed of the difficulty. Only when he was leaving did Cranford tell the sister casually, almost off-handedly, purposely deflating its importance, that he would be away for a few days. 'An international medical congress, Sister. It means my Tuesday operating list is cancelled, and possibly Thursday's, but I'll let you know.'

'And if you're wanted, Mr Cranford?'

'My registrar at the St Bede's will be on call. Good night, Sister: keep everyone happy.'

81

He left the clinic, walked the two blocks to Harley Street, where he signed his letters and reports, and instructed his secretary to make the necessary postponement of appointments. He rang Khouri and told him what to do. Finally, he put through a call to Shinglestrand.

Bateman was waiting as requested, with the car, at six-fifteen, and as the Bentley weaved expertly through the traffic in the Park, Cranford felt for the first time for many months a glow of exhilaration. It seemed it wasn't so difficult if one grasped the nettle firmly.

When he came into the centrally-heated elegance of the hall, he called out to Eve that he was home on time for a change. He hoped she noticed the warmth of affection in his voice in place of his more usual tired apology for being late. Then he saw the two ivory-handled walking-sticks lying along the top of the chiffonier. He picked them up and put them where they should have been left, inside the cloakroom. Out of sight.

Chapter Twelve

WILLY LOWERED THE 'phone, holding it lightly with his finger-tips, releasing his grip suddenly so that the receiver dropped the last half-inch into place. He used the same movement when putting a pile of chips on zero *manque* and *noir,* his favourite stakes at roulette. He sighed because he was tired of making calls and also, as it occurred to him, because his circumstances made visits to Crockford's sadly infrequent.

'No reply,' he yawned.

'What about Bernard and Dorothy?'

'Out. I'll try again this evening.'

He settled himself back in the silk-upholstered bergère, and watched his sister with pleasure and admiration as she described graceful, complicated arcs of movement with the scent-spray.

'I think you ought to go now, Willy,' she said.

'Why?'

'Alex'll be home soon.'

'Should that worry us?'

'He might be tiresome if he found you in my bedroom.'

'What utter presumption. I'm more closely related to you than he is.'

Eve laughed and put down the spray on the mirror-topped surface in front of her.

'Not in the eyes of the law, darling.'

'Who cares about the law?'

'Alex does. I should hate him to invoke it, and have you banished from our portals.'

Willy snorted contemptuously.

'He'd never dare. Like all his class, he's terrified of scandal. Look at the fuss he made last year when he found out you'd smuggled that Leica through the Customs for me. . . .'

'And the cigarette-case. And the cuff-links,' she reminded him.

'But he never did anything.'

'He made quite a scene.'

'Oh, yes, he threatened and puffed and blowed; but that was as far as he got. Besides, it was all for his benefit, the miserable ingrate. We saved him duty on what he'd already paid out to you, to buy for me.'

Willy chuckled with satisfaction, but the sound went on too long, reminding Eve that such cheap victories were to her brother important battles won against the unkind world, from which, since they were very young, she had tried to protect him. He would be lost without her and yet, paradoxically, she depended on him too, as a mother depends for love on the tyranny of a spoilt child. She crossed the room and turned her back towards him.

'Come on, Willy,' she ordered gently. 'Up you get and do this zip. Then you must go.'

Willy struggled out of the deep chair.

'You're a beast, Evie,' he complained. 'Always trying to shoo me away, aren't you?'

'That's not true.'

He pulled up the metal tag, and deftly fastened the eye-hook above it, caressing her neck as he did so.

'It is. You might at least pretend sometimes you're not ashamed of the family monster.'

'Stop talking nonsense. It's just that . . . well, you and Alex hardly hit it off, do you?'

'And whose fault's that? I've bent over backwards trying to make him feel an equal.'

'Really, Willy. That's the sort of remark which causes trouble between you. Do try and behave. When you don't, it's hell for me. I particularly want to avoid any friction just now. I'm not feeling up to dealing with it.'

She smiled, kissed him, and moved away again, the silk jersey of her dress delineating subtly her body.

'God, you're a dish,' he said.

'You like it?'

'Christ, Alex doesn't deserve you,' he exclaimed. 'No one does. I go stark crazy once in a while when I think . . .'

'Willy, stop it! I had to marry someone, sometime.'

'I know, I know,' he sighed forlornly and hobbled over to the bed, sitting on a corner of it. 'But it's not the same any more. You know what I mean—us. You promised it would be.'

She fitted a diamond clip on the neck-line of the dress, then changed her mind and put it back in the jewel-case.

'You'll always be closer to me than anyone else. You know that,' she reassured him quietly. 'How can it ever be otherwise? We're the same, aren't we?'

'That's a bloody laugh,' retorted Willy. 'Like the one I bet father didn't give when they showed me to him an hour after you. I know exactly the expression there must have been on his stupid military face. The same hard-lipped grimace which he produced when the chestnut gave birth to that stunted foal, remember? He'd like to have said the same thing, too: "Shoot it".'

'Shut up, Willy.'

'But he daren't because of mother. And when she died he'd still have farmed me out somewhere abroad if you hadn't cried like mad for me.'

'Father's dead, Willy. Please don't go on. He can't hurt you any more.'

Willy stood up and taking support from her arm, walked towards the door.

'Sorry, darling,' he smiled. 'But I have to indulge my little outbursts of self-pity with you. I can't with anyone else.' He kissed the top of her shoulder. 'God, you look fabulous,' he repeated. 'Who cares about me?'

'I do.'

Eve opened the door as the 'phone rang. She went back and lifted the receiver, but before she could speak she heard Cranford's voice on the living-room extension. She covered the mouthpiece.

'It's Alex. He's back.'

She signalled urgently to her brother to go. He made an elaborate shrug of indifference, but started off through the doorway. Eve lowered the 'phone carefully so as to minimize the tell-tale click of re-

84

placement, but the unmistakable distortion of a female voice through the instrument tugged at her curiosity, and she raised it again.

'Good of you to ring. You've found the address?' she heard Cranford ask.

'Yes . . . yes, I think so . . .' said the voice.

She recognized it immediately. Norah Britt. Ringing Alex?

'Good. Hold on, I'll get something to write on.'

She listened to the sound of the receiver being laid on the table. The voice continued.

'Isn't Eve there . . . ?'

'Yes I am, Norah,' she whispered forcefully. 'What the hell are you up to?'

She heard the intake of breath at the other end of the line before the recovering gurgle.

'Eve, darling, how are you?'

'Ring off, Norah, and call me straight back.'

'But, darling . . .'

'Ring off!'

There was a pause and then a click and then Cranford again.

'I have it now. Go ahead . . . Hello . . . ? Hello, are you there . . . ?'

She heard him rattle the connexion bar, curse, and timed her movement so that they both replaced their instruments at the same moment. She noticed her hand was trembling slightly as it hovered over the 'phone, waiting for it to ring. She let the bell have two bursts and then snatched it up again.

'Hello?'

'Eve?'

'Yes?'

'Norah.'

'Hello, Norah. Nice to hear from you.'

Cranford's voice broke in.

'Hello?'

'Hello, darling. It's for me. Alex, give Willy a drink, will you? He should just have made the bottom of the stairs by now. I've been showing him some of the things I brought back from Paris,' she poured out glibly, and sat down with relief when the receiver dropped back in place.

'Well, Norah dear, you'd better start explaining,' she began.

The reply tumbled out excitedly, breathlessly.

'It was all too awkward, darling. I met Alex in the street quite by chance, and out of the blue he asked me for the name of, well, you

85

know who. I hadn't a clue what you'd told him or what he knew so I dithered a bit and said I'd look up the address and ring it through. I could have expired when he answered the 'phone himself just now.'

'I'm glad I picked it up,' Eve observed, coldly.

'But, darling, I'd never have let on. You know that. How did he find out you'd been to a doctor, anyway?'

'I looked pretty wan last night when he met me at the airport. Alex doesn't miss much like that. I had to say something.'

'How frightful. What are you going to do now?' The anticipatory pleasure of scandal in the question was barely hidden.

'I don't know,' replied Eve, and began to feel a deep uneasiness as various solutions rapidly presented themselves, only to be rejected as too unconvincing, devious, dangerous. The burden of deceit was not so much the guilt of it, as the demands it made on ingenuity, the strain it exerted on memory, the wearing toll it took of energy, which had to bolster it up here, plug a leak there, while all the time its false structure grew fresh subterfuges, sprouted new lies, until, teetering on the edge, the whole worm-eaten edifice seemed ready to crash down.

'I'll think of something.' She tried to impose an off-hand lightness into her voice as if by so doing the sound itself would reassure her, 'It'll be all right. Provided you don't throw out mischievous double-edged hints, when you see him on Saturday.'

'Darling, I ought to resent that,' Norah giggled back. 'It would be absolutely terrifying if he found out. Being a surgeon he'd probably cut you to pieces.'

The joke had a sick mirthless underslant which flicked at the place in Eve's mind where she kept a bundle of fears, tied and labelled, like letters hidden in a drawer, always painful to re-read, but impossible to throw away. There was the fear which had led her to Paris for an abortion, because even the mere contemplation of conception filled her with nausea and horror, making her shrink from its ultimate pain and deforming inevitability; the fear that there must be some terrible flaw in her personality because she could not, like other women, surround the revolting procedure of birth with an aura of romantic fulfilment; the newer fear of Alex making love to her because never again, after what had happened, could she trust the defences she had used; never again rely on the assurance of infallibility in this or that design of cap or diaphragm, this or that brand of pill. Nothing seemed to work with her. Nothing was really safe, which all led up to the fear that ultimately Alex would demand, with all reasonability on his side, that she have a child; the fear of his inevitable rage at her refusal; the fear of what he might do if he discovered he had already been cheated.

Norah Britt's voice jabbed at her ear.

'Anyway, Eve, don't worry. I shan't be seeing either of you on Saturday.'

'Oh, can't you come? Willy said . . .'

'Not me. You, darling.'

'What nonsense. Of course we shall be there.'

'Not according to your husband.' The amusement bubbled along the line. 'Really, Eve, you and Alex ought to tell each other things sometimes. I'm sure you'd find life much less complicated.'

'But much less interesting.' Quickly, defensively while she sought for the reason for his change of mind. 'I expect we have to go to some medical dinner he's been roped in for.' But she knew that wasn't the answer. Alex detested such functions. 'Did he tell you why, by any chance?' she said, putting a casual lilt to the question with difficulty.

'No, darling. And I didn't like to ask. As a matter of fact he sounded rather, well, madly sinister, if you know what I mean.'

The word, flippant, conversational, inexplicably created ripples of uneasiness, which gained amplitude until they lapped against her as waves of apprehension, making her feel suddenly cold in the warm softly-lit scented bedroom.

'Hello? . . . Eve . . . ? Are you still there?' squeaked the voice in her hand.

'I must go now, Norah,' she said and put the receiver down abruptly, pushing the 'phone away from her as though the instrument itself was the cause of her mounting anxiety.

She shivered and then sat a moment, stuffing the docketed fears back in their drawer, summoning her wits and courage to aid her in the task. She stood up and looked in the mirror, mutely beseeching its reflective mantle of youth and beauty to warm her again and instil confidence. The glass discharged its duty with adulation, so that her poise and composure had completely returned by the time she had reached the end of the passage.

Unhurriedly, gracefully, she walked towards the sound of the male voices down the elegant curving staircase.

Chapter Thirteen

'IT'S ALL A matter of taste, my dear Alex. You're either born with it or you're not. You can collect objects of splendour, surround yourself with art-treasures, even buy a beautiful woman, but they'll none of them do anything for you if you're a philistine at heart. The situation is universally commonplace; the self-made man confusing possession with culture. Once established you can never eradicate the fish and chips mentality.'

Cranford let the prattling dissertation, with its false premises, erroneous conclusions, and mannered delivery, flow over him without comment. He could shoot the argument full of holes in a few seconds, but the effort would be pointless, in a way, cruel. Life had dealt Willy two devastatingly bad cards: a title without riches, and a crippling deformity. The combination was overwhelming. The pox Britannica with knobs on. Both were incurable.

'Another Martini, Willy?' he said.

'Yes. You make them quite professionally, Alex. If I owned a restaurant, I should put you behind the bar.'

Ignoring the barb of condescension in the praise, Cranford picked up the mixing-glass from its bed of ice. But for Eve, he would never submit in silence to such wearisome provocation. As it was he often wondered at his restraint. He walked over to the couch, where Willy lay sprawled in exaggerated relaxation, a posture which proclaimed a message, plain and unequivocal. 'Not everyone can boast a peer as a brother-in-law. Those who can should be grateful for the privilege.' Willy edged his glass forward, and when Cranford had poured the drink, he sipped at it superciliously.

'Admirable,' he observed. 'And you serve it so nicely.'

'I'd love one too, Alex.' Eve closed the doors behind her and, smiling serenely, came over to them. 'You're home early, darling. Lovely surprise.' She kissed Cranford lightly, pushed Willy's legs off the couch and sat down beside him. 'How did you manage it?'

'I had the sudden notion I'd done enough. So I came home,' Cranford replied, and began making some more martinis.

88

'Haven't you heard, Evie? Alex has finished with surgery. Chucking it up.'

The piece of ice Cranford was holding shot out of the tongs and splashed into the mixer.

'What gives you that idea?' he jerked out; but the frivolous answer reassured him.

'We're going into a restaurant partnership,' announced Willy. 'Nothing spectacular. Small club membership. I shall supervise the cuisine, while Alex serves the drinks. Of course he'll also be responsible for sharpening the knives and carving the joints, so as not to waste entirely the skills of his old trade.'

'What fun,' laughed Eve. 'Can I put on black fishnet stockings and kinky boots and sell cigarettes and fluffy dogs from a tray?'

'Of course, darling.' Willy patted her thigh. 'Alex'll be useful again there. He can treat your bruises.'

'What bruises?'

'Where all the filthy businessmen will pinch you.'

'I shan't allow that.'

'You must, Evie. It's what they'll really come for. We'll charge them a pound a pinch.'

'Make it five.'

'Too much.'

'I shall strike.'

'All right. Five. That'll keep it exclusive.'

'What name do we give the place?'

'How about "The Surgeon's Rest"?'

'Sounds like a pub.'

'Not if it's spelt Rest. with a full stop. That'll show there's food as well as drink.'

'Too subtle for our sort of customer. Besides, I'm the main attraction, not the food.'

'Very well. We'll call it "Eve's Buttock". And advertise it "Where Top People find the Absolute Bottom".'

They dissolved into laughter. Cranford turned and watched them. Completely absorbed in each other, and the infinitely variable game of 'Let's pretend', their childlike glee was unselfconscious, oblivious of his presence. That he was vaguely the butt of their joke was forgotten in the satisfaction of their intimate pleasure. As he stood, holding the cold-frosted glass in his hand, he saw them as they must have been as children, playing together in the nursery on wet winter afternoons. Eve in a pretty flowered dress, her golden hair combed out and hanging below her shoulders. Willy, in shorts secured with a striped snake-buckle belt, accepting with unconcern, at that age, the special boots for his talipes. Eve, bewitching, with the sure promise of the beauty to come, the dominant of the two, but protective and tender. Willy, mischievous, a bright little fellow, happy, with no hint of later bitterness, as yet mentally unmaimed by the world outside the rain-streaked window. Both of them creating inside their own affectionate secret universe, which ever after would bind them closely.

The laughter subsided and they were talking again, but he didn't hear what was said. Cranford had the uncomfortable fleeting sensation of being lost, like waking from an anaesthetic and finding familiar faces unnameable and oddly menacing. His wife was there, but he didn't know her. This elegant room was his own but strangely unrecognizable; his place in it bewilderingly inexplicable. Then the scene came into focus and he saw that Eve was scribbling on the pad where he had left it by the 'phone. He went over and put the martini in front of her.

She took the glass eagerly and swallowed most of the drink, closing her eyes and making a sound of satisfaction. Then she ripped off the top sheet from the pad and handed it to him. Guarded truth, freely given, was often the best defence. Cranford looked at the slip with a Paris address on it.

'Kurt Christencrendler?'

Willy sat up.

'Who?'

Eve gave her brother a reassuring glance and then smiled disarmingly at Cranford.

'I believe that's the name you wanted from Norah Britt.'

'Was that her again on the 'phone?'

'Yes. Her first call was cut off.' Eve noticed he was briefly disconcerted and pressed her advantage quickly. 'I hope Norah's spelt it out properly. It sounds vaguely like the little doctor who came round to the hotel, but I couldn't swear to it,' she said, deliberately casting doubt on the information. Willy picked up the stratagem.

'Norah's a sweetie, but a complete scatterbrain,' he laughed. 'It could easily be the name of her fortune-teller, or furrier.'

Eve looked gratefully over her glass. Cranford's shrug, as he folded the paper and slipped it into his wallet, seemed rewarding. His reply destroyed the illusion.

'I can easily check the name in the French Medical List,' he said, and went back for his own drink.

Willy was staring at her questioningly. She pressed her knee against him. It didn't matter. She intended additional precautions anyway.

She finished her martini calmly, and then tested out her suspicion against the other piece of information Norah had given her.

'Poor Norah. Always getting hold of the wrong end of the stick. She's under the impression, Alex, that you told her we wouldn't be at Willy's on Saturday.'

Cranford picked up a cigarette and lit it.

'Quite right. We shan't.'

'What! Why not?' Willy exclaimed.

'We're going away.'

She saw Cranford looking at her, gauging her reaction, and the warm smile sent a chill of apprehension across her skin.

'That's the weekend after next, darling. Not this.'

'It was, but it occurred to me that we owe ourselves more than a weekend. So I made a snap decision.' He flicked off some ash into the fire. 'Spontaneity gives a certain extra lift to anticipation. I must say I'm looking forward to it.'

'Yes, of course, Alex, but . . .'

'Charming, delightful, I'm sure,' Willy tried to rescue her. 'But what about me? The arrangements are all made, people invited. . . .'

'You don't have to cancel anything because we won't be there,' said Cranford.

'Really, Alex. Sometimes I despair of your social sense. The whole party's impossible without Eve. There must be a hostess. I need her.'

'Sorry, Willy. So do I.'

Cranford took a drink, put his glass on the chimney-piece, and stood with his back to the fire. A log slumped in the grate behind him, sending up a shower of sparks. Eve cut into the lengthening pause.

'Perhaps I could join you, Alex, on Sunday. How would that be?'

Cranford shook his head.

'Get Norah to do the honours. She's unattached, I gather, at the moment.'

'But that isn't the point . . .' Willy objected with bleating emphasis.

Cranford shrugged irritably.

'You can have another wretched party later on, can't you?' Then he said to Eve, 'We'll go tomorrow. It's all fixed up. Officially I've left for an international conference. Only Khouri knows where I shall be. Otherwise the damn 'phone would spoil everything.' He turned back to Willy. 'You see, I've made my arrangements too.'

'With rather peculiar haste by the sound of it. What's happened? All your patients died?'

Cranford measured the petulant insolence in Willy's expression. It was hard to resist the temptation to wipe it off his features with one simple satisfying action. He wondered if it was charity or disgust which on other occasions had deterred him. But he suspected it was the sheer inequality of the contest, or perhaps because the two of them, sitting there on the couch in front of him, looked so alike. He was conscious as well of the pathetic consequences of the microscopic fault in one chromosome whose untainted pair had given the flawless beauty of Eve. He thrust his hands in his pockets, ignoring the increasing urge to scratch them, and said:

'I should be interested to know, Willy, how you square that remark with your earlier observations on good taste.'

Willy ignored the gibe.

'Eve, darling, you want to come to my party, don't you?'

'You know I do, but . . .'

'Then there's no more to be said.'

'Oh, isn't there . . . ?'

'My dear Alex, even in this plebeian day and age, you must try and remember that a certain class still exists where the conventions of society are observed. I asked her first. She accepted. My claim on Eve, therefore, takes precedence.'

'You've no claim on Eve, whatsoever.'

'He *is* my brother, Alex.'

'And you're my wife. And it's about time Willy understood that.'

'He does. Don't you Willy?'

'Unlike his, my time is precious,' Cranford went on. 'With some difficulty I've managed to arrange this little break for us. I'm not going to have it altered or postponed because of a quite unimportant gathering of extremely boring people.'

'My parties are always important,' Willy shouted indignantly. 'And how dare you say my friends are boring?'

'I've met some of them.'

'You're glad enough to have their custom.'

'Good God,' said Cranford. 'From the size of my waiting list, it's the other way round.'

He pushed his anger back, refusing to let Willy's effrontery pitch him into a rage which would overspill into the next day and the important days after. He smiled at Eve, and said:

'If you want the truth, Eve, it'll be quite wonderful not to see a patient or a nurse or anyone for a few days. Except you.'

Willy sensed his sister respond to the simple confession of affection. A sickening disgust burnt into the back of his throat.

'If you want the truth, Alex,' he sneered, 'Eve will be bored to ob-

92

livion with just you, at your folksy little pub, or wherever you're taking her.'

'Willy . . .' Eve stood up.

Cranford smacked his glass down and swung round.

'Now listen to me, Willy. I've put up with a lot from you one way and another. If my wife weren't your sister, I wouldn't suffer your presence for longer than I could show you the door. . . .'

'Alex, it's all right. Of course I'll come tomorrow. . . .'

Eve put a hand on his arm, but he brushed it aside, continuing at Willy.

'You drift in here whenever you please, loll about drinking my liquor, talk down to me with your precious condescension, and expect me to be glad of the privilege. . . .'

'So you should be,' bleated Willy, edging back on the couch. 'Our family is one of the oldest in the country. . . .'

'Your family?' Cranford snorted. 'What kind of a specimen has it produced in you?'

Willy's face puckered in disbelief. He gestured ineffectually with his hand towards Eve.

'Don't let him speak to me like this,' he implored her.

'It's time someone did.'

'Alex, he can't help being . . .'

'A cripple? Of course he can't,' shouted Cranford. 'But there are thousands worse than he is. All decent people, making the best of it, most of them doing useful jobs. They can't help it either; Willy can't help it. But he can help being an idle, arrogant, sponging, insufferable snob.'

'Evie! Stop him!' shrieked Willy, and flung himself backwards on the cushions, rolling his head from side to side.

Cranford walked over to the couch.

'Get up,' he ordered.

Eve ran after him, pulling at his sleeve.

'You can't . . . please, Alex . . .'

'Don't worry,' said Cranford. 'I'm not going to hit him.' He looked down at Willy, whose eyes were shut tight, took hold of his coat collar, and pulled him up into a sitting position. 'Cold water is usually more effective with hysterics.'

Willy flinched and opened his eyes.

'I shall scream,' he said.

The pathetic hopelessness of the threat suddenly drained all Cranford's anger out of him. Poor sod, he thought; and letting go of Willy's collar, walked back to the fire and finished his drink.

'I think it might be wise if we didn't see each other for a time, Willy, don't you?' he said quietly.

Willy sat rigid, clenching his jaws, staring in front of him. Cranford stood a moment, undecided. Then he went back to the couch where Eve was still standing, and kissed her on the cheek.

'I put his sticks in the cloakroom. Bateman'll drive him home,' he said.

He walked out into the hall, called for the car to be brought round, and went upstairs to deal with the torture in his hands.

Willy's face was ashen, and as she coaxed him to his feet Eve felt the quivering impotent fury in his body. He muttered and spoke disjointedly, like a man sentenced, trying to grasp the reality of the gallows.

'Kicked me out. Me. Your brother. Did you hear what he called me? He can't do that. I could kill him, Evie. Kill him.'

'No, Willy, no,' she said softly, putting her arm round him, helping him towards the hall.

'He's a barbarian, Evie, your husband. A savage. Not safe to be near. You're not safe with him. You know that? Look what he did just now.'

'Willy,' she said, smiling and straightening his tie. 'He didn't touch you.' She left him standing by the chiffonier and fetched his sticks from the cloakroom.

'I shall never forget what he said to me. Never,' continued Willy.

'Well, you did provoke him. I've asked you not to, but you go on. . . .'

'*I* provoked *him*? That's rich. Very rich,' Willy stumped indignantly away towards the door. She followed him, wanting to soften the loneliness and despair she knew he would feel when he had gone.

'Darling, try not to brood while I'm away,' she said. 'When we get back, I'll . . .'

Willy turned round in amazement.

'You're not going with him? After this?'

Eve opened the door and the frosty air touched her bare arms.

'After this, I have to, Willy,' she sighed. 'If you hadn't . . .'

Willy caught hold of her hand.

'Don't go, Evie. Leave him.' He glanced down the flight of stone steps to the Bentley. Bateman saluted and started up towards them. 'Come with me now. We can get money from somewhere. He's no good to you, Evie. You can marry someone else.'

She looked at him, and laughed indulgently.

'Who? You?'

Willy's face suddenly crumpled and he turned away.

'I didn't mean that, darling . . . I . . .' she said.

'Mind the step, sir,' said Bateman, and helped him down to the car. Willy didn't look back, nor did he return her wave. The car made a wide circle and sped away down the drive.

She closed the door and stood leaning against it, consciously telling herself to keep calm and clear-headed and unafraid. Now, tonight, tomorrow, and for however long was necessary. She sought assurance from the warmth and light of the house which was all about her. Distantly, where Mrs Bateman would be executing to perfection her orders for dinner, came the soft background music of the kitchen radio. Tray-bearing with used glasses and an ashtray, Rose crossed the hall from the living-room without noticing her, and silently melted out of sight. Gradually the luxuried, pampered comfort took hold of her nerves, until at length she felt relaxed and alert and purposive.

She went to the foot of the stairs and listened for the muffled sound from above of water gushing from a faucet into a bath. Satisfied, she went into the living-room, picked up the 'phone, and asked the operator for a Paris number.

Chapter Fourteen

BY ELEVEN-THIRTY in the morning they were beyond Ipswich, and making for that flat tongue of the Suffolk coast between Aldeburgh and Harwich. Cranford had suggested they went in Eve's Mercedes instead of the Bentley. He wanted her to drive, to involve her as an active partner in the expedition, rather than take her as a reluctant passenger. She had acceped the assignment without argument. Neither of them had made reference to the tensions of the previous evening, and the journey began, if not on a note of bubbling enthusiasm, at least on one of acceptable neutrality. It seemed, by tacit agreement, they were both on their best behaviour.

With every mile covered, Cranford's mood lightened. Now, as they sped through the spring-green acres of pasture-land, interspersed with fields of dark, fertile, arable earth, the road undulating between lowdyked hedges tufted with embryo leaves, it made a first tentative breakthrough into optimism.

He allowed himself a proprietary sideways glance at his wife's classically proportioned profile: straight chiselled nose, high sculptured cheeks, lips full-painted, chin firm-tilted. He had first seen it on the front of a glossy fashion magazine brought to him by a patient with the formidable and impossible demand, 'Make me look like that, Mr Cranford, and I'll kiss you.' 'Look like that, and I'll kiss *you*,' he had replied with doubtful discretion, and somehow the remark had been relayed until, a few months later, when they had first met at a dinner-party, Eve had asked him, with amusement, when he intended to carry out his threat. He had done so the following week and from then on, in spite of the familiarity of two years of marriage with all its off-guard moments, her features had never failed to cast over him their initial electrifying spell.

In all her varied garbs and roles—the gracious hostess, the gay mischievous guest, the dutiful wife, the glamorous unattainable model—her looks gave to them a certain quality of perfection seldom encountered. Now she was playing the part of the dream-girl, the super blonde in the super sports-car; wind-teased headscarf, Kashmir sweater, provocative dark glasses. Against the background of a fine day, blue sky, and time to be together, it was a prescription for happiness. The imagery was persuasive, and for the present Cranford was prepared to let it persuade him.

'This part of the country hasn't changed for a hundred years or more,' he observed. 'No new towns, no industry, no fast new roads. Just the old ones leading to nowhere.'

Eve pulled up at an unprotected cross-roads and quizzed the signpost.

'Thursday Street, Grobblegock, Nightshade Hill,' she read out. 'Which would you like?'

'Straight on.'

'How do you know?'

'Instinct.'

She returned his smile agreeably and the car shot ahead. Soon they had to cut down speed as the hedges edged in closer and the bends became sharp and unpredictable. Because of the flatness of the landscape there were no distant glimpses of the coastline to indicate they were near to it but presently, when the road escaped from a spinney, Cranford sniffed the air appreciatively.

'Smell it?'

'What?'

96

'The sea. Three miles and we'll be there.'

With increasing awareness Eve noticed that the surrounding countryside had taken on a bleak and derelict character. The trees thinned out, to be replaced by wind-bent thorn bushes, and the fields lost their demarcations in favour of areas of rough, springy turf, and patches of salt-marsh. The sky rose up, dominant with billowing cumulus, reducing the earth below it to a narrow ochre strip, as in a John Crome or Arnesby Brown. Apart from a farmer's cart and a boy on a bicycle they hadn't seen any traffic for ten minutes. Cranford sensed her uneasiness and anticipated her question.

'Last time I was here it was dark with a thick sea-mist. But I found the place all right,' he laughed reassuringly. 'In truth I wasn't really looking for it. Ran right into it might be more accurate. I thought I was on the outskirts of Colchester.'

'So much for instinct,' remarked Eve.

'Turn right at the next fork.'

She followed the instruction obediently. After a hundred yards the car wheels set up a brief hollow pounding as they crossed an iron bridge over a small tidal inlet. On the other side the road climbed up a gentle gradient to a low bluff.

'There it is,' exclaimed Cranford. 'The martello tower. Make straight for it and we'll park for a few minutes.'

The road ran level for half a mile, and then angled abruptly a few yards from the old stone cylinder, one of many dotted around the island, built as a defence-post against Napoleon's flat-bottomed barges. As in 1940, the men who had looked out from it across the grey waste of water a century and a half ago had taken their turn on guard, grumbled and joked, played cards, talked of beer, leave and women. But the enemy never came, and when the danger was over, they went back to their homes, leaving the gulls to cry unheeded warnings over the damp windswept English marshes.

Cranford got out and, taking Eve's hand, led her up the grass-covered bank to the base of the tower. Only then did the sea come into view, the thump of the breakers bursting upon them, punctuating the long, sighing exclamation of the shingle, as the savage undertow sucked it back for mile on mile up the bare featureless coast.

Eve gazed at the scene, first with dismay, and then with frank disbelief. Surely this dreary deserted stretch of pebbles and uninviting salt-water couldn't be the place he had brought her to? She looked with puzzlement at Cranford, eyes narrowed against the wind, his glance ranging back and forth, his expression, incredibly, one of boyish enthusiasm.

'Well, what do you think of it?' he shouted.

She searched vainly once again the expanse of white horses galloping to the horizon, the steeply shelving bank of a myriad smooth round stones, the weathered surface of the disused watch-tower, for some redeeming feature.

'I think it's . . . quite frighteningly awful,' she answered.

To her surprise, he roared with laughter.

'That's what I knew you'd say.'

'Do *you* like it?'

He took her arm and, pointing, turned her with him, as his finger described a complete circle around them.

'Look, Eve, no boats, no traffic, no smart restaurants; no dim-lit night-clubs, no romanticized expensive surroundings, no babble of sophisticated boredom. No people. Nothing. No one.' He took hold of her shoulders firmly, without roughness, and pulled her towards him. 'Except you and me.' He lifted her up on to her toes, until her face was close to his. 'Which is why,' he said, his voice suddenly thick with a tenderness he had no wish to disguise, 'I could grow to like this Godforsaken place more than anywhere in the world.'

The obvious sincerity of his confession moved her. Passively at first, she let him kiss her, his tongue finding hers, filling her mouth, her throat, her stomach, the whole of her, until at length, unbidden, her body responded. Then a white bird screamed above, stabbing her with awareness of the hardened pressure against her belly, making her break from his embrace.

'Eve . . . !'

She saw his look of resentment and quickly, lest it change to anger, turned her compulsive movement of escape into a coquettish gesture of propriety.

'Really, darling. There may not be any people about, but what will the gulls think?'

Cranford stooped and picked up a pebble.

'Observant creatures,' he said. 'You can't fool them either. On present showing, they won't mistake us for lovers.'

He flung the stone as hard as he could with a low flat trajectory. It cleared the first wave, bounced twice, and then lost itself in the green underflank of an oncoming breaker.

'Where's the hotel?' she asked.

He pointed to where the beach turned back towards the marshes.

'It's about half a mile away. You can't see it from here because the shingle further down is piled up much higher.'

'Oh,' she said, and tried unsuccessfully to make the word sound as if, because the shingle was in the way, everything on the other side of it was wonderful.

'I've an awful feeling I'm going to hate that too.'

'You haven't seen it yet,' he retorted.

They walked back against the wind towards the martello tower. It was going to be worse than her most pessimistic imaginings. Urgently she tried to invent some excuse, at this late stage, not to stay, to get back home, where evasions were so much easier to arrange. Cranford supported her elbow as they climbed down the bank to the car. And then, because she looked bewildered and unprotected, he was suddenly ashamed of his ill-humour.

'You'll be quite comfortable, Eve,' he said. 'I've organized a few special extras for you. You might even enjoy it.'

'I just can't imagine what we're going to find to do down here,' she complained.

'We've a whole lot of things to talk about.'

'Surely we can talk just as well at home.'

'But we never do, Eve.'

Round the top of the tower the gulls were spinning like flakes of coconut in a child's snowstorm ball.

'I don't have to be back for several days. A week. Longer even,' he said.

The time stretched away like a long harsh sentence. She struggled against it instinctively.

'But won't that be bad for your practice?'

'Possibly,' he said. 'But other things could be worse.'

'What sort of things?'

He glanced down at his hands. He was tempted to tell her about them, to explain that to give them a rest was why he had been forced to take this time off now, and not later. But he didn't, because that wasn't the whole of the truth. The other side of the coin, her side, was important too. Perhaps more so.

'Things like our so-called home over the last few weeks,' he said.

'What's wrong with our home?'

'Nothing on the surface. It's elegant, it's beautifully run, the service is quiet and unobtrusive. People come and go, admire it, covet it, use it, or jealously run it down. But it doesn't seem to have anything to do with us. Lately we've been like two guests, passing the time of day when we've happened to cross on the stairs.'

'But, Alex, you're so busy . . . I've lots of friends. . . .'

'I'm not busy down here. Down here you've no friends. Down here

99

none of these unimportant things can come between us,' Cranford smiled at her. Her expression was serious and withdrawn and he wanted it to be gay and enthusiastic. He put his arm round her shoulders, and turned her face towards him.

'Darling, almost since our wedding, as people, we've been swamped somehow by a surfeit of civilized living. Lately it's made me disgruntled and irritable with you, with my work, with everything. I want us to be together without all the veneer and the trappings.' He made a vague, encompassing gesture with his arm, 'I want to give the earth and the sea and the sky a chance to work on us. Will you let them, Eve? For a few days? Or does that sound odd and perverse? Or simply square?'

Eve shook her head, wondering how to resolve the half of her which agreed, understood and went out to him, with the other half which cringed away, fearful of the implication.

He opened the car door and, as if on cue, the sun escaped from a dark bulk of cloud, flooding the tower and the shingle and the bright cellulose of the Mercedes with a tempting brilliance in advance of the season. Cranford looked up at the sky and purposefully shut the door again.

'Now I'm going to be plain eccentric,' he said.

He went round to the boot and took out a small canvas bag. Then he ran up the bank with it.

'What are you going to do?' she shouted.

'Come and find out,' he called back and disappeared into the martello tower through a broken part of the wall on the landward side. Burdened with heavy misgiving, Eve made her way dejectedly up the slope. Cranford came out of the tower as she reached the top. She looked at his brawny swimming-trunked figure incredulously.

'Alex! You're not seriously going to swim, are you?'

'Well I haven't put these on just to give you a thrill,' he said.

'In this weather? In that sea? You must be mad.'

'Looks worse than it is.'

'But why? There can't be enjoyment in it.'

'Oh yes there can,' he said. 'The enjoyment of finding out if my body can still do what I tell it.' He kissed her on the cheek. 'Or perhaps I feel it's necessary sometimes for a forty-year-old man to show off to his twenty-three-year-old wife.'

The shingle made short explosive crunches, stinging his bare feet as he ran down the steep sloping beach, until the sound was lost in the hiss of the foam-crescents which swirled round his ankles at the water's edge. She watched him wade a couple of steps, hesitate briefly when a low wave slapped round his thighs, and then plunge under the creaming summit of the first eight-footer. Seconds later he surfaced past the next crest and she saw him swimming vigorously away from the shore in the grey trough beyond.

Cranford turned on his back to take a breather as the initial numbing shock of the April North Sea relinquished its hold. The swell lifted him up and he picked out her slim figure, diminutive, by the stone pepper-pot building. He raised his arm and glimpsed her answering signal before a bubbling comber thrust its way under him, and sluiced him down again into the hollow behind it, cutting her off from view. He felt oddly triumphant and, before the cold could get a real grip, he rolled over and with immense satisfaction settled down to an easy, powerful crawl.

It seemed as though her feet were taking her unprotesting, following their own set purpose down the grass bank to the car. She couldn't stay, couldn't go through with the hours and days ahead. She hadn't the will left to tell him, to argue, to plead, to try and make him understand. Something would have to be done, a conclusion reached, but not here.

She got in the driving-seat, and her hand stretched out to switch on the ignition. With dismay she saw the empty key-hole. Then she remembered he had taken the key out when they had first stopped. He was always warning her about leaving it in, leaving the car unlocked, leaving her jewel-case open, caring for her, protecting her, but it didn't change the way she felt; just added another layer of guilt to the thick cowl which weighed her down daily.

She jumped out and scrambled up to the martello tower. She snatched off her glasses in the must-coloured gloom within, casting round for his discarded clothes. She found them strewn over an old beam. Hating herself, she began searching through his pockets. But there were no keys. She stood a moment, biting her lip, and then, as the gulls screamed defeat, she picked up his towel and walked out once more into the sunlight.

Resignedly, listlessly, she started down the shingle to meet him. She had gone several yards before she realized he was nowhere in sight. No bobbing head relieved the monotony of the foaming waste. No laughing figure was scrambling up the shingle towards her. She scanned the scene with mounting panic and a different kind of fear sucked at the pit of her stomach. And then she was shouting his name and pounding aimlessly over the stones to the edge of the water.

Exhausted, Cranford stumbled out of the sea a good two hundred yards from the martello tower. He sat down and clasped his knees, his shoulders heaving, until at length his requirement of air assumed more manageable proportions. Then the shivering took hold of him and, pulling himself up, he began the wearying trudge back to the place whence he had started; where the deceptive vicious current had nearly borne him away, out beyond the point, past any hope of rescue.

She saw him as soon as he began moving and the two figures converged, the one running, slithering, calling, the other plodding laboriously. She flung the towel over his shoulders.

'Alex, whatever happened?'

'Bit of a current, that's all.'

'Well, I hope that'll teach you a lesson. I really thought you'd been drowned.'

'At fifty I would have been,' he smiled, and slipped his arm round her waist, and they climbed back to the martello tower. She waited for him to dress and made no comment when he opened the small zip-pocket of his trunks and tossed the ignition key to her.

As soon as The Admiral Benbow came into view, Cranford watched her face for tell-tale reaction, but she gave no hint until they had pulled up on the gravel in front of the rambling low-built inn, and Bill Field, the landlord, was taking the bags out of the car. There was a muddy Ford shooting-brake parked by the door. Cranford didn't know exactly what he expected her to say but when she spoke it was clear the battle of persuasion had only just begun.

'Is there anyone else staying here?' she asked.

'Bless you, no,' chuckled Field. 'Us 'as only room for one couple.' He walked a pace or two and then continued with enthusiasm. 'You'll like it here, Mrs Cranford. Nothing to do, of course, unless you play darts or shove-halfpenny.' He gave them a toothy, sly smile. 'But people usually find their own amusements.'

Cranford, warm again and thirsty now after his gruelling bathe, said:

'We'll have a drink before we see the room.'

They went through the white-washed porch, down the flagged passage and into the saloon bar. It was as Willy had accurately predicted. The oak beams were there, horse-brasses, a ship's binnacle, a stuffed chub in a glass case and even a smoky fire with an inglenook. The reminder of Willy made her feel more desolate and trapped than ever. But she hadn't the resistance to struggle any longer. Her attempt at escape had exhausted her initiative, and she drank the large Scotch Cranford brought for her with a meek unprotesting gratitude.

A burly bald-headed man at the end of the bar looked her over slowly. What he saw was the most exciting thing he'd come across for many a day, but she sensed, in spite of it, he found her too thin for his country tastes, and certainly too expensive for comfort. He nodded at Cranford.

'Is it raining, then?'

'No,' replied Cranford, puzzled, and then, realizing the man was looking at his still-wet hair, explained 'Sea-water. First dip of the season.'

'You must be bloody fond of it,' the other laughed. 'And a strong swimmer, too. By God, it's risky when the tide's going out. There's a hell of a current.'

'I know. I felt it,' said Cranford.

'Some fool couple went in last summer on a rough day like this. One got herself washed up a week later ten miles down the coast where the water runs back into the estuary. Never found the other.' He smiled tentatively at Eve. 'I see you didn't try the briny, lady?'

'No. I'm afraid I only like warm water.'

'You won't find any of that here. Will she, Mabel?' he asked the landlord's plump wife behind the bar. 'Except in the beer, eh?'

'Seems to suit you all right, Fred,' she replied placidly.

'What is it to be?' asked Cranford.

'Mild and bitter.'

'Two pints and another large Scotch, please.'

'That's very civil of you. Bishop's the name.'

The man thrust out his hand, and Cranford shook it. He introduced Eve, and the drinks came and he began to feel curiously contented. He smiled at his wife and, because she responded, he believed that he would succeed after all in transferring his contentment to her. Eve let the whisky take its effect, trying to insulate herself from the surroundings, the conversation, the prospect before her. Bishop was saying:

'The bathing's too dangerous for kids and there's no sand. The Council won't allow caravans; not while I'm on it, anyway. And the land belongs to the farmers, such as me; and it's too valuable to mess up with a bloody row of bungalows. That means drainage, power lines, roads, then shops and buses and the rest of it.' He drained his tankard, stood up and grinned at Eve. 'We like our visitors to be few and very select. I hope you enjoy your stay, Mrs Cranford.'

'I hope so too,' she replied automatically.

'It's as quiet as the grave, down here, but you'll be well looked after at The Admiral. Won't she, Mabel?' he said, cheerily.

'That's right, Fred,' Mrs Field winked at him. 'As the last visitors we had said, "It's an ideal place to write a book or make love."'

'Or do a murder,' laughed Bishop. 'I'll be in again tonight. Goodbye all.'

He went out of the bar. Eve finished her drink in silence. Cranford put his hand on her arm. She smiled and nodded and let him lead her up the narrow carpeted staircase to the room above.

Chapter Fifteen

STILL MRS FIELD lingered by the open door. Her work-scrubbed hands clutched the tray piled with used plates and the remains of the meal she had served them. Oysters, tender beef of the best cut, vegetables fresh and unspoiled by freezing, food within the ambit of her wholesome skill, and no fancy nonsense. Still she talked, sprinkling an endless shower of inconsequence about her, the habit of a lifetime, serving its purpose now of prolonging proximity to the imagined magical world of London, of the films, of T.V. advertisement glamour, miraculously brought near enough to touch, to smell, to savour and recount later with embellished detail; all embodied in Eve, brushing her shining hair, waiting in diaphanous apparel for her distinguished handsome husband to come upstairs from the bar below, to make rapturous romantic love, through hours of ecstasy. Not like Bill Field, rough and quick and easily satisfied.

'You enjoyed your meal, then?'

'Very much. Good night, Mrs Field.'

'There was enough, was there?'

'Quite enough.'

'Did your hubby like it?'

'Yes, thank you. Good night.'

'You've had sufficient?'

'Quite sufficient.'

'You enjoyed it, then?'

'Yes, I did.'

Eve shut her eyes, gripping the hairbrush, wanting to scream, praying for the woman to go. Goggle-eyed and good-intentioned, Mabel Field hesitated, shifting the weight of the tray between her hands.

'Well, I'd best say good night.'

'That's right.'

'You've got everything you want?'

'Yes.'

A final stare of adulation and an audible sigh.

'Good night, then.'

'Good night.'

At last the prayer was answered and she was gone. Eve put the brush down. She took off her rings, dropping them into the open jewel-case. The stones twinkled the firelight back at her. She glanced round the low-ceilinged room, at the clean white-distempered walls, the two-hundred-year-old beams, the crackling open wood-fire, the warming-pans, the simple oak gate-leg table, the Jacobean rocking-chair, the canopied Georgian four-poster. It was a veritable haul for a wandering dealer from the Portobello Road. It was charming; it was genuine. It was the romantic setting for a misty-eyed honeymoon virgin in which to make fumbling love. But to Eve's hard clear eyes it was a hackneyed cloying, oppressive prison. She hated the relative discomfort, the beastly serviceable little bathroom across the passage, the unsophisticated isolation. She felt a burning anger that she had allowed herself to be brought on such a mad, pointless escapade. She was unmoved by the great bowls of spring flowers Cranford had ordered to be put there. She resented the insult to her intelligence, that such artificial ruses could affect her, change how she felt. Nothing, no one ever could.

She looked in the mirror and watched her lips set firmly and defiantly. She submitted to sex, oh yes, and she was vaguely glad if her submission gave Alex, or any other man, pleasure; but she, Eve, would remain whole forever. Beyond that lay the nightmare country where her body could be invaded by an alien, revolting parasite. Nausea followed the thought, so that she had to repress the desire to retch. Cheerful beery accents filled the night air outside the window as closing time emptied the bar. The sound made the sickening sensation slide away into fear, itself compelling protective action.

Quickly, she went to her suitcase, opened it, and plunged her hand into the fabric side-pocket for the small square cardboard box. Cursing, she closed the lid and opened the other case, half-full because the chest of drawers was woefully inadequate for the two of them. She turned over the clothes, feeling underneath them along the silk lining. She slammed the case shut and stood undecided, going over in her mind the motions of the morning when she had packed her things.

With growing panic she snatched up her handbag, emptying it on to the table. A glance was sufficient to tell her there was no box. Distraught, she began searching the wardrobe, feeling in pockets, opening and shutting the drawers of the commode, knowing it must be somewhere, yet knowing it couldn't be where she was looking.

'Sorry I was such a time . . .' said Cranford.

Eve spun round, trying to figure how long he had stood there watching her urgent search.

'. . . But it's impossible to avoid the pressure of hospitality in a place like this.'

His expression told her nothing, exhibited no sign that he had noticed the disarray of the room. He put a new, unopened pack of cigarettes on the table beside the scattered contents of her handbag.

'Not that one wants to,' he went on. 'We're an exciting event down here. Especially you,' he smiled. 'You should have seen the faces fall when I said you wouldn't be coming down for a drink.'

'I was doing my stint up here with the landlord's wife. I gave her enough hints, but would she go? She's got a hide like a dinosaur.'

'She's tough all right,' he laughed. 'Puts twice as much work into the place as her husband.' Cranford noticed the open jewel-case and began fitting the rings she had discarded into their velvet grooves. 'Our Mabel's a good cook, a good wife, and a good mother. She has two sons, you know. One's in the Navy. The other's just started up as an accountant.'

'Well, bully for her. Bully for all of them.'

Cranford frowned. Eve closed the drawers, wondering where to look again, uncertain now as to whether she could have left the thing behind after all.

'How do you always manage to sound so condescending, Eve?' he asked.

'I'm nothing of the kind. But I'm naturally bored by Mrs Field and her strapping family. What could there be about them to interest me? Though I'm sure she's a very worthy, honest soul.'

It was useless. Like Willy, there was an inborn error of attitude, a class cataract, a social deaf-mutism, which only a radical operation like a revolution or a bomb would ever cure. Or kill. He set about arranging the expensive trinkets in some semblance of order out of the careless jumble Eve kept them in. All his years of striving and effort were crystallized in these pretty stones and the pretty girl across the room they were bought to adorn. The casual way she kept them angered him.

'You should have left all these behind in the safe,' he said. 'In a place like this they could so easily be stolen.'

'By honest Mabel?'

'Of course not. But anyone could walk in and . . .'

'Anyone could walk in at home. We let the Batemans and Rose off for a madly gay weekend too, remember?'

He ignored the jibe.

'I think you ought to treat them with more respect. In this mess you'd never notice if anything was missing until you come to wear it.'

'Wouldn't I just? Anyway, they're insured, aren't they?'

'Yes,' he said quietly. 'So am I. You can always get your money back.'

The flick of sarcasm was lost in her renewed search through the suitcases. Cranford placed an emerald bracelet carefully alongside its matching clips. He remembered her profusion of affection on their first anniversary. Each piece photographed for him an occasion, her looks, the dress she was wearing, what she said and the pleasure he had felt in the giving. Or was the pleasure pride, and his generosity a mockery, a foolishness which made her into a spoilt rich child he could no longer control? One emerald bracelet, matching earrings, three brooches, two necklaces, a pendant, six rings, four clips, and a partridge in a peartree. Five rings. No, six. Surely there were six?

'Where's that square-cut sapphire, Eve?'

'What?'

'The ring I gave you for Christmas?'

The question jabbed her into preoccupation, jerking her concentration from one evasion to a new one.

'Are you wearing it?' he asked.

'No . . . No, I'm not.'

'Well, it isn't here. Where is it?'

Her fingers trembled as she closed the case and opened the second one, hopelessly now, for the third time, trying to conjure a rescuing lie out of it. With relief it came easily, soft and silken like the garments she was aimlessly turning over, and her hands became steady again.

'One of the claws was loose,' she said. 'I took it back to Aspreys. They're fixing it for me.'

She waited for him to say something, tensing for the next question, already preparing the counter to it; but she heard him close the jewel-case, and the immediate danger was past.

Cranford looked at his wife with curiosity.

'Eve, why did you bring all your jewellery down here?'

She sat on the bed, suddenly exhausted, her mind back on the old problem.

'Why not?'

'You can't have thought there'd be occasion to wear much of it.'

'I like to have them with me, that's all. It gives me pleasure just to know they're there. Is that so peculiar?'

'No. No, it isn't,' he replied after a pause. 'I suppose that's what's meant by treasuring something. Or someone.'

'I suppose so.'

She nodded and smiled at him, weighing the relative plausibility of a headache or some vague pain.

'Worthy of a nod or a smile,' he said, getting up. 'But nothing more demonstrative. Is that it, Eve?'

He came over to the bed and took hold of her hands, but she withdrew them instantly. For a moment he thought there must be something in his own which had repelled her, but he knew there was nothing to be seen except by the trained eye. He became aware that she was shaking.

'What's the matter?'

'I'm cold,' she said.

Cold and beautiful and distant.

'Are you? It's like an oven in here.'

'I think I must have caught a chill on our walk this afternoon.'

'Then you should get into bed.'

He took hold of the sheets and pulled them down, but she stood up quickly.

'I've a headache, too. Did you bring any aspirin?'

She went round the bed to the fire and he watched the light from the flames silhouette her body through the flimsy négligé. Amongst the litter from her handbag he noticed a half-full tube of veganin tablets. He closed his hand over it.

'So it's aspirin you were searching for so diligently?'

His question was like a gift, a ready-made excuse. She clutched it eagerly.

'Yes, I usually have some with me, but . . .'

'You still have.'

She turned and saw his hand open, disclosing the tube. She cursed herself for the slip, but his smile appeared to be one of amusement, not suspicion. She took the tube from him and went to the wash-stand for the carafe and tumbler.

'Thank goodness,' she said. 'I was looking everywhere for it.'

'No, you weren't, Eve.'

'What?'

'You were looking everywhere for this.'

He produced the square red box from his pocket, and held it up like an accusatory exhibit. She stared at it dumbly, repressing her fury at his having tricked her so easily. With a supreme effort she summoned her ingenuity, pretending innocence and dragging up, God knew how, a laugh of gurgling unconcern.

'That's right. I was looking for that as well. It's nice of you to own up to stealing it.' She held out her hand. 'Thank you.'

He shook his head.

'No. Not any more,' he said. 'It's time this contraption literally stopped coming between us.'

He turned and lobbed the box into the fire.

'No, Alex! Don't . . .'

She ran forward, but he caught her arm and held her to him. Round his shoulder she saw the box burst into flames before it became lost in the red interior of the fire as a log crumbled and smothered it, sending up a cascade of sparks.

'Let me go,' she ordered.

'I don't want to, darling,' he laughed, and tried to kiss her, but she twisted her face away, struggling to free herself. Still holding her, he allowed the momentum of her escape to take him with her until they were by the bed. He clasped her wrists, forcing her back on to it, finding her mouth, obliterating her cries of protest, until he felt her resistance disintegrate. Suddenly he released her roughly, because her total passivity was more effective a rejection than a laugh or a sneer or a blow. He watched her breasts rising and falling as her breathing became less laboured. At length she opened her eyes, but her gaze remained averted, travelling back and forth along the creosoted woodworm-dotted beam above her. He touched her hand gently, but she recoiled as if he had struck her. She sat up and leaned back against the bed-head.

'Why, Eve? Why?' he whispered.

'Because it isn't any good.'

Her reply was flat, matter-of-fact, final. He looked at her for some moments before he said,

'No, it isn't. This isn't any good for you, for me, or for our marriage. You see, Eve . . .'

'Oh, please. Please don't start one of your conjugal lectures.'

'I wasn't lecturing. I was talking. We've got to talk.'

'For God's sake! I told you, I've a headache.'

'No, you haven't. You've only an excuse. You're full of them, Eve. When one lets you down, you invent another. You needed a headache as an excuse not to make love, because you lost that bloody bit of rubber in the fire, which itself was an excuse not to be a mother.'

'Why should I be a mother?'

'In order to have a child.'

'I don't want a child. Is that so impossible to understand?'

'Yes, without a reason.'

'I dislike children, that's the reason. Some people do, you know. Some people hate dogs, or cats, or horses, or cream cheese, or geraniums. I hate children: what's so wonderful about them? They're messy, dirty little beasts. They're a worry and a bind. You can't talk to them for years, and when you can, they don't want to talk to you. So why should I have a child, if I don't want one?'

'Perhaps because I want one.'

'Then *you* have it.'

'Don't be funny.'

'It may be funny to you. But I don't find it at all amusing to make myself ugly and go through all that discomfort and pain, subject myself to the disgusting revolting procedure of becoming a mother. Why should I? Just because you want to be a father?'

'Yes, Eve. If there's no other reason. Just because of that.'

He spoke quietly, searching her face, but she turned away, avoiding his scrutiny.

'I never said I'd have a child,' she said truculently.

'You married me.'

'There were no promises about children.'

'We talked about them.'

'You did.'

'And you said, perhaps in a year or two . . .'

'All right, I'll say it again, if it'll make you any happier. "Perhaps in a year or two . . ."'

'We can't go on evading this.'

Cranford stood up and went over to the window. The moon had risen, and dimly he could make out the line of the shingle bank and beyond it a metallic sea-strip. When he turned round she was in bed, the clothes drawn up around her. With surprise he saw that she was smiling at him puckishly.

'We can have lots more fun without children, darling,' she said.

The provocation of her physical attraction threw him into renewed anger.

'Fun! Is that all that marriage means to you?'

'No, Alex. It means you. You and me. But not a family of screaming brats.'

'And what do I mean? Money and clothes and diamonds? Why did you pick on me? Anyone else with the means would have done.'

'I never wanted to marry anyone else.'

'I wonder why . . .' he said bitterly.

'Chemistry. Hormones. Sex. You should know all about that. Why did you marry me?'

'I loved you.'

'Loved? But you don't any more?'

'I didn't say that.'

'It's true, though, isn't it? Your love for me depends quite simply on my having children.'

'Children mean love.'

She looked at him a moment and then threw her head back, and the cold, silvery well-bred laughter danced round the room, mocking the warm flickering light from the fire.

'Oh, Alex, you're very sweet,' she said. 'Under that shining modern professional armour of yours, you're nothing but a rather bewildered old-fashioned sentimentalist.'

He stood still, letting the words hurt him, absorbing their particular searing sting, observing through them the blue slanting tilt of her eyes, the moist fullness of her lips, framing the porcelain regularity of her teeth. He took a step forward, and the sound stopped as if he had already struck her, and suddenly he knew her laughter and the things she had said were a fake, a bravado, another tactical move in her all-consuming strategy to keep him off. Illness, protest, passivity, sweet reasonableness, and now derision, belittlement: all were weapons of defence. He let his rage blur the image of her features, and in its place he released once more the clear focus of his desire for her lissom flawless body which squirmed now in movements of retreat under the bed-clothes. Purposefully, he took off his jacket, and unloosened his tie.

'No, Alex, no . . .' she said huskily.

'Get back into bed,' he ordered her.

'Alex, I can't. Don't you understand? Try and understand how I feel, darling. I can't help it, I tell you . . . I'm afraid . . . Alex, please . . . please . . .'

The tears started to come then, the last defensive supplication, the ultimate bastion of excuse; but he lifted her firmly from her knees.

Before he could cover her lips she screamed, and the knocking on the door swung him round. He waited for the sound to be repeated before he let her fall back, sobbing, on to the bed.

'What is it? What do you want?' he rasped out.

The landlord's voice came, respectfully muffled, from the other side of the oak panel.

'Can you come down, sir? Telephone from London. They said it was urgent.'

He looked at Eve, face buried in the pillow, her shoulders moving convulsively as she continued to weep, and all his purpose ebbed away, leaving him sad and depressed and sorry for both of them.

'All right. I'll be down,' he said.

'Thank you, sir.'

He lit a cigarette, put on his jacket and went out of the room, going to the top of the staircase, past the disappearing chink of light as the listening Mabel closed her door.

Eventually Eve stopped crying, and pulled the clothes over her. She moved to the far side of the bed and stared at the fire, dying in the grate. Shortly she heard his footsteps along the passage again. She lay still, listening to his movements as he took off his clothes and got into bed beside her. He didn't touch her, and gradually the tension left her as she knew at last that the few inches of space between them were as effective as a thousand miles of cold turbulent water. At length, he said:

'You'll have to see a psychiatrist, Eve. And if that doesn't work, then we'd both better find a solicitor.'

He turned over and switched off the light.

'What did they want?' she asked.

'It was Khouri. We shall be leaving first thing in the morning. You'll like that, won't you?'

She tried to keep her breathing even as the miracle reprieve spread a warm and comforting balm through her body.

'What's happened?'

'One of my patients. Major Wharton. There'll have to be a post-mortem.'

She stayed awake for some time, but eventually sleep overtook her. The last thing she remembered was puzzling over the soft repetitive vibration of the bed as restlessly Cranford continued to scratch his hands late into the night.

Chapter Sixteen

As soon as Cranford's overcoated figure appeared, Khouri excused himself from Sister Garland and Doctor Birley, and hurried down the corridor to intercept his chief.

'Morning, Khouri.'

'Sir. I am inevitably sorry you have been brought back. . . .'

'Can't be helped. You did quite right.'

'I thought it was wise to inform you, in the circumstances.'

'What are the circumstances? You'd better tell me. All of them.'

Cranford took the case-folder from him, and turned over the pages with his gloved hand, checking the pulse and temperature chart, the nurses' reports, the drug sheet, while he listened to his registrar's summary of Major Wharton's last twenty-four hours.

'I examined the patient as a matter of routine, yesterday morning. He had a headache, there was half a degree rise in temperature, but no positive signs. Completely absolutely.'

'Did you disturb the plaster?'

'There was no indication, sir. But at six o'clock Sister very properly 'phoned me, as by then the patient had a fever of a hundred point two, and was complaining bitterly of his head and also of some vertigo.'

'Any nystagmus?'

'Definitely not. Nevertheless I removed the plaster, but there was no sign of any local infection, so I redressed the operation area. . . .'

'Did you take swabs?'

'Yes. The culture, when it comes through, could be definitely interesting, I am thinking, sir.'

'So am I,' said Cranford drily. 'Go on.'

'I also had his chest X-rayed—perfectly clear—and withdrew a sample of blood for count and prothrombin.'

'Is the result back?'

'This morning.'

Khouri handed a green slip to Cranford. His eyes ran down the column of figures. A slight alteration in the polymorph-lymphocyte ratio. Otherwise negative.

'Nothing there,' he said.

'Inevitably last night I could not know that,' continued Khouri, 'so as an absolute working precaution I supplemented the antibiotics.'

'Good.'

'There was no change until ten p.m., when the Major vomited. Neck rigidity had developed, and the Kernig test was positive.'

'You did a lumbar puncture?'

'At the precise moment of preparing for it, he became unconscious, had a sudden convulsion, and died.'

Cranford dropped the slip into the cardboard folder and closed it. The story screamed its message at him. Operation Wednesday night: introduction of infection. Spread by lymphatics to the meninges, Thursday and Friday. Saturday: natural defences overwhelmed. Acute encephalitis. Convulsion. Death. Obviously some antibiotic-resistant organism. It could happen to anyone. No one to blame. A remote risk in any operation. But it had to be his operation, his action, his hands. He clenched them firmly round the folder, refusing to acknowledge the burning which had plagued them inside the leather gloves as they had shaken the hand of Bill Field, controlled the wheel of Eve's Mercedes all the way back from Shinglestrand, returned with suitable recognition the salute of the doorman of the Bulstrode Clinic, until now, when the irritation seemed more implacable than ever.

'What's your diagnosis?' he shot at Khouri.

He saw the olive-skinned eyelids flicker and the brief hesitation in the lips, noting the younger man's sensitivity, his wish not to embarrass his senior by a too-quick, too-accurate answer.

'Er—cavernous sinus thrombosis, sir?'

Cranford smiled at his considerateness. It lay like a bond of respect between them but, with Khouri's ability, the error was transparently deliberate. He shook his head.

'With a low fever and no signs? Try again.'

Still Khouri attempted to soften the blow with circumlocution.

'His fever was not high, agreed, but nevertheless with certain types of organism this could be so, and inevitably an acute meningoencephalitis . . .'

'As a post-operative complication?'

'It is a possibility which is hard, sir, to keep out of my mind.'

'It'll be hard to keep out of everyone else's too,' Cranford growled. He glanced down the corridor. 'Who's that talking to Sister?'

'Major Wharton's G.P. He has recently been showing considerable excitement.'

'I'll bet,' said Cranford. He handed the folder back to Khouri, thrust

114

his hands in his pockets and shrugged. 'Well, the post-mortem will tell us all. Has Whittaker started?'

'It is not Dr Whittaker, sir. He is at the moment in bed with influenza. Dr Munro is doing . . .'

'Munro . . . !' Cranford made a sound of exasperation. 'That's all I needed.'

They began walking towards the lean grey-haired man engaged in earnest conversation with the white-bonneted Sister. Hurried footsteps behind caught up with them.

'Hello. I've only just been told,' said Berenger breathlessly.

'What have you been told?'

'About Wharton.' Berenger fell into step beside them and for no obvious reason gave a short laugh. 'What . . . what was the cause?'

'You can't be a success all the time, Berenger.'

'You mean . . . something's happened in my department . . . something pulmonary . . . ?'

The anxious tone made Cranford mitigate his mildly sadistic observation with faint reassurance.

'I shouldn't think so,' he said. 'But brother Munro is unlikely to leave us in any doubt.'

As they reached the lift-doors, Dr Birley stepped forward.

'Mr Cranford?'

'Ah, yes, Dr Birley,' Cranford nodded. 'This is Dr Berenger, my anaesthetist. You know my registrar, Khouri. We didn't meet, doctor, over Major Wharton, but we spoke over the telephone, I believe.'

'This is a terrible business. Shocking, tragic,' said Birley. 'His wife's in a state of collapse. She didn't even know he was having this done. Thought he was on a business trip.'

'Not an uncommon situation in my particular field,' replied Cranford.

'It's put me in an uncommon situation, I can tell you. She blames me. As you know, I advised him strongly against it.'

'What, dying?' asked Cranford irritably.

'Against the operation,' Birley spluttered. 'A perfectly fit man in his prime, nothing wrong with him except an occasional touch of dyspepsia for which I treated him with simple measures, and now . . .'

'Don't distress yourself, Birley. Major Wharton had a mind of his own. Neither you nor anyone else could have changed it. He wanted this operation.'

'He didn't want to die.'

'You mean he didn't want to be killed? Is that your thesis?'

Birley blanched and shifted on his feet uncomfortably.

'Well, now . . . I'm not suggesting that there has been any negligence. . . .'

'There hasn't,' said Cranford.

'It's just that . . . well, I think he rushed into an unnecessary—an unjustified risk. . . .'

'As you may be rushing into an unnecessary, unjustified conclusion, doctor. It's a human failing. Let's accept just that for the time being, shall we?'

The lift-doors opened. The four of them followed each other in awkwardly, and plunged down to the basement in silence. Cranford felt the sweat inside his gloves sticking the lining-material to his fingers. As they filed along the short passageway to the mortuary, where a draught of colder uncentrally-heated air made him glad of his overcoat, Cranford braced himself against the expected findings of the postmortem, against a further outburst of unprofessional emotionalism from Birley, against Munro, but above all against the nagging illogicality of conscience and the erosion of success. 'Expect success, Alex. It's half the battle. You've everything on your side, darling. Look at me and listen, Alex. You're going to be handsome when you grow up. Like your father in a way. But he was so shabby and untidy. He didn't care. And that spoilt the whole effect. Appearances are so important, Alex. They're the other half of the battle.' The mortuary doors slapped to, behind them. Let battle commence.

The long red-rubber apron accentuated Munro's short stature. He stopped his dissection until his spectators were distributed round the glazed drainage slabs. He held a blood-stained sponge in one hand and a broad-bladed post-mortem knife in the other. With deliberation he put them down and wiped his gloves on a towel. This was his show and he wasn't going to hurry it. Using a probe as an indicator, he turned to the organs already removed, where they lay displayed for inspection on shallow flat trays.

'To recapitulate the findings so far, gentlemen,' he began, 'this is the body of a fifty-year-old man, well-nourished, moderate rigor mortis, no external abnormalities save amputated fourth and fifth left toes, and . . .'

'He lost those at Dunkirk,' said Birley. 'He had a fine record as a soldier. . . .'

'And,' continued Munro, quelling the interruption with a glare, 'the obvious recent operation trauma in the nasal area which I'll come back to. Thorax . . .'

He picked up the heart which he had cut open, demonstrating the smooth shining walls of the atria and ventricles.

'Heart not enlarged. Weight 290 grams, pericardium, chambers, valves normal. Coronary vessels show no atheroma. Good for another thirty years,' he added, shaking his head.

The comment was irrelevant, valueless, except, as Cranford guessed, in building up the impression of a strong stalwart individual who would still be alive but for some misfortune, such as falling into the hands of a cosmetic surgeon.

'Get on with it, Munro,' he snapped.

The pathologist looked at him levelly and then took hold of a lung, and squeezed part of the lower lobe between his finger and thumb expressing a frothy pink fluid.

'Apart from the slight tendency to emphysema, the lungs are healthy. This is merely terminal oedema.'

Berenger sighed audibly and the grin of relief on his face changed to self-satisfaction. The anaesthetic was in no way contributory. Berenger was in the clear, and Berenger, the expression declared, didn't give a damn about anything or anyone else.

'Abdomen,' announced Munro. 'Spleen, kidneys, adrenals, pancreas, liver O.K. Stomach. Now this is interesting.'

He stretched the mucous membrane near the pylorus and held it out for them to see.

'Here is a single chronic gastric ulcer, about two centimetres across, floor smooth. But look at this, d'you see? The edge is just beginning to build up at this point and I have no doubt that on section we shall find early malignant change.'

Cranford glanced at Birley.

'So much for the touch of dyspepsia and the simple measures, Birley,' he whispered.

'I'm . . . I'm surprised,' mumbled the older doctor, 'very surprised.' He looked earnestly at Munro. 'It couldn't have contributed to . . . ?'

Munro shook his head.

'I'd say not for a year or two, and that assuming it didn't declare itself before. Which is mighty unlikely. Then, of course, an operation could well have been successful in time.'

'Provided it wasn't advised against,' remarked Cranford.

'And so we come to the head, Cranford,' said Munro. 'Taking into account the history of the case, obviously the seat of mischief!'

Cranford let it ride and walked round the table so that he could obtain a clear uninterrupted view. With a few deft taps of the mallet on the chisel, Munro carefully eased up the bone of the vault of the skull, which, after a little difficulty, separated in one piece from the encircling saw-cut he had made earlier, revealing beneath the duramater, the strong outer membrane covering the surface of the brain. As anticipated, this showed no abnormality. It was in the delicate pia and arachnoid meninges at the base where Cranford knew the tell-tale evidence would lie.

Munro worked quickly with practised strokes, raising the frontal lobes, dividing the cranial nerves successively with a scalpel as they appeared. He cut through the spinal cord as low as it could be reached, severed the tentorium and, with a gentle persuasiveness, gathered the whole brain into his hands and delivered it out of its bony prison in a sure, graceful movement. He let it slither into the scalepan, noted the weight and, turning it over to expose the under-surface, placed it on a fresh tray. He picked up his dissecting scissors and a pair of forceps.

'Now, gentlemen,' he said, smiling malevolently at Cranford, 'let us see if we can find out where the trouble came from.'

He slit through the dura and folded it back. Then he made a small cut in the pia-arachnoid. Thin, blood-stained fluid gushed out. Here was no thick, sticky, exudate, no infective process, no surgical complication. Cranford saw Munro's smile fade, heard Birley's gasp of surprise, observed the puzzlement on Berenger's features, and felt the tenseness in his own chest and back and limbs ebb away, as the blood and cerebro-spinal fluid ebbed away, making pink rivulets across the white surface of the tray.

'Sub-arachnoid haemorrhage,' exclaimed Khouri, with enthusiasm. 'Congenital aneurysm of the circle of Willis. A slow leak of blood over two days prior to the final rupture of the vessel. It explains all the signs. I am bitterly self-critical I am not thinking of this before, Mr Cranford.'

'Nothing you could have done. The important point is the discovery now.'

Cranford turned to Munro, who had extended the excision and was busily dissecting out the ring of vessels on the base of the brain. 'Is my friend's diagnosis confirmed, Professor?'

'Aye,' grunted Munro. 'Here's the bloody little sac.'

He directed a stream of water on to the artery to show the bubble-like expansion of the aneurysm, where the blood had spurted out, ploughing up the adjacent brain-tissue, killing Wharton as surely as a bullet.

'Amazing to think he could carry a time-bomb like that around with him all his life,' managed Birley.

'Which proves a number of things,' observed Cranford.

'Such as what?' rasped Munro.

'They should be self-evident. But the master one is the value of an excellent post-mortem demonstration,' Cranford replied magnanimously. 'You'll deal with the death certificate, won't you?' He addressed Birley. 'Now that we know the cause, it should make your task of consoling Mrs Wharton a lot easier.' He shook Birley's hand. 'I shall not be sending in an account for the operation.'

'Why not, Cranford?' barked Munro. 'Surely that defeats the purpose of doing it?'

Cranford felt his hands clench but forced them to open again as he looked at the embittered man in the rubber apron.

'Probably,' he smiled. 'But at times it pays to be generous. You should try it sometime, Munro.'

He heard Berenger's sycophantic snigger and, taking Khouri by the elbow, led him back to the lift. They got out on the ground floor, and Khouri accompanied him out to the Bentley in Bulstrode Street.

'Well,' he said, 'it's a case of "as you were".'

'Will you be going back to Shinglestrand, sir?'

Cranford didn't need to consider the question. The abysmal disappointment of the previous night remained with distasteful clarity.

'I'm not sure,' he lied. 'I'll keep you posted. I'm at home today, anyway.' He turned the ignition key and touched the starter. 'Good of you to cope with this extra work for me. Don't think it isn't appreciated.'

Khouri nodded solemnly.

'I am completely aware that it is, sir. I am grateful, too. It is all experience.'

Cranford smiled.

'Let's hope the experience of Major Wharton won't be repeated.'

'I hope not, but the case was immensely valuable because it poses an interesting question, I am thinking, sir.'

'Oh, what's that?'

'Supposing it had been possible to know that Major Wharton had an aneurysm. Would the operation have been done? Would it have been right to be done?'

'Probably not. So?'

'Then the remote possibility of the operation precipitating, by some undetectable mechanism, the bursting of the aneurysm, is implied in your answer. Am I correct, Mr Cranford?'

'Remote possibilities, undetectable mechanisms, right to be done?' exploded Cranford. 'What's the matter with you, Khouri? That's metaphysics, not surgery.'

Khouri pondered, and then smiled.

'You are quite right, sir. One of my most difficult faults is that often I cannot seem to separate the two.'

Cranford held his glance a moment, then gave a nod of dismissal, and drove away. As he turned right into Welbeck Street, he caught in the driving-mirror the reflection of a white-coated figure still standing on the pavement, lost in contemplation.

The image stayed with him as he parked in Cavendish Square, and went into his bank to cash a cheque. He took out a couple of hundred. There was still the vague possibility that Eve might be persuaded to go away somewhere. He came out of the bank and pointed the car up Wimpole Street towards home. Khouri's words repeated themselves again, spreading their doubt and implication about him so that his attention wandered for a sufficient fragment of time to make him shoot the red light into Marylebone Road. A horn shrieked in his ear, he jammed his foot on the accelerator and swung the car round in a squealing curve. The wheel banged the opposite kerb, and then he had corrected the skid and was narrowly ahead of the cross-stream of vehicles which poured over the intersection behind him.

The moment of danger, now past, released an arctic wave of relief under the skin on his back. The sensation repeated itself, making him continue to grip the wheel with unwarranted intensity. He became aware of a clamminess round the collar and the cuffs at his wrists, and the rapid, forced excursion of his respiration. That such an incident should produce so much reaction unnerved him and, for safety, instead of going into the Park he turned down Harley Street, and pulled up outside his consulting rooms.

He sat still, ordering himself to relax, but his fingers refused to release the wheel. As he increased the effort to straighten them, pain built up in the joints. At length he managed to extend his thumbs and pull his hands free. He coaxed the digits into movement, but they felt like overcooked sausages trying to burst through the leather covering the gloves. Panic flicked at him. He got out of the car and went up the two steps to the door. He was still fumbling with the key, trying to insert it in the Yale lock, when a greeting from the pavement behind, broke his concentration.

'Alex, my dear fellow, how nice to see you.'

For a moment Cranford couldn't place the well-fed features beneath the fashionable bowler, but the voice and the ready smile took him instantly back thirty years and across half a dozen counties to afternoons together at Bradgate, chasing Meadow Browns over the bracken with fine-meshed entomological nets to the sinister almond-like whiff of cyanide from the poison bottle; to the deep-felt envy for the other's Swallow-tail, pinned in a glass-topped drawer all to itself, afterwards discovered to have been bought at Watkins and Doncaster in the Strand and not, as claimed, taken on the wing; and then twenty years ago to the mud-slithering, muscle-straining, crowd-waving battle of a varsity football game and the drunken night-club ragging which followed. And, ten years back, to an old boys' dinner, suitably solemn in comment as befitted the attainment of the first promising rungs of a career in medicine and at the Bar respectively. And nearer still, to an encounter one June outside the Casino at Cannes, both modestly in luck, and the happy squandering of it in an eating, drinking, marauding four days along bronze-skinned beaches, on mimosa-scented terraces, and amid the animal stimulation of all-night jazz-filled bars, youth-clogged to capacity.

'Henry,' he said. 'When was it, one, two, years ago?'

'More like three. What have you been doing? No, don't tell me, I know. Getting married, getting on, getting older. Sorry I couldn't make your wedding.'

'Yes, that was a pity.'

'You've never invited me to meet the beautiful Eve. How is she?'

'Beautiful,' replied Cranford and meant it.

Galbraith laughed.

'Well, don't look so depressed about it, old boy.' He shot a legal-eagle, intuitive glance at his old friend. 'What's the matter? Teething troubles?'

'No. Not at all,' he heard the aggressive denial break through.

'No patter of tiny feet yet?'

'No.'

'They'll come along soon enough.'

'I expect so,' he agreed. He wanted to say, 'But not if my bloody beautiful bitch of a wife has her way. Tell me what to do, Henry. Am I unreasonable? How would you tackle it?' Instead, he turned abruptly, and thrust the key at the lock, getting it in first time.

'Look, Alex. We must meet for an evening. It's ridiculous letting these long lapses occur. Come and dine with me in the Temple.'

'Yes, I'd . . . I'd like that. Good idea,' said Cranford. He had the door open now, and could see the fifteen yards of tiled flooring to his room.

'Well, what about next week? Thursday?'

'Next week?' he frowned, because next week had an ominous hopeless ring about it.

'All right; the week after?' persisted Galbraith.

'Thanks, Henry. Fine. I'll ring you.'

'Mind you do.'

The handshake made him wince, and he saw that Galbraith noticed something.

'You're working too hard, Alex. Don't overdo it, old boy.'

With a final puzzled glance over his shoulder, Galbraith strode off down the street on the same springy, bouncy feet he remembered as a boy.

Cranford closed the door on the sunlight and went into his room. Free from observation at last, he undid the mother-of-pearl wrist buttons. He eased the leather tips of the fingers away from those of his own inside, and then, holding his breath, wrenched the gloves off in two painful movements.

Immediately he saw that his hands were swollen. In places the outer layers of the epidermis had rubbed off where the tops of the vesicles had broken, leaving patches of red, weeping tissue, criss-crossed by the scratch-marks delivered in the abandon of half-wakefulness the night before. He slumped down in the chair behind his desk and stared at his hands, the essential, irreplaceable tools of his craft, of his livelihood. He felt a conflict of emotions, which eventually condensed into a kind of desperate fury. This was the dreaded end-result of weeks and months of anxiety, of putting off anxiety, of refusing to take action earlier, of muddling on, of acting, in fact, in a fashion quite alien to the ordered, objective regimen of his training. Why, why, why? He didn't know the answer, but it was too late now for recrimination, for hiding any longer behind the pride which had prevented his seeking expert advice. He'd left the whole bloody thing too late. And yet, bad as it seemed, wasn't there still a chance that something could be done with speed and skill and know-how?

He opened a drawer and took out some gauze. He wrapped a length of it round each hand, and followed it up with a crêpe bandage, leaving the tips of his fingers which were least affected, projecting, as if from mittens. Manstein was the man. Sam Manstein, dermatologist at St Freda's. He'd never met him, but the grapevine in pill-island tipped him as the best. Like Cranford was tipped as the best if you wanted a couple of hundred-guinea wrinkles removed.

He secured the bandages with safety-pins and went to the directory-holder. Saturday; Manstein would be at home. Where did he live? Somewhere in Surrey. Warlingham, wasn't it? He picked up the Surrey volume and riffled through the pages. Macgril, Mair, Mann, Manning, Mannheim, Manstein Sam. S., S.A., S.A.B., S.A.G., Samuel, M.R.C.P. That was the boy, 51, Langland Crescent, Warlingham 5131.

Cranford put the book back and then clutched the receiver with a bandaged hand and dialled the number. Tensely he listened to the ringing tone from the instrument twelve miles away. Eventually it was interrupted.

'Hello. Is Doctor Manstein there?' he asked.

'Daddy's not in. Who is it?'

The young voice was clear and distinct, with an attractive enunciation. He guessed at a girl about ten.

'This is Dr Cranford. A colleague of Daddy's. Do you know where he is?'

A pause for diplomatic consideration.

'He's in the garden.'

'Well, would you ask him to come to the 'phone, please?'

'He's awfully muddy.' Laughter and then, as instructed, 'Is it urgent?'

Cranford saw the open window, the little girl in jeans and a sweater, the early daffodils under the hawthorn, and the contented shirt-sleeved man coming out of the tool-shed.

'Yes,' he said. 'I'm afraid it is.' And waited, listening to the running footsteps as they died away. Somewhere, distantly, there was another child's voice and, nearer, a bird was singing.

Chapter Seventeen

'SIX CHICKEN SUPREME JEANETTE, three dozen oyster patés, three dozen Dublin Bay prawns in aspic, two dozen curried eggs mayonnaise, two veal pies, salad, two ice-cream puddings, peaches and strawberries Romanoff, petit-fours. Would you like to check them, sir?'

'I'm not a butler. That's why I've hired you. What about the drinky?'

'Two cases of magnums. Krug "55".'

'That should float it all down very bravely. Ice me a bottle now, will you?'

'My instructions were not to leave or open anything . . .'

'Until you'd got your filthy money, is that it?'

'Yes, m'lord. Here's the bill.'

Willy snatched the tissue-thin envelope, stumped over to his desk, and took out a cheque-book. The man from Garrods hovered behind him, like a bird of prey.

'I was instructed, sir, that payment would be made "Cash on Delivery".'

Willy flung the cheque-book down.

'My God, what infernal impertinence.'

'Those were my orders. Take it or leave it. It's up to you.' The tone was suddenly insolent.

Willy glowered, and his rage mounted as he caught the man exchanging a grimace with his assistant, who stood listening in the open doorway.

Angrily Willy took a roll of notes from his pocket and threw them on the desk. He watched the short stubby fingers count out the appropriate amount.

'Thank you, sir.'

'Get your nails cleaned,' said Willy.

The man looked at his hands, shrugged and went towards the door.

'When I've changed, sir, I'll open the champagne.'

'Do that,' snapped Willy. 'And watch your manners. If a servant had spoken to my father as you've done to me, he'd have thrashed the hide off him.'

The man turned, smiling.

'He wouldn't be able to get away with it nowadays, though, would he?'

'You . . .'

'The name's Johnson, sir, and this is Watts. We shall do our best to see that your guests get the impression we've been in your lordship's employ for some time. That's the idea, isn't it?'

'Get out!'

'Thank you, m'lord.'

Willy picked up his stick, but the grinning face disappeared superciliously behind the door, and he recognized his own gesture as one of impotent defeat.

Eve closed the flat door behind her, and dropped her key in her bag.

'Is Lord Binfield in?'

'Yes, madam. Very much so.'

Snickering, the men disappeared into the kitchen. She listened to the staccato sounds coming from Willy's room, and knew as she went in how she would find him, pounding at the leather-covered pouffe with one of his sticks.

'Willy, darling, don't!'

He turned round, and the child-like fury left his expression, and an equally child-like smile of welcome, unfettered for the moment by any other consideration, took its place.

'Evie, you're back.'

'Of course I'm back. I always come back.'

She put her arms round him, and kissed him, and he hugged her, and for a time they said nothing, and the scene was the same as it had always been; after she'd come back from skating on the lake, Willy immured by the nursery fire; back from school for the holidays, Willy term-tied to a succession of unsatisfactory tutors; back from her first dance, Willy uninvited; back from Paris or Rome or New York, heady with success as a top model, Willy resentful, but proud at the same time and in his way near to being happy; and now, back from her husband with the desperate need she had for Willy too, because in his pathetic love for her was an understanding Alex could never give her.

'You'll be at the party?'

'Yes, I'll be at the party.'

'Hooray! That's one in the bloody eye for bloody Alex,' Willy chuckled. 'He climbed down, you see. They always do. I've won, haven't I, Evie? I've won.'

'Oh, Willy, it isn't a game any longer. I'm not having any fun.'

She got up, and he watched her go over to the window and take a cigarette out of the alabaster box.

'I'm sorry, darling,' he said. 'It was very sweet of you to come back. Was he cussed awkward?'

'No. One of his patients died.'

'So it wasn't because of me . . . ?'

'I'd have been home today, Willy, whatever had happened.'

'What did happen? Evie, you're all right, aren't you?'

'Just about.' She turned and laughed suddenly. 'I wonder if, technically, a husband can *rape* his wife?'

Willy shut his eyes.

'Don't say things like that. I told you not to go. I begged you not to. . . .'

'You were right, darling.'

She sat on the pouffe and he took hold of her hand.

'It was all about as ghastly as it could be, my dear, I can tell you. The dreary place, the dreary people, the frightful food, and Alex so hearty, swilling beer with the locals, swimming . . . in *this* weather, and actually enjoying it all.'

'Showing off, darling, showing off. As a class they have to do it. You must have wanted to vomit.'

'And then, in the evening, up came the same old one-track long-player, but crafty and cunning, you know. A dirty little trick really, and I was stuck there, pushing him off until I was so terrified, yes, terrified, and then mercifully they called him to the 'phone. God, it was hell, and yet all the time I could see how he felt. Willy, it can't go on much longer. Why am I so bloody fertile? Why doesn't anything work with me? What am I going to do?'

Willy stroked her neck with his finger. There was only one thing to do, but first he fed her an alternative, tempering her resolve so that, when it hardened, it would be true and sharp.

'You *could* divorce him, I suppose,' he said. 'We might just manage on your baubles and furs until we had the alimony. Then you could try someone else—an American or one of these management boys. They couldn't be worse than Alex, and far more dough.'

Eve sighed and drew on her cigarette irritably.

'Doesn't divorce appeal to you?' he asked.

'On what grounds? Because Alex wants a child, and I don't? He could ditch *me*. And he will, unless I . . . but I can't, Willy. I can't and I won't!'

Willy brushed his lips over her hair. Then he said quietly,

'You won't and you needn't, if you do what I've asked you to do all along. It's quite simple.'

'What do you mean?'

'Ring Christencrendler. Now. I'll get him for you. . . .'

'No, Willy. . . .'

'Why not?'

Eve looked away and stubbed out her cigarette, continuing the prodding movement long after all the fire had been extinguished.

'It's so final . . . irrevocable. . . .'

'Final irrevocable safety. What could be better than that?'

She shivered suddenly.

'I'm afraid.'

'Of what?'

'I don't know. So many things.'

'Evie,' he said, 'it's only Alex you're afraid of, isn't it?'

'Willy, if he ever found out . . .'

'He can't. Christencrendler is completely discreet. Surely he made that clear to you on the 'phone the night before last?'

'How do you know . . . ?'

'I called him. Shortly after you'd warned him not to let on to Alex. Well, it was an obvious precaution, darling.'

Eve smiled, and the smile became a chuckle, born of a lifetime bond of mischievous conspiracy.

'Willy, you're quite ruthless.'

'So is Alex. Look, darling, once it's done, you need never worry again. Afterwards you can be nice to him. Give him a good time. I don't really mind. If I know you're safe. It'll be fun in a way watching him begin to doubt himself, questioning his virility, wondering, worrying.'

'You really hate him, don't you?'

'Of course. It's a good emotion, hate. One of the few I have left. Far better than love. It never lets you down.'

'But you love me.'

'You're different. You *are* me. And you've never let me down. You won't now, will you, Evie?'

'Alex said I should see a psychiatrist. Perhaps, if I did . . .'

'Mother saw one, remember?' his voice pitched higher, and the words burst out. 'All the other doctors said she shouldn't have another child. But that didn't matter a damn to Father. Oh, no, he shopped around until he found a crackpot headshrinker to say it really would be the best thing for her, even if there was a risk. God knows what he paid him, but then Father was buying what *he* wanted most. A licence to have another son, so that he could forget I ever happened . . .'

'Willy . . .'

'Well, he didn't get one, did he? He was stuck with me after all, because the baby died and then Mother died too. Or rather she was killed. He killed her. Yes he did, Evie, he killed her. . . .'

'Stop it!'

Willy heaved himself up on his two sticks and walked over to the window.

'I'd do anything to stop your being killed like that,' he said hoarsely. 'Just so that Alex Cranford can satisfy his vanity.'

Outside, in its Saturday afternoon desertion, the Mayfair street looked drab, stripped of its weekday bustling glamour. Most of the high heels, the minks, the My-dears and the Oh-darlings, the Bentleys and the surreptitiously spitting chauffeurs had gone on their high-speed weekend migration to air-conditioned cottages and tax-loss farms, leaving only a few ill-bred dogs to foul the pavements unimpeded. What a pity, thought Willy, that Wolfenden hadn't concentrated on faeces instead of fornication.

He turned and looked at his sister, and saw the small convulsive movements of her shoulders. She'd always cried like that, silently, hiding it from him, protecting him from hurt, from his father, from the real world which clearly had no use for him. What a terrible burden he must be to her.

'Don't cry, Eve,' he said.

'I'm . . . I'm not crying. I just hate your talking like that. It doesn't do any good, Willy. To you or me.'

She blew her nose, and the absurd harsh little sound toppled the pebble of pity he had for her into the deep pool which was the pity he had for himself.

'The only good I could ever have done you was to have fallen down somewhere, and broken my neck,' he said.

'No, Willy, no.'

She looked round as he knew she would, wiping her cheeks dry with her finger, and came over to him as he hoped she would, and said what he wanted to hear her say.

'Never, never feel like that, darling. You'll always be more to me than anybody in the world.'

'Anybody?'

She smiled and kissed him on the mouth, knowing suddenly she had reached a decision.

'Willy, while I try and restore my face, why don't you put through a call to Paris?'

As he watched her pick up her handbag and disappear into the bedroom, he was filled with a sensation which he recognized only after he had spun the dial and had given the operator the number, probably because he so rarely experienced the elation of victory.

Distantly Eve heard his fluent idiomatic French, and then the tinkle of the bell as he put down the receiver.

'Any luck?' she called, and wondered what sort of luck she meant, and if for her it was about to run out.

'He should be ringing back in half an hour.'

Half an hour, and the first step would be taken, and then the next, and the next and, Hell! she'd be the same woman, wouldn't she? Always the same. Entire, inviolate, undivided. What did a little internal rearrangement mean? It meant no more messy, chancy, manoeuvres, no more anxiety, she told herself. It meant, in fact, glorious uninhibited freedom. The thought excited her, and the relief of final decision combined to swing her mood unexpectedly into light-heartedness.

The renovation of her make-up complete, she returned to the living-room as Johnson, his expression now as professionally impersonal as his tails and black tie, came in with an ice-bucket, tray and glasses. She watched Willy indulgently as he went through the ritual of tasting the wine and curtly approving it. Johnson brought her a glass, but the bow was overdone, and the 'Thank you, Madam; thank you, m'lord' an almost ridiculously obsequious caricature, as he disappeared again.

'Insolent bastard,' said Willy, and raised his glass. 'To gynaecologists in general, and little Christencrendler in particular.'

Eve laughed and took a long drink of the cold, biting fluid, and put her glass down on the desk. The notes lay where he had thrown them, careless, blatant.

'Willy, what are you doing leaving all this money lying about?' She picked them up and began counting.

'I had to pay those disgusting menials in cash. It's getting absolutely intolerable the way . . .'

'But there are over three hundred pounds left. I thought you said you were flat?'

'I was, darling, I was.' Willy helped himself to more champagne, pouring too fast so that the bubbles surged up and over the edge, sliding down the outside of the hollow stem, making a frothy pool on the black marble of the table. 'Blast,' he said, and sucked at the wine noisily.

'Where did this come from, then?'

'Angel sister, adorable twin, my other half, come over here, your glass is empty.'

'Willy, I want to know.'

'Do stop being cross and peevish. This is such a lovely bottle. . . .'

'You can't have borrowed all this on the ring. . . .'

'You're dead right I can't. Not from that revolting little Jewboy.'

'Who did you go to, then?'

'Don't remember his name, offhand. But he gave me a very decent price, I thought. About three times the pawn sum.'

'You mean . . . you sold it?'

'Yes.'

'To someone you don't know?'

'Well, yes. . . .'

'Oh, my God!'

Eve dropped the notes back on the table.

'What's wrong? He was a charming fellow. An O.E., actually.'

'What's it matter if he went to Eton or Manchester Grammar . . . ?'

'Of course it matters. . . .'

'You must be off your head to do such a thing.'

'Why, for God's sake? It was a straightforward business transaction: quick, civil, and profitable, instead of a mealy-mouthed loan at exorbitant interest.'

'But we can't get the thing back, you idiot!'

Eve went to pick up the bottle, but Willy took it and filled up their glasses. He smiled sheepishly up at her.

'You don't really need the ring, Evie, and I *do* need the money. You'll get it all back, I promise. I'm going to win next week. I'm bound to. I've had such lousy luck lately.'

'Don't you understand, when Alex finds out the ring has gone . . .'

'He'll never notice.'

'Willy, he *has* noticed.'

'What! When?'

'Last night. You know how property-conscious he gets at times. I said it was at Asprey's having a claw fixed. Sooner or later he'll ask if it's been done, and then what shall I tell him?'

'Oh, tell him you've lost it, tell him you sold it, tell him the truth if you like. What's it to do with Alex, anyway?'

'He bought it. He gave it to me.'

'Exactly. *Gave.* It's yours. To do what you like with. So you gave it to me.'

'I didn't. . . .'

'Darling, I said I'll pay you back.'

'You know you won't.'

'Oh, hell, have some more champagne. Don't you like it? I bought it specially for you.'

'Liar; you didn't know I was coming.'

'Well, I bought it anyway. . . .'

'With Alex's money.'

'Christ, can't you forget him for a single minute?'

'I have to live with him.'

'Then why don't you stand up to him? God, how long are we going on creeping about, worrying what Alex will say, what Alex will do . . . ?'

'As long as we're dependent on him, I imagine.' Eve sighed, drank some more wine, and sat down again on the pouffe.

'Love champagne, Willy. It was nice of you to get it for me.'

'I *am* nice.'

'So am I, then. If you're nice, I'm nice. We're just the same, Willy.' She kissed him, and began stroking the back of his neck.

'That feels fabulous, darling,' he said.

'Does it? I feel fabulous. I *am* fabulous. Fab. I'll always be fab. I'm getting squiffy, Willy.'

'Don't stop.'

'I won't.'

'You can do anything you like, Evie.'

'Anything *you* like, you mean.'

'Well, why shouldn't I?'

'Oh, God, that's lovely . . . !'

'It's stupid to be afraid of him, isn't it?'

'Who?'

'Alex.'

'I'm not afraid of him.'

'Then I'm not afraid of him. Don't let's be afraid of him any more.'

'We're not.'

'Of course we're not. And you know something?'

'What?'

'I'm going to stand up to my husband and if he doesn't like it . . . he can go to hell.'

'Hooray!'

Eve picked up the bottle, poured out some more, and let it slosh back amongst the ice.

'Better, now?'

'Christ,' said Willy.

'If you want me to look nice for you tonight,' she said, 'I'll have to go home and change soon.'

'I've got to change, too.'

'*And* have a bath.'

'Am I stinking?'

Eve giggled.

'No, I'm the one who's stinking. Silly old Alex. Must go Willy. Must go.'

'No, Evie, stay . . .'

'What about your bath?'

'I'll have it now, if you'll stay.'

'Willy, that's naughty,' she smiled. 'Do you want me to bath you, darling?'

'Would you?'

'Well . . .'

'You haven't done it for ages.'

Eve got up.

'All right, then. You've been very good buying the champagne.'

Willy picked up his sticks and struggled to his feet. She helped him towards the bathroom. Willy began laughing.

'What's the joke?' she asked.

'Alex. He'd think even this was frightfully perverted.'

'Well, it is. And if he knew, he'd probably kill me.'

'Then I'd kill him,' said Willy.

'Darling, how fabulous, would you?'

Their laughter enveloped them in its own private cocoon, and, as they left the room their voices and the sound of it became fainter, and mingled with the echo of running water and gay explosive splashes so

131

that the telephone had been ringing for some little time before either one of them heard it.

Chapter Eighteen

'Fifty-one, Langland Crescent. Detached. Four bedrooms, sun-lounge with French windows, loggia, spacious hall, dining-room with serving-hatch, modern kitchen, Aga cooker, half-acre garden, garage. This desirable freehold residence . . .' Mentally composing the estate-agent's advertisement, Cranford surveyed with distaste the curved row of houses, identical save for the variation of paint-colour, curtain-colour, porch-lights, door-knockers, garage-shapes. Desirable by whom? Manstein, presumably, and his wife and his children, and his dog and cat, his ox and his ass, his manservant and maidservant; coveted and re-coveted, bought and sold and astonishingly lived-in with Betjeman-like glee. He got out of the Bentley, which looked out of place parked next to the Morrises and Fords and Austins, like a pedigree Labrador, aloof amongst a litter of assorted terriers.

He walked up the short path to the front door. He looked for and found the expected mazooza nailed diagonally just below the right lintel, pressed the bell-push, and heard the expected door-chimes of the 'Blimey-Imey', and anticipated the faint smell of vinegar and Kosher frying-oil, offsetting the obsessional fussy tidiness, as he would sit and wait in a cut-moquette covered chair by a light walnut side-board, next to a chromium standard-lamp. Almost as soon as he had formed the imagined impression, he had castigated his own conde-scension, and stamped on his inbred, illogical anti-semitic prejudices. He tried to swallow his arrogance but, even in his present distress, it stuck half-way. He suspected it was because Cranford the renowned, the spectacular, disliked seeking advice from a modest colleague whose praises were relatively unsung, in spite of being one of the best dermatologists in England. He heard sounds on the other side of the door, and tried hard but unsuccessfully to don the humility appro-priate to a patient disturbing a hard-worked doctor on his free subur-ban afternoon.

The door opened on a domestic pandemonium of shouting children, a barking spaniel, a doe-eyed beauty in gold slacks and black breast-bulging sweater, record-player blaring away somewhere. He was sucked into the maelstrom, down the hall into the living-room littered with books, the walls covered to the ceiling with paintings, a 'cello in the corner, a mini-piano, cushions and broken-down chairs, and flowers all over the place, and laughter and unaffected hospitality, coffee on the tray waiting and, in the centre, leaning happily against the chimney-piece, Manstein, fifty, beaming, pipe-sucking, old grey flannels but an immaculate open silk shirt, exuding supreme content-ment in the midst of this, his own personal bedlam.

'Cranford, we haven't met. Always wanted to.'

His brown eyes darted over the bandaged hands, skilfully avoiding the handshake, and Cranford was eased gently into a low uneven chair with a castor missing. Someone turned off the record-player.

'I apologize for disturbing your weekend,' he said.

'You couldn't,' Manstein laughed. 'What could you do to a weekend? My whole life is constantly disturbed by these women. And look at the mess. And what does it cost me? I'm very badly treated.'

'Daddy . . . !' from Sharon, nine, long lashes, her mother's eyes, intelligent, bursting with vitality.

'Daddy . . . !' Jackie, seven, a faintly lisping echo of her sister, less plump, a little wistful.

'He's miserable here. Can't you tell? Every day Manny's going to run away. Sugar?' His wife Samira, radiant, warm-hearted mouth, putting the sugar-bowl by his cup, each child proffering a plate of biscuits, the spaniel following their movements with salivating intensity.

He didn't want a biscuit, or coffee; he wanted this thing over—diag-nosis, prognosis, treatment, immediate, effective. He had not driven out nearly twenty miles late on a Saturday afternoon for smalzy domes-tic banter.

'If you don't mind . . .' he began, but the four bright smiling eyes gazing down from a little above him were irresistible, impossible to disappoint, and he changed the end of the statement into a question '. . . may I have two?'

'You can have three.'

'You can have four if you like . . .'

'Or five . . .'

'Or six . . .'

'Or sixty-six.'

'Or six hundred and sixty-six.'

'Silly, he couldn't eat six hundred and sixty-six.'

'He could if he stayed until tomorrow.'

'I shan't be able to do that, I'm afraid,' said Cranford.

'Have you come to see Daddy about your hands?'

'Sharon! Don't ask personal questions.'

'That's all right. Yes, I have.'

'Daddy'll cure it. Is it warts?'

'I don't think so.'

'He cured my warts. I had six.'

'So did I. I had more than you.'

'How many did you have?' Cranford asked the young girl. 'Sixty-six?'

'No. . . .'

'Six hundred and sixty-six?'

'No!'

The laughter bubbled up and infected the dog, and the barking mingled with it.

'With six hundred and sixty-six warts, there wouldn't be any room for me!'

Manstein knocked out his pipe.

'But there *is* plenty of room for you in the garden. Now buzz off while Mr Cranford and I have a talk.'

'*Mister* Cranford? I thought he was a doctor?'

'He's a surgeon. They call surgeons "Mister".'

'Why? They're doctors too, aren't they?'

'Some are,' said Cranford. 'I agree it's very confusing.'

Samira got up. 'Come on, girls.' She shooed them towards the door. 'Let me know if you want more coffee. Say goodbye now.'

'Can't I show him my rabbits?'

'I've got a tortoise. Would you like to see him? He's ever so sleepy.'

'Sharon. Jackie.'

'Yes, Daddy. Goodbye, Mister Doctor. Goodbye.'

The door closed and the chatter faded and the room was very quiet, but it was a quietness which the deep-piled luxury of his own home never possessed. Cranford wondered at its special quality, a paradoxical tranquillity which waited with pleasure on its own disruption again by the gay expectant voices with their inquisitiveness and candour and nimble inconsequence. It was quite unlike the disinterested childless silence of the elegant house in Highgate.

Manstein observed his gaze of appraisal round the walls.

'My escape,' he said. 'But like all hobbies, obsessive, and rather selfish. Runs away with most of the jam on the bread.'

'Quite an investment, though,' observed Cranford. He had spotted two Sickerts, a Nicholson and a Nash.

'Here and there,' Manstein shrugged. 'But it's sometimes difficult to persuade a woman that a Proktor is better than a bit of mink or a diamond cluster ring.'

A nude on the far wall caught Cranford's attention. The pose, kneeling back, weight supported on the hands, head turned away against an almost dazzling blue, the coral glow of the skin in the curve of the neck and breasts, repeating the pattern of rounded bole-like shapes in the background, had a disturbing familiarity which he could not place. He got up and went over to the picture.

'Not that Samira is like that,' Manstein continued. 'I do her an injustice. She's as keen as I am. So are the children. They all try and wield a brush. Interesting, some of it,' he laughed. 'But I'm hopeless as a creator. My defence is criticism. I do some reviews for the *Statesman* and the *Argus* from time to time.' He came up behind Cranford.

'I wondered if you'd notice that,' he said.

'I've seen it before. . . .'

'Of course. It hasn't the confidence or the technical sureness of the later work, but it's all there, that indefinable quality of life which some of the Old Masters had, the bones, the vessels, the nerves, unseen but all functioning somewhere inside the paint. And the colour-singing. I imagine he was that rare kind of painter who smiled while he worked. Was he?'

'Who?'

'Maxwell Cranford. . . .'

The picture jumped out at him, suddenly illuminated by the flash-bulb of memory, his mother parcelling it up with all the others, a look of sadness on her tired face as she paused in her task, briefly studying it. 'Don't you like that one, Mummy?' 'I did, Alex . . . I do.' 'Then why are you making a face like that?' 'Like what?' 'As though you had a pain or something.' 'Happiness lost and remembered is painful.' She had strong fingers, like his own, and she pulled the picture-cord tight round the bundle, knotting it capably. 'If only your father had painted portraits of important people, people who matter, then we should have had something to live on.' Distantly, snatches of argument overheard from his bedroom. 'But I don't like their faces, Alice, so why should I paint them?' 'Because they pay . . .' 'God, what a reason for art!' 'It's been good enough for better artists than you.' 'You're a mercenary insensitive bitch . . . a social bum-sucker . . . a . . .' 'You're drunk, Max.' 'Yes, I am, thank God. Why aren't you? Why don't you ever get pissed? Might make you faintly bearable. . . .' 'Keep your voice down. You'll wake Alex . . . !'

'He was your father, wasn't he?'

'What . . . ? Yes,' said Cranford. 'And that was my mother.'

Manstein was disconcerted by the other's dry, clipped revelation. He said:

'She must have been a beautiful woman.'

'I didn't know her then. Before my time.'

Cranford turned away from the picture abruptly.

'Are you going to look at these hands of mine?' he asked curtly.

'Of course. Of course. Come through into the lab. Very inconsiderate of me . . . I was carried away. . . .'

His voice trailed off as Cranford gave him no help. Manstein led him across the hall into a small room on the other side, its meticulous order making a remarkable contrast with the haphazard carefree atmosphere of the rest of the house. Shelves, pathological specimens neatly labelled, bound volumes of medical periodicals, filing-cabinets, cases of slides, reagents, stains, porcelain-topped work-bench, X-ray tube, oil-immersion microscope, centrifuge. Manstein, too, seemed to alter as, pipe away, he slipped on a white coat. His movements became quick and precise, almost pedantic. The two halves of the man, work and play, balanced, mutually complementary.

He told Cranford to take off his shirt. He looked at his hair and scalp without comment and then slit up the bandages with scissors, exposing the swollen, weeping palms and fingers. He wiped some of the exudate away and used a hand-lens on the dried surface. He scraped some epithelial scales off with a scalpel, floated them into a spot of *liquor potassae* on a slide, dropped on a coverslip, and put the slide under the microscope. He searched carefully for two minutes, then came back to Cranford.

'Can't see any fungus. No mycelial threads,' he said, 'but we'll try Wood's light. It might pick something up.'

Manstein drew the blind which cut off the fading daylight outside the window as efficiently as in any photographic dark-room. He switched on the lamp, holding Cranford's hands under it. They showed up faintly in the purple glow, but there were no tell-tale spots of green fluorescence to indicate the presence of small-spored ringworm. He snapped off the light again, raised the blind, and then sat on a stool opposite Cranford. He took out his pipe and began filling it. The unhurried deliberation of the action snapped Cranford's patience.

'What is it?' he asked irritably, and added rudely, 'Do you know?'

'Yes, I know.' Unruffled, contemplative.

'Well?'

'I could give it a lot of names—cheiropompholyx, dermatitis, eczema —but you realize as well as I do: they're only descriptive terms. It isn't

136

a name we want: it's an aetiology. Why, after serving you without complaint for forty years, should the skin of your hands suddenly rebel? Against what?' Manstein looked again at the angry confluent lesions. 'And in no uncertain manner.'

'You tell me,' retorted Cranford. 'You're the expert. I detailed to you, on the 'phone, everything my hands have been in contact with.'

'Almost everything will make it worse—soap, detergent, even water —but they're not the cause.'

'Then what is?'

'This,' replied Manstein, pointing with the end of his pipe at the pink, sodden skin, 'is a battlefield. The outward and visible sign of an inner hidden conflict.'

'My God, is that all you've got to say?' Cranford exploded. 'The typical physician's escape-route. If you can't explain it, label it. Psychogenic!'

'It's a useful term. It indicates causation.'

'Look, Manstein, I'm a surgeon, not a neurotic woman. . . .'

'You could be a neurotic surgeon.'

Manstein smiled at him. Cranford checked the abusive retort which was his immediate response. He had an impulse to get up and dismiss further consultation as a waste of time, but an uneasy flash of insight made him remain where he was. He retreated behind a shield of superiority to which his reputation, he knew, entitled him. He smiled back.

'How far do you think I'd have got, if that were true?' he asked.

'Where you are. At the top. Perhaps that's what worries you.'

'Why should it?'

'You can't go any higher. The only direction you can take is down.'

'I don't have to move at all. I can stick where I am.'

'With those hands?'

'Obviously not, if they stay as they are. That's why I've come all the way out here. Listen, Manstein, either you can do something for me or you can't. . . .'

'You haven't got a simple infection, Cranford, like scabies, or impetigo or erysipelas, to be dismissed with an injection or an antibiotic. This state of your skin is the final declaration of an underlying disturbance. . . .'

'Oh, for God's sake, you're not a psychiatrist! Stick to practical dermatology, will you? Can you give me something for this bloody mess, or not?'

Unperturbed, Manstein nodded agreeably.

137

'I can clear up the acute reaction, dry up the exudate, remove the itching. . . .'

'How soon?'

'In a few days. . . .'

'Fine . . . that's all I want you to do.'

'Then the skin will be more or less normal to look at. . . .'

'Good enough.'

'I said normal to look at. It won't *be* normal.'

'What do you mean?'

'In its reactions. This can all break out again. And again. Unless you take pretty rigorous precautions.'

'Such as what?'

'No soap, no irritants of any kind. If possible, keep your hands out of water. Use olive oil for cleansing. No friction. No extremes of temperature. Some ultra-violet. Better still, a careful ration of natural sunlight.'

Cranford catalogued the details, fitting them into circumstances.

'That should be possible to arrange,' he said, 'for a week or two.'

Manstein shook his head.

'I'm afraid it'll need to be for longer than that.'

'How much longer?'

'Hard to say. That depends on you. The mental conflict, as you so properly reminded me, is not in my sphere. The practical dermatology is. The régime is fairly easy to adhere to. After a year or two, perhaps three, the skin should completely lose its hypersensitivity.'

Cranford stared at him with incredulity.

'Do you know what you're telling me?'

'Yes,' he nodded. 'The situation as I see it.'

'As you see it?' Cranford jerked his head back scornfully. 'As I see it, you're telling me I'm finished as a surgeon.'

'Not at all. You'll just have to stop operating. . . .'

'What's the difference?'

'Stop operating, temporarily.' Manstein got up and began searching along a shelf of jars and bottles. 'If you do as I say, you'll be able to get back to it.'

'You call two or three years: *temporarily?*'

'It is, in a life's career.'

'And what the hell do I do in the meantime?'

'You're still a doctor, Cranford.' Manstein smiled at a recollection. 'Interesting the way Jackie made that point. You can still heal the sick. Isn't that what we all go into medicine for?'

The question hung there in the room, rhetorical, accusatory, like a

Very light, suddenly exposing him, unprotected in the no-man's-land of his conscience. Don't answer. Don't think. Cranford froze his mind and features, knowing that immobility was his only protection, until the light faded. In the after-dark he could move forward against the enemy, who was only a man like himself; was himself. He watched Manstein bring a jar and spatula back to the bench. He sat down again on the stool opposite him, and Cranford allowed him, without comment or resistance, to spread the cooling thick white paste evenly over his palms and fingers.

'You'll find this will stop the irritation pretty quickly.' He produced from a drawer a pair of surgical gloves. 'Put these on, and don't take them off for four days.'

Manstein saw the impassive expression break into sudden laughter, eyes cold with the sharpness of flint.

'I shall enjoy that,' said Cranford. 'Congratulations on a nicely pointed ironical touch. I can always pretend I'm wearing a mask and gown too.'

He pulled on the gloves and slipped the rubber bands round the wrists.

'This will be the quickest way back into harness, believe me,' said Manstein quietly.

'On the contrary,' replied Cranford. 'It may be something else entirely.'

He got up, put on his shirt and then fixed his tie in the mirror, the stiffness of his fingers inside the rubber gloves making him fumble a little. Manstein scribbled a prescription and handed it to him.

'I doubt if you'll need more than one application, but in case you do, here's the script. It's nothing exotic. Anyone can make it up. Ring me if you're worried.'

Cranford took the piece of paper.

'That's what I always say. "Ring me if you're worried." Thousands of doctors dishing out the glib formula every day. All part of the game of healing the sick, isn't it, Manstein? Mostly, of course, it means "Don't ring me if you can possibly help it. I'm just mentioning it, to salve my professional conscience. I really hope you won't ever bother me again. I've much more interesting things to do, like playing with my children, or watching T.V., or collecting paintings." Is that why you went in for medicine?'

Manstein hesitated. 'I don't think so,' he said. 'I started rather late. After I came out of Buchenwald.' He opened the door and ushered Cranford down the hall.

'Goodbye,' he said. 'I'm sorry you've got such a long way to go.'

Cranford held his eyes a second, and then, with a crisp 'I'm obliged', walked down the path and out to the car, and suddenly the two girls were waving at the gate and the spaniel was barking, and he swallowed hard, and couldn't wave back, and he kept his eyes off the mirror and accelerated away fiercely, the tyres kicking up the gravel of the curved suburban road.

It was dark by the time he reached home. As he pulled down the garage door he noticed the fresh dent, where the cellulose had been stripped off, on the nearside rear wing of Eve's Mercedes.

Chapter Nineteen

'I HAVE MY driving licence and the insurance certificate here, constable. I can read out the number, would that be good enough . . . ?'

Eve held the receiver in one hand, and turned over the pages of the red paste-board covered booklet with the other.

'In the next three days? . . . I can't possibly do that, I'm flying to Paris early tomorrow. . . .'

The policeman at the other end of the line was respectful but irritatingly tedious in his dogged insistence. Over the parrot-like recitation of pedantic regulations she heard a door slam, recognizing it as the one leading from the garage into the kitchen. A moment later, a glimpse of Cranford crossing the hall into his study suggested a way of avoiding this boring, ridiculous formality. As he had questioned her after the accident, she remembered the young man's boyish features peering with absurd sternness from under the dark-blue helmet, belying his obvious susceptibility. She pouted her lips into the mouthpiece and her voice took on the quality of soft runny caramel.

'Constable, you were so terribly sweet and helpful a few minutes ago when this silly thing happened; couldn't you possibly be a darling again and call round here to look at the licence yourself?'

The pause lengthened, and she could see him licking the toffee off the words.

'What about on your way home, then . . . ?' Effortlessly she added a lie as sugar-coating. 'I'll be all on my own.' A moment's silence and the spurious sweet had been swallowed. 'Heavenly . . . I knew you were an angel. I'll have a drink waiting for you. . . .' She brushed aside the hesitant formal protest. 'But you won't *be* on duty, will you, constable?' She laughed and let the receiver drop back easily into place, then walked across the long elegant room.

She walked carefully because she was still lightheaded from Willy's champagne, a state fortunately undetected by the policeman, but the exhilaration she felt was more than could be induced by a million bottles of bubbling wine. She was going to be free, free, free of fear, free to give herself without the fear that followed the giving, free to take, free for the taking. Dear sweet Willy. Poor dear Alex. Both should be satisfied. Clever little Christencrendler, you can make me a very generous person to everybody. Generous and fearless. Fearless of anybody. The decision is made, made, made.

His decision was made, Cranford suspected, even before Eve had opened the door, but he was daunted by it as he looked up from the desk, and saw anew—as it always seemed, wondrously new—the dazzling radiance she could switch on, as now, with capricious but totally persuasive effect. God, what a possession!

'Alex, darling, may I interrupt a moment?'

'Interrupt what?'

'Aren't you working?'

'No,' he said, 'I haven't any work to do.'

As he watched her close the door and come over to him, he noticed his voice had a ring of elation, of defiance, instead of the appropriate dismay it should have had.

'I thought, as you were sitting at your desk . . .'

'Habit,' he said. An old broken habit. New habits for old.

'But you *are* staying in tonight?'

'Yes. . . .'

'Oh, good. A nice young policeman will be calling later on. Be an angel and show this to him.' She held out the driving licence. 'I'm afraid I've made rather a dent in the rear wing of the Merc.'

Cranford took the licence, checking that it was current.

'I saw it. What happened?'

'Some idiot pulled out from the kerb as I was passing. . . .'

'Were you hurt? Was anyone hurt?'

'No,' she laughed. 'Don't look so censorious, Alex. It wasn't my fault.'

'Of course not. How fast were you going?'

'I've no idea.'

'Did you tell the police that?'

'Really, darling, it isn't serious. Don't let's waste time talking about it.'

Time wasted, life wasted, love wasted. What a futile exhausting struggle ambition turned out to be.

'All right.' He put the licence on top of the pile of *British Medical Journals* at his elbow. 'How would you like us to waste time?'

She looked at him, briefly serious, before she remembered that the habit of defence was no longer necessary. Smiling, she came round the desk to him, savouring the pleasure of playing Tantalus.

'Dear, sweet Alex,' she said. 'If you want to know something, we've been ridiculously extravagant with time. We should never waste it—ever again.'

She put her arms round his neck, the action, by its unexpected display of affection, compounding the future for both of them. Disbelieving, he let her embrace him, smother what he had been told that afternoon by Manstein and the measuring up to the shock of it; let it erase the failure of the previous evening at Shinglestrand; let it defy the feeling that everything had gone sour, that everyone—Munro, Khouri, the dead Major Wharton—was standing round him in fell critical crescent, waiting for the kill. The magic of her fingers on his neck, in his hair, released, like a gush of oil, all the tangled-up puzzled love he had for her. He took her and kissed her, overwhelming her with a savage tenderness, keeping his own words back, not letting her speak, until the kiss itself, renewed and reborn, and renewed once more, at length escaped from between them.

'Eve,' he said. A statement summarizing existence. He could give up work, career, even the hope of children, if he still had her. Through his selfish desire for children he had nearly lost her. Eve. A word. Eve. A *raison d'être*. With blinding clarity he suddenly knew she was all he needed, all he had left, all he wanted.

'Dear, passionate Alex,' she touched his lips with her fingers, and then teasingly, 'That was fun. We must have a lovely drinky to celebrate it.'

'You're ahead of me, aren't you?'

She laughed. 'That's where I like to be.'

She went to the end of the desk and opened the concealed cabinet, the bottles and glasses surfacing like miniature rockets from a hidden silo.

'What will you have?'

'Eve, I'm sorry about last night. . . .'

'Don't let's worry about last night. Don't let's worry about that any more.'

142

'That's what I mean. If you don't want children, I don't mind any more.'

She stopped pouring the brandy, clattered the decanter down on the mirror-top of the cabinet, tilted her head back and let the laughter take hold of her. He watched the throbbing movement of her breasts with incomprehension.

'I'm serious, Eve. Don't you believe me?'

'Yes, darling. I believe you,' she got out. 'I believe anything you say. You're a very believable person. Of course you're serious . . .' She broke off as the joke caught her again in another of its facets. 'But you don't know how funny you are as well.'

'No, I don't,' he said.

Still shaking, she picked up the syphon and carelessly squirted soda into the brandy, the first shot wide of the target, sending a shower of spray on to the desk.

'I was just going to tell you,' she giggled, 'if you wanted some children, I'd have some for you.' She grinned at him. 'That *is* funny, isn't it? How many would you like, darling? Two, three, a dozen? *Fait votre jeu, Monsieur?*'

He watched her, suspicious of her inconsequent gaiety, not believing, yet desperately wanting to believe, like trying to make sure he had read his name on the examination pass list. He got up and went over to her.

'What's made you change your mind?'

She tilted her head and eyed him coquettishly.

'I could ask you the same, dear Alex. I'm just a changeable, unstable, frail little female. But you, Alex. Why have *you* suddenly changed your very strong, clever orderly mind . . .' She was laughing once more. '. . . on such an important and serious question?'

He took the tumblers from her and set them down.

'I couldn't begin to tell you all the reasons,' he said, 'but your happiness was the best one.'

He kissed her gently, and the laughter, which was still inside her, gave way to a tenderness towards him, tempting her to make a clean total confession. She broke from him in order to overcome it, because the emotion was fleeting and because she knew what she had at last decided to do was the only way to preserve whatever it was that existed between them. And between her and Willy, and Willy and the world.

'Your happiness is most important to me, Alex, too,' she said.

He kissed her again and the happiness she spoke about did not sound to him like a worn-out conventional cliché, but seemed fresh and true, and enveloped him in a way he had never quite experienced before.

'We will drink to that,' he smiled.

He gave her her glass, raised his and drained it, closing his eyes because he wanted to etch on his memory the softness he imagined he saw in hers, playing a childhood game: 'When you're not here at night-time, Mummy, I'm not afraid, because all I have to do is to close my eyes, and then I can see you.'

'Alex . . .'

He opened them and noticed that her glass was still untouched, still half-raised to her lips.

'Yes?'

'Alex, why on earth are you wearing those gloves?'

Instinctively, he turned away, hiding his hands from view.

'I have a . . . dermatitis,' he said. 'It's been coming on for some time. Today it flared up. I saw a skin specialist this afternoon. This is part of the treatment.'

'Oh, I see,' she replied lightly. 'I thought you'd become absent-minded, and forgotten to take them off after operating.'

Her casual acceptance of the situation, her unconcern, stung him. He turned and put his glass down.

'I shan't *be* operating again,' he said. 'Not for a very long time. If ever.'

'You're joking, of course?'

He held up his gloved hands in front of her.

'Do you think my sense of humour is as sick as this? I can't operate: do you understand? I'm trying to get used to the idea. You'll have to try, too.'

She stepped away from him as if his hands had indeed struck her. He let them drop to his side.

'Eve . . . I'm sorry,' he said, hoarsely. 'Sit down . . . I want to tell you about it.'

She swallowed her drink and then obeyed his request, still clutching her empty glass.

'But if you can't operate, Alex . . . what are you going to do?'

Cranford paced up to the door and back again.

'When Manstein delivered his prognosis, my first reaction was a blind fury, a blind refusal to accept it,' he said. 'I wanted to run out and tear up and down Harley Street until I found someone to swear he was wrong. But he's right. I know that. He's one of the best. As I drove home, I knew I had to learn to live with what he'd said.'

He clenched his hands, trying to persuade himself that the irritation was growing less, that the treatment was already beginning to take effect.

'It isn't easy, Eve, to accept suddenly at forty that you're finished as a surgeon. Operating has been my life. To give it up is a kind of dying. You can understand that, can't you?'

Eve nodded, and the implications of what he was saying, what it would mean to her, to Willy, were chasing in panic turmoil round her head.

'But surely you don't have to give up everything?'

'No. I'm still a doctor. I can go back ten years and work my way up as a physician; I could do research, be a G.P. Heal the sick, don't you know? Well, it wouldn't work. Not for me. I wouldn't be able to heal them. I'd just grow to hate them.' He laughed suddenly. 'You can't ask the prima donna to return to the chorus. That ends up with a bottle or a gun.'

He put some soda in his empty glass and drank it down.

'No. I've made my mark in medicine. Let it rest there. Let it speak for itself. That's how I feel, you see?' He smiled. 'I never could quite swallow the mushy sentimentality, the pious self-righteousness of the Hippocratic oath. I can say it now. It's about as practical as a vow of celibacy or life-long fidelity.'

'Is it practical to talk and think like that?'

'It can lead to something practical. Besides, it gives me a feeling of release, of euphoria in a strange kind of way.' His voice became excited, younger. 'It isn't really a tragedy, Eve, that this has happened at forty. It's a blessing. There'll be time for living now. Days, weeks, years of time, not just a few snatched moments—for me, between cases; for you, between parties. Time for living with each other; for living together.'

She got up and poured herself another drink.

'How can we live, if you don't make a living?'

He saw her hand trembling as she held the expensive crystal tumbler.

'We can, if we settle for modest necessities.'

Her head jerked up.

'What does that mean?' she swallowed some brandy, and heard herself beginning to slur. 'I hate necessity. I hate modesty, for that matter.' She steadied herself and sat down again. 'Alex, you're not making sense.'

'I'm trying to make a plan.'

'For what?'

'For me—for us—for the future.'

145

'It doesn't sound very rosy. Not from over here.'

'It could be just that, Eve.'

'Without any money coming in?'

'I have a few investments.'

'Enough to live on?'

'Without so much going out, we could manage. If we're both deter-mined we can make it work.'

'Make what work, for heavens' sake?'

'A new sort of existence. Perhaps a better one.'

'Better? How . . . ? Where . . . ?'

'We can sell this place for a start.' He looked round the room she had furnished for him with such abandoned disregard for cost. He wondered how he had indulged her so immoderately. 'And all the gaudy contents,' he added.

Eve drew in her breath audibly.

'Gaudy? Don't be so insulting. They're gorgeous. . . .'

'Let's hope we can recoup the gorgeous price,' he retorted.

'I don't want to recoup it. I like it. Just as it is. I like this house. I like everything in it.'

'It's out of the question, Eve. I can't keep up a place like this now.'

'Well, what sort of a place can you keep up?'

'Something small and unpretentious. And cheap.'

'And where do you imagine you'll find that?'

'I don't know, exactly. Somewhere in the sun. There's plenty of choice. Away from the high-priced fashionable places it's possible to pick up a small villa for about the price of a short lease on a four-roomed flat in Maida Vale.'

'Who wants a four-roomed flat in Maida Vale?' she said, illogically, and held out her empty glass. 'Same again, Charlie.' He took the glass and put it back on the tray.

'Any more and you'll be as high as a kite.'

'That'd be a nice place to live. Right up in the sky.'

He turned away sighing with a sudden weariness.

'All right, Eve. We'll talk about it tomorrow.'

'Talk, talk. Alex, why do you always want to talk? Is that what we'd do in our cheap little villa?'

'Why not? After a time we might even find something to say to each other.'

'And when we'd said it, what else would there be to do?'

'Oh, for God's sake, Eve . . .'

'Sorry, Alex. I'm being bitchy. Tell me, darling . . . I'm listening. Really I am.'

He hesitated, and then as the picture developed in blue and white and the sound faded in with waves on a shore, he could suppress his enthusiasm no longer.

'We'd have a bit of land, a few fruit trees, our own grapes—not for wine of course, just for eating—a boat to catch some fish. We could sell some produce and haggle at the market—not for profit, just for fun. We could swim, and cook and eat and sleep. I could try and write a little. You could read. And of course you couldn't help looking beautiful. Isn't that what most people dream of retiring to? But most people put it off and off and die in the process. Those that do get there find it's too late to adapt, and the dream turns sour and that kills them too. But it needn't for us.' He looked at her earnestly. 'Well, Eve, how does it sound to *you*?'

Her face was blank for a few seconds, and then the smile became laughter and the sound became words, and each one flicked and stung, and he knew what he'd just said was his last appeal, and it was all over, and there was nothing left after all.

'Shinglestrand! It's Shinglestrand all over again! With heat and flies instead of cold and woodworm. That's how it sounds to me, do you hear?'

She was on her feet, and the room spun round, and she felt sick, and when it steadied she was leaning on the desk and he was sitting there, looking at her dumbly. And the nausea cleared and for the first time she saw him as a pathetic, defeated man. And rage came because on her terms he had let her down, and that meant Willy too, and he was of no use to either of them any more.

'Listen, Alex, you can go to your romantic little place in the sun, with the simple life, and the homely virtues, but don't expect me to come with you. I'm not that sort of person. I like comfort and money and luxury and parties and people. I hate lonely, drab little places. I love cities and lights and I don't feel the slightest shame in admitting it. I need a heap of money, Alex. So does poor Willy. We were born to it. I don't mind admitting that either. You haven't nearly enough for us, even now. It's such a bore having to eke out my miserable allowance by pawning and selling my jewellery. Yes, you might as well know. That ring isn't at Aspreys. Willy sold it to finance his party tonight. It's sad, I suppose, but you see, Alex, unless you can give me the sort of life I must have, you have nothing to give me at all.'

He kept his anger down, pushing away the moment when the bitter hopeless failure of everything he'd striven for and cared about would envelop him.

'Thank you, Eve, for being honest,' he said. 'It's prettier than finding out one has been deceived.'

She laughed, then, and she couldn't control it and she didn't care if she could or not, because that was funnier than anything she had heard for years, the two years of her life she had wasted with him, trying to make herself be something she never could be.

'You know, Alex,' she said. 'You're the sort of person who somehow encourages deception. It might be useful to remember that, when I'm not with you any more.'

Concentrating on the geography of the room, she found the door.

'I'm sorry about your hands,' she said, and went out leaving the door open.

He listened to her laughter fade as she made her way up the stairs. He broke, then, and with a blinding furious movement, swept his arm across his desk, scattering the ormolu and onyx inkwell, the tooled-leather blotter, the Lalique lamp, and the pile of journals, on to the floor, knowing that the action was symbolic of the ruin and full stop his life had come to. He tried to prevent the blurring of his eyes and the thick hotness in his throat as he stood still looking down at the jumbled mess around his feet.

Gradually he realized his eyes had cleared, and he was staring at the cover of a journal of surgery. The print of one line of the 'Contents' leapt up at him, jangling a spot in his mind, turning it inside out in suspicious revelation. He stooped and lifted the magazine, and quickly turned up the article.

'"A new technique for the insertion of intra-uterine contraceptive rings" by K. Christencrendler, Chef de Clinique, Hospital de Saint Saens, Paris.' He took out his wallet and read the name on the slip of paper in Eve's handwriting. Christencrendler. What the hell was a gynaecologist doing, treating her for food-poisoning? A cold clamminess broke out on the back of his neck; the neck of the sort of person who encourages deception.

He went to the bookshelf and found the French Medical List. The name was there all right and the 'phone number. This was a deception which could be checked straight-away. He snatched up the receiver.

'Yes, darling, of course I'm coming. . . .' Eve's voice and running bath-water, and Willy's, and then Eve's again, 'I'll tell you all about it when I see you. . . .'

Cranford put the receiver back. Up the stairs, along the softly-lit passage, across the perfumed bedroom and through the mirrored door until he was looking down at her, the blue water rising around her in the bath, her slender fingers holding the blue receiver to her ear.

'Eve,' he shouted, over the sound of the water.

She turned towards him with unconcern.

'Just a minute, Willy, Alex wants me. Yes?'

'Christencrendler's a gynaecologist. What did you see him for?'

'Really, Alex, what does it matter now? I'm having my bath. Besides, I'm talking to Willy.'

He snatched the instrument out of her hand.

She stood up and tried to grab the 'phone from him, but he held it out of reach on the long cord, clutching it with both hands, smothering the mouthpiece.

'Tell me the truth, Eve.'

'Give me that back. . . .'

'He fitted you with a ring, didn't he?'

'No.'

'And you had a haemorrhage. That was what happened, wasn't it?'

She swayed a little, holding on to the hand-bar behind her for support.

'All right, Alex; you didn't have to know, but I'll tell you.' Her voice became hysterical with tears and anger. 'I've been through hell for you. Hell, because all you really wanted me for was to produce a screaming brat for you. . . .'

'That's not so. . . .'

'Oh, yes. Well, I didn't want it, so dear little Doctor Christencrendler took it away from me. Satisfied?'

The shock of her admission transfixed him, staring at her, nude, beautiful, defiant.

'You mean you were pregnant . . . ?'

'Naturally.'

'With my child?'

'Oddly enough, I haven't deceived you in that way.'

'And you deliberately . . . destroyed it?'

'Do you think I liked doing it?'

'But you did it. You murdered . . . my . . .'

'Yes. And I'm going back to Christencrendler next week. Do you know what for? To be sterilized. So that I can never be pregnant again. By you or anybody. Never. Never. Never . . . !'

She shrieked the words out, and all he wanted was to stop them. His eyes blurred and he raised the 'phone to strike her.

'Don't, Alex . . . Willy . . . Willy . . .'

She slithered down into the water. A bleating sound in his hand arrested its movement. Willy. That was where her love was, always had been, always would be. An exclusive, sick kind of love which, like twin serpents, the two of them had twisted round his own, so that now it was strangled and utterly finished. Suddenly all he felt was an overwhelming revulsion, an imperative urge to escape.

The 'phone squealed hysterically. With a gesture of disgust he threw the receiver into the chair where she had dropped some of her clothes, and went out through the door, back through the bedroom, and into the silence of his own room.

For twenty minutes he sat on his bed trying to get his thoughts into some order, but the task was too much for him in his present mood. He couldn't stay in this house; that was at least certain. He decided to go to a hotel and try in the morning to work out what he should do. He threw some things into a case. He switched off the light, blotting out the fiery-eyed animals in his father's picture, and walked along the passage past Eve's door. Downstairs he went through the kitchen towards the garage, but a noise outside the window arrested his hand on the door-knob. He could see the water tumbling down from the overflow-pipe above. Even in his present mood of despair, the irrelevant untidy wastefulness of the sound irritated him, until suddenly its significance had spun him round, and sent him running back into the hall. Dropping his case at the foot of the stairs, he mounted them three at a time. For the second time that evening he hurried along the passage and into her bedroom.

The bathroom door was open as he had left it. The tap was still running. Eve was in the bath with her face downwards. One leg and an arm were hooked over the edge. Round the slim, perfectly-shaped ankle was looped the telephone cord. Her hand still clutched the receiver. A continuous buzzing sound came from the earpiece.

Chapter Twenty

FOR A SECOND, or part of a second, the shock of his discovery paralysed him, fragmenting time and thought and memory and intention into a myriad stinging particles, like the dazzling suffocation of a blizzard.

He saw the scene as if he had been there and watched her reach for the 'phone, Willy's voice wailing and sucking her towards destruction. But Cranford was part of the action too: he had left the instrument out of reach. Eve, as well, with the unsteadiness of champagne and brandy: all three had contributed to the tragedy as she had slipped. Stunned for only a moment, perhaps, yet it had been long enough to let her take the first unconscious inspiration of hot, perfumed water. Even then there must still have been hope, but the alcohol coursing through the blood had locked it out, damping the centre at the base of the brain which controlled the protective cough reflex, allowing the second deadly intake and then the third and the fourth, until the delicate pink alveoli of the lungs were filled and swamped, frothing helplessly, cut off for ever from the air of the heated room which was life.

The heart would have gone on pumping wildly for a time, forcing the blood, blue and darkening as the haemoglobin changed its colour, to the cells of the brain, itself faltering, using up the lost oxygen, transmitting in ever-weakening salvos the impulses necessary to keep the diaphragm moving, until at last, with a few apologetic beats, the strong muscular chambers would have become still and silent, like a ship's engine-room at the end of a voyage.

Half an hour now and no possible chance of resuscitation; half an hour while he had sat in the next room, licking his own misery and disappointment, letting her die.

It seemed to him that her death completed his total desolation. He wanted to kneel and gather her up and kiss her and, by some skill beyond the craft of science, restore her for a moment so that at least he could tell her that whatever she was, or had done, or would have done, he had once loved her. Instead, like a robot following the programming of its computer, he went about the automatic trained verification of her death, as though the tragedy of it were in a separate world, apart from him, without significance to past or future. He unwound the cord and lifted the leg over the side of the bath, turning the body face upwards with infinite gentleness, so that it lay decently, with undiminished beauty, in the place where it had luxuriated so often. He turned off the tap and replaced the 'phone.

Instantly it rang, the sound pounding against the dazed armour of grief which held him briefly protected, until he registered its protest, and lifted it again.

'Hello . . . hello . . . Is that Highgate 2197? . . . Hello . . . ?'
'Yes?'
'Engineer here. Your line has been reported out of order. Would you replace the receiver please and we'll test-ring the number.'
'Not necessary,' said Cranford. 'The thing's been off the hook.'
'Right-y-o. Sorry to have troubled you.'
He put the instrument back, and at once he heard the door-bell

ringing distantly. He stood, disinterested by the sound, wanting to be alone inside his armour, not ready yet to strip it off and expose himself to the sad, aimless emptiness which was now his life. On and on the jingle stabbed and then became continuous, as some unknown finger pressed on the bell-push relentlessly, until to Cranford it seemed to be pressing on his skull, cracking it open, prising up his private solitude with outrageous effrontery. He ran through the bedroom, along the passage, down the stairs and across the hall, flinging open the door aggressively.

The cars were parked carelessly in the drive, headlights cross-lighting the scattered group, splashing the women's dresses with colour, silhouetting the men's dark suits against the reflecting chromium and cellulose, all faces turned towards him. They looked like some modern Raphaelesque fresco, the lines of composition leading the eye to the central figure, each arm supported by a chinless youth, each hand clutching a stick, one stick reaching the ground, the other's ferrule rivetted to the bell-push.

Willy grinned, swaying against his supporters.

'Good evening, my man,' he said.

It was a drawling, slurred condescension, summoning from behind him sniggers and, 'Do listen to Willy, isn't he frantic?'

'Don't just stand there.'

'Run in and get her, old boy.'

'Stop being beastly; how can the poor darling run?'

'Good old Willy!'

Cranford knocked the stick away from the bell-push with a swift upward movement of his arm, as though he were parrying the thrust of some weapon.

'What do you want?'

'My sister,' replied Willy, and walked forward, helped by his idiotic bearers, stumbling against Cranford, so that before he could prevent it, he had stepped back, and the whole gabbling, giggling crowd were following on top of him into the hall. For a moment all thought of Eve, and the fact that she was lying dead upstairs, was lost in fury at Willy's insolent trespass.

'How dare you push your way in here like this?'

'Because it's unlikely that you'll invite me in.'

More sniggers and voices from behind.

'Not very friendly, your brother-in-law, what . . . ?'

'Funny sort of chaps, these sawbones. . . .'

'Look, he's got rubber gloves on. . . .'

'Does he operate here?'

'Only abortions, I expect. . . .'

Giggles.

'Don't laugh. Good quacks are useful to know, Moira.'

'Hello, Alex. Aren't you coming to the party, darling?' Norah Britt drunkenly leering at him.

'No!' shouted Cranford.

Perhaps because he was a big man, perhaps because the desperate tension of the last few hours made his voice crack, and his whole body tremble with rage and anguish and sadness, the sea of faces round him dropped their supercilious, empty smiles, perceptibly flinching. Cranford faced them, somehow keeping back a compulsive urge to fling himself at them, to go berserk. The whole idle, superior, parasitic bunch of them, entrenched behind their privilege and money and ludicrous outdated snobbery, appeared to him as the authors of his own total destruction. But through the rage there welled up a new fury at himself, a fury tinged with shame that he had mis-directed his God-given skill to take his place among them, accept their values, their symbols, tend their vain needs, marry one of them . . . Eve. But Eve was beauty and there could, somehow, have been love and respect and children. If there hadn't been Willy; but there was Willy, and it didn't matter any longer, because Eve was dead. Eve, his wife. Yes, that made her his. His and not theirs, and all he wished was to be left in peace to mourn her. His eyes pricked and he turned away, knowing in that moment that he wasn't going to tell them that she was dead and how she died. At least he would salvage, from the wreck of their life together, a memory of her which would be untarnished by wagging mischievous tongues and sordid newspaper speculations.

'Eve's not coming. She's staying with me. Now will you please, all of you, go?' he said, and the quiet passion of his tone was more effective than any aggressive threat of ejection.

There was a brief silence and then a shuffling and murmuring.

'Come on, Willy. . . .'

'We'll go back. . . .'

'I said it wasn't a good idea. . . .'

'You didn't, you said . . .'

'Oh, shut up and come on. . . .'

'Goodbye, Alex. Sorry to have missed you. . . .'

Willy's voice broke through.

'All right, go if you want to, you rotten bastards. But I came here for Eve, and I'm not leaving till I've seen her.' He banged one of his sticks petulantly on the floor and shouted up the stairs. 'Eve! Darling . . . ! It's me, Willy! Where are you?'

153

The door through which his friends had vanished was still open behind him. For a second Cranford felt a compassion for the half-man which was Willy, a vague fleeting bond because, without Eve, half of him too had died with her.

'She won't answer, Willy,' he said.

'Why not?'

'Because she's asleep.'

'Asleep? Why?'

'Sleeping it off.' Her life, all of it.

'But she promised me on the 'phone she was coming to my party. . . .'

'When she promised she was pretty drunk.'

'But she promised . . . she promised. . . .'

It was a forlorn, blubbering cry, the agonized refusal of a child to believe that a grown-up loved-one could let him down.

'Well, she's broken it,' shouted Cranford. 'She's not coming, do you hear? So go away, Willy, go away. Grow up. Live your own life, but get out of mine.'

Willy stood, trying to speak through his anger.

Cranford turned in disgust from the puckered features and quivering lips. His foot caught the suitcase, knocking it on to its side, making him stumble. He righted it, clumsily. Through the open door a voice called, 'Come on, Willy,' and another, 'We can't wait all night,' and 'Willy, come on.' A car horn sounded raucously. Willy pointed at the suitcase with one of his sticks.

'What . . . what's that doing there?'

'Mind your own bloody business,' said Cranford. 'Go on. Get out. Get back to your party. Your precious friends are calling for you. There's nothing for you here. Goodbye, Willy.'

Willy's eyes flicked from the suitcase to Cranford's and back to the suitcase.

'Why are you . . . you're going away, Alex, aren't you?' he said.

'Yes, I'm going away . . . now for the last time . . .'

'Why? What's happened? Why couldn't I get through?'

'The 'phone was off the hook.'

'But why, why was it off? I heard you arguing, and then . . .' he broke off and stumped to the foot of the stairs, and called again, 'Eve . . . Eve. . . .'

Cranford caught his arm and swung him round.

'There's nothing for you up there, Willy. Nothing. Nothing ever again.'

Willy stared at him, wincing at the strong grip on his arm.

'What . . . what do you mean, nothing ever again?' he whispered.

A car engine started up, and the sound of the tyres on the gravel came through the door to them.

Suddenly, the full implications of his position swept over Cranford in a gut-tightening shock of realization. The interrupted phone-call; the knowledge he had of Christencrendler which supplied the motive; whatever Eve might have said to Willy before he had snatched the receiver from her; Willie as witness; the body drowned in the bath; his gloves, not to cover a skin-condition, but to leave no finger-prints, and finally his case packed—with him caught in the act of leaving—to make the whole affair look like an accident, which it was, but which nobody would believe in face of the mountainous weight of circumstance around him. Yet what did it matter now? His wife was dead, his career finished, there was only an airless vacuum left to live in. The answer came, rapid, certain, building up its own web of action and decision. If his life was over it was not going to end in miserable resignation, with his defending it, trying to prove its innocence, letting it wallow through the degradation of public scandal. No. It would end with dignity. His reputation, such as it was, would stay as it was.

'I mean,' said Cranford, 'that tonight Eve had to make a choice. Between you and me. Our marriage and your dependence. Well, she made it, Willy. We're going away again together. As soon as Eve has slept off her hangover, we're going back to Shinglestrand. I was just taking this case to the car.'

He marvelled at the calm delivery of the words and with satisfaction saw them strip the incredulity from Willy's face, watched the lie kick away the supports of his fragile ego. It was the ultimate rejection. He let go of Willy's arm and picked up the case.

'But she . . . she said . . . ?'

'She said to let you know she'd changed her mind. That's why she doesn't want to see you. It would only hurt more.'

The car horns jabbed away outside the door again. Willy's mouth was moving, but no words came. Abruptly it snapped to and the jaws clenched. The venomous hatred in his eyes fenced with Cranford's a moment, and then he spat straight at him and, whipping round, limped laboriously out of the house to the clamorous empty welcome beyond.

Cranford felt the saliva still wet on his cheek when the last car had gone.

Chapter Twenty-One

'WHATEVER YOU DO, boy, do it because you want to. Submit to no one, nothing, boy, only the dictatorship of your soul. Dictatorship. Difficult to say when you're drunk. Say it, boy. Dictatorship. That's it. Your father's drunk, Alex, and your mother's lying upstairs alone between the sheets, sober, tense, soulless, trying to pretend she'd be better off dead than with me. And dead she is to me. Dead because we've never seen anything in the same colours. All roses to her are black. And I'm rotten black inside, too. So she's dead and I'm drunk. Go to bed, boy, go to bed, and let's all smile at breakfast.'

As he slammed the door and ran back up the stairs, his father's words churned up the images of then and now. Cranford reacted now as then, with cold withdrawal.

Escape lay, then, in order, in the careful graded arrangement of the cherished objects in his little bedroom, in an obsessive tidiness of the mind, which even within its ten-year-old compass made him do, not what he wanted, but follow a breath-holding compulsive determination to make his mother happy. And tidiness, rightness, correctness, made her happy. And who could be more tidy than a surgeon? And who could be more happy than your mother? 'Your father would never have made a surgeon, Alex.'

In her bathroom Cranford snatched up the 'phone and demanded the number. As he waited for the East Anglian accent to come on at the other end of the line, the fire inside his gloves began to lessen. He glanced round the glistening walls. This gaudy palace he had built around him had no meaning or attraction any longer, now that the deity of the shrine lay dead. It could all go, and he could go too and never return. The warm water in the bath had preserved the pinkness of her skin. He looked at her, motionless, but was no more stirred to emotion. Eve had gone. This wasn't her. And this body was just another object to be tidied away out of his life like Willy, and operating, and the race for riches. He took hold of one of her ankles and gently bent the knee. The joint moved easily without resistance. The warm water again, holding off rigor mortis. That was important. A thing to be held off as long as possible.

'Hello . . . is that you, Field? . . . Alexander Cranford here. Look, Bill, I find I'm able to resume my holiday after all. Is that room we had still there? . . . Good . . . There's a party going on, so I'm not sure if we'll get away tonight. . . . Anyway, if we're coming, we'll be with you before midnight . . . but tomorrow definitely . . . Oh, several days, can't tell . . . Fine. Thank you. Goodbye.'

Goodbye, goodbye. God be with ye. The end of the road. But before reaching it all good men put their house in order. Method, logic, detail, no turning back. No waiting for Willy's hysterical cry of 'Murder'. Action this day.

He felt the temperature of the water. Eve must be kept soft and pliable. He pulled out the bath-plug, ran a few gallons off, and topped up again from the hot tap. Her eyes gazed past him emptily, without lustre. Like the snapping off of a light, his grief had gone, leaving a strange, leaden dissociation. But decency should remain. The goddess must be hidden from vulgar stares. He closed her lids gently with his fingers, and covered the bath with one of her outsize blue, mono-grammed towels.

In the bedroom he worked his way down the long row of mirrored doors, a dozen of them, which fronted the fitted wardrobe, itself form-ing one side of the room. Her clothes were in colours, soft, subtle, se-ductive, with flashes here and there of daring primaries to give that conversation-stopping impact; materials sleek, silk, satin, but also rough-woven, clinging, deceptively simple; day dresses, street dresses, dresses for cocktails, dresses for the grand evening; coats, casual, belted, short, three-quarter-length, ocelot, mink, leather, suède, casuals, faintly fetishist creations, and shoes, shoes, delicate, spindle-high, iridescent, to raise her above the adoring earth they so lightly trod on. This was the wanton ephemeral envelope he had gladly helped to fashion. And because it had covered beauty, pointed it, adorned it, he had mistaken its equation with love and truth, only to find now that the symbols were wrong, the formula spurious. The sweet reek of perfume, which belched through each door as he opened it, smelt of deception and death.

He packed two cases for her with infinite care, choosing logically underwear, slacks, a sweater, a tailored suit, two warm long-sleeved dresses, a couple of scarves, bed-jacket, nightdress, toilet-bag, slippers. In the top of the second case he put the most extravagant of Eve's evening dresses, a silver lamé, a pair of stiletto-heeled diamanté san-dals, and closed the lid on them. He shut the wardrobe doors and carried the cases into the passage. He went back into the bedroom and took a brooch and two rings and a necklace out of the jewel-case, leaving the rest.

In his own room he packed a second case for himself: an old sweater, grey flannels, his gardening jacket, old hat, raincoat, two pairs of golf-shoes. Into the pocket of his raincoat he put the rings and brooch and necklace and most of the cash he had drawn from the bank that morning. He filled the remaining space in the case with two towels. He folded his own swimming trunks into a convenient neat nylon square which hardly bulged the pocket of his suit.

He was breathing heavily by the time he had carried the three cases and his original one, which was still at the foot of the stairs, through the kitchen to the garage. He put one of his and one of Eve's in the boot of the Bentley, and the other two on the rear seat. He opened the garage doors, started the engine and switched on the car-heater. It was essential to get the interior of the car warm and keep it so. He left it to heat up and went back into his study with a brush and pan. He swept up the broken glass, and tidied the periodicals from the floor, putting them back on the desk. He collected his spare surgical bag and took that to the car. He emptied the contents, instruments, dressings, local anaesthetics, antibiotics into his second suitcase on the rear seat, locked the empty bag, carried it upstairs and flung it in the lumber-loft.

All this had been easy, a methodical ordering of events and inanimate objects, like the preparation for any normal holiday. The next part was another matter. He caught his own reflection in each of the mirrored doors on his way across Eve's bedroom. He perceived the tense preoccupation in his expression, and thought he saw an older man glance back, tired and ready to relinquish the strength-sapping demands of ambition; a man who had settled for things as they were. The game was over bar the shouting, and the crowd was restless and ready to go home. Consciously he braced himself, correcting the inadvertent stoop of his shoulders.

He found a drawer full of her swim-suits and bikinis. He selected one which he had always liked, and then discarded it for another. Any sentimental faltering now could unnerve him, crack his resolve, and his resolve must be final and for all time. He took the swim-suit into the bathroom.

He stood still a moment, aware of the sweat covering his face. The only way he would be able to accomplish what he had to do was to notch his mind into its well-worn groove of professional detachment. Concentrating, he hypnotized himself to don the surgeon's armour of competence, and knowledge and skill which had become second-nature to him. As he took the towel off the bath and laid it on the floor, he fancied he heard the deferential tone of the theatre sister's voice: 'We're ready, Mr Cranford.'

He lifted her body out, light and limp and warm, and placed it face downwards on the towel, observing with relief the absence of post-mortem staining on the buttocks and shoulders. He dried the back thoroughly and then turned her over, and gave meticulous attention to neck, armpits, breasts, limbs and abdomen. He patted her face and rubbed her hair as dry as he could. He sprinkled the flawless skin with talc, and lubricated the inside of the swimsuit with more powder. Thus prepared, it proved easier than he had imagined to fit on to her body. This done, he took a fresh warm towel from the heated rails and swathed her in it like a mummy, leaving her head free.

He paused, still on his knees beside her, resisting an idiotic thought that he might be discovered there like some slave-worshipper in an attitude of obedient prostration.

He found the hair-dryer on a shelf, and when he had used it, he combed her hair carefully, leaving it loose and cascaded on to her shoulders. Then he fetched cosmetics from the bedroom, and set about the final attention to detail—eyebrow-pencil, eye-shadow, mascara, lipstick. He stood back and regarded her, oddly pleased with his skill. Faces, after all, had been his working medium, and this one was the most beautiful face of all. His macabre reflection flipped over into sudden remorse and desolation, and before he could stop himself, he had gently kissed her lips, and then escaped headlong into the bedroom, fighting an overwhelming desire to cry out.

At length he recovered, and it was with renewed precision that he snapped the clasp of the emerald bracelet round her wrist and inserted the gold hooks of the matching earrings through the fine pierced holes of her earlobes. He tied a silk scarf round her head, let the water out of the bath, and fetched her full-length sapphire mink from the bedroom. Having unwound the towel, he slid her arms into the sleeves of the coat and let the warm fur envelop her, in the manner to which it was accustomed. He picked her up, switched off the bathroom light, hooked his finger through the jewel-case handle on the dressing-table as he passed it, and carried his burden of riches, his life and death, his conscience and pride, with solemn decorum down the fine curved staircase.

Reaching the car, he positioned her in the rear in an attitude of exhausted sleep, tucking her legs up and leaning her against the two suitcases, putting the cushion from the driving seat under the face. He tucked the camel-hair travelling rug securely round her and across the seat, attaching the ends of it to the rear window-handles on each side. He placed the jewel-case on the empty front seat, slammed the door from the kitchen into the garage. In the tool-box on the work-bench he found a rusty nail and put it in his pocket. At last he got in the car. From the dash-locker he took out his driving-gloves and slipped them over the rubber ones. He glanced in the driving mirror at his wife. Poor Eve, tired out, and asleep after the wild extravagances of her dear brother's party.

Cranford checked the dash-clock. Ten-fifteen. There'd still be traffic, but negligible, once he was away from the North Circular Road. He switched on the headlights. The sudden glare made the policeman coming up the drive on his bicycle dismount immediately.

Chapter Twenty-Two

LIKE A THOUSANDTH of a second exposure, a high-diver glued to the air, a raindrop impacted on the surface of a puddle, a rifle-bullet stuck in the muzzle, Cranford froze in arrested action. Panic urged him to accelerate down the drive and ignore the officially raised hand or the command to stop. Logic made him switch off the lights and engine, get out of the car and walk towards the helmeted figure, who was now removing his trouser-clips.

'Good evening, Constable. Can I help you?'

'Doctor Cranford?'

'That's right.'

'It was your wife I wanted to see, sir.'

The past tense, the colloquial turn of phrase, unknowingly hitting the truth. But it bounced off, soaring away, as he remembered the dent in the Mercedes. A simple formality, an easily circumvented obstacle.

'Ah, yes, she told me about her little argument with some fool who shot out from the kerb without warning.'

'Is that what she said, sir?'

'Isn't that what happened?'

'No. It was your wife who pulled out. The other car hadn't a chance.'

Eve, lying, even about a triviality such as this.

'I must have got it wrong. Anyway, there's not much damage. Lucky no one was hurt.'

'You've got that wrong too, sir. The vehicle struck a pedestrian refuge. The driver's in hospital. Concussion. He's come round now. I've just been along to see him.'

Why couldn't she have told him that? Big ones, little ones, hundreds of them. A kind of game. A lie a day keeps the doctor at bay.

'Skull fractured?'

'No.'

'He should be all right, then,' said Cranford. 'I gather you want to check my wife's licence and insurance certificate?'

He remembered where it was. He'd put it back on the desk by the side of the periodicals. He could take the fellow round to the front of the house and go in that way.

'Yes, sir, but now I've been able to talk to the driver, I want to check a couple of other things.'

'Oh, what things?'

The policeman rested his cycle against the low wall skirting the drive.

'That *is* your wife's car, sir, by the Bentley?'

'Yes.'

'I wonder if I could have another look at it?' He moved off towards the garage. Cranford leapt after him.

'You won't be able to see much in there, I'm afraid,' he said. Not much, my God, not much.

'How's that?'

'The garage light's fused.'

The lie to hide the lie to conceal the lie.

'It's all right, sir. I've got a torch.'

Cranford pushed ahead of him.

'I'll back the car out for you. That might help.'

Cranford began to squeeze between the Bentley and the Mercedes, but the torch went on and a restraining hand pulled him back.

'You needn't trouble to do that. If you'd let me come between the two cars, I can see all I want.'

Eve, you bitch, reaching out with your dead slippery coils, tripping my life up, bringing me down, discredited. The indecency of failure. The ragged end to the story, instead of the neat surgeon's knot.

He stepped backwards, and helplessly watched the other man stoop down unhurriedly to inspect the damaged rear wing. When the idiot stood up he'd turn towards the Bentley and his torch would shine through the rear window, illuminating the carefully made-up face, peaceful, above its sea of mink. Safe for a casual glance on the road, but not for close scrutiny. It was only a matter of time, creeping seconds to the climax, certain, inevitable. Discovered in the bath there had been a chance, but this was a compound of the truth putting him beyond even a theoretical shadow of doubt. What a crazy mess.

Split-second inspiration shot him round to the other side of the Mercedes. He took out his keys and, covering the sound with a cough, he jabbed the point of his latchkey against the cellulose and felt it gouge a six-inch scar into the opposite wing.

'Constable . . . ?'

'Yes?'

'Look at this. Have you seen this?'

Tensely, he waited for the man to straighten up. The torch swung away from the Bentley towards him. Ponderously, the policeman came out from between the two cars, and relief gushed through Cranford like the surge-water from a dam.

'On the rear wing,' he said.

The torch-light made the mark he had just manufactured glisten like a wavy silk thread. The constable smiled.

'I don't think you'll be able to swing that on the insurance, sir. Nothing to do with the accident.'

'It wasn't there this morning.'

Anything, keep talking. Anything to get him away from the garage.

'Did you notice it just now, sir?'

'Yes.'

The constable switched off his torch. The silver scratch was invisible in the darkness. Cranford cursed himself for digging a hole and then falling into it. He scrambled out again.

'I saw it in the reflection from the headlights . . . just before you came.'

He waited, rapidly calculating the next question, the next answer, the twisting whirligig of words, but he need not have bothered. Only the guilty, and the neurotic, forever read suspicion in the wind. The young man put his torch away.

'Looks as if a kid scratched it while it was parked somewhere. They can be little devils, some of 'em.'

'Yes,' said Cranford. 'Yes, they can.'

'Have you any children, sir?'

The smile, the human interest, the bond of family men, the meek attempt to break the class-barrier.

'No.' Emphatic, washing the slate clean, demanding withdrawal. Pursue the topic at your own risk.

'I've one boy. He's just pushing three. Peter.'

'Really.'

Let the last disinterested comment foster embarrassment, force retreat.

'Well, I needn't trouble you any more, sir. Do you think I could have a word with Mrs Cranford?'

They rushed at him, the wild answers, the delaying tactics, the spurious postponements. She's not in. She's at her brother's party. She's gone away.

'Now?'

'She suggested I should call at this time.'

'My wife's in bed. She was naturally rather upset about all this. I had to give her a sedative. Won't tomorrow do?'

'It would, but I understand she's flying to Paris early in the morning.'

Cranford clenched his hands, but then killed immediately the notion that he could secure escape by a quick blow at the fatuously unimaginative face under the helmet. That could only seal his defeat in the game of chess he appeared to be playing with a corpse who could still move pieces.

'The trip's off,' he said. 'She's not going.' Objective truth.

'I see.' The young man frowned. 'I won't disturb her, then.'

He bent down to put on his cycle-clips, and Cranford knew he had taken the Queen with his Bishop, and that there were only a few skilful devastating moves left, and that all of them were his.

'I'll call round in the morning about ten. Will that be a convenient time?'

Cranford smiled. 'Why not make it eleven? Sunday, you know.' Ten, eleven, twelve, anytime you like, old boy.

'Very good, sir. Eleven o'clock. I can see the licence at the same time.'

'Fine.'

'I'll be off then, myself. Good night, sir.'

'Good night.'

Cranford watched him mount his cycle, and pedal unhurriedly down the drive. In under half an hour he'd be in bed with Joan or Doreen or Betty or whatever his wife's name was. Peter would have been asleep hours ago.

When the red rear-light had flicked off as the cycle turned out of the gate, Cranford went back to the garage. He moved the Bentley out, shut the garage doors, and drove away without glancing back.

Chapter Twenty-Three

THE ROTATING FIGURES on the trip-counter told Cranford he had travelled six miles since the needle on the fuel-gauge had last budged off the empty mark. Which meant he had four to five miles in hand, six at the most. He marvelled at the chance events of existence which could alter the course of a life, seal the fate of a country, fire the destiny of a people; Fleming's mould, Hitler's real name, George the Third's obstinacy. Errors of omission, flaws in the personality, failures of communication, they operated in a chain of circumstance which ultimately involved the whole world and myriad personal worlds within it. He had not thought of checking the petrol. Bateman always looked after it. But Bateman was off for the weekend. And Bateman wouldn't have been off if he, Cranford, hadn't planned Shinglestrand, and then the petrol wouldn't have mattered anyway and he wouldn't have been rushing now down the green-white tunnel of the headlights, his wife dead on the seat behind him, cursing the chance events of existence.

Stop. He must stop and look at the map which might, or might not, help, because he didn't know precisely where he was, to give himself an accurate fix in this black damp wasteland of fields and ditches and dykes. A reflection of black and white snapped into view ahead where the dual beams converged. He switched off and free-wheeled to the sign-post. Every drop of gas was going to count. He looked up at the names. They were the same ones Eve had read out the day before. Thursday Street, Grobblegock, Nightshade Hill. But they didn't sound the same. The quaintness, the intriguing quality, had somehow gone, and in their place was a ring of doom.

Under the map-light, as he searched for the particular criss-cross of yellow second-class roads at which he had stopped, his eye was diverted by the irrelevant petty details and inventions of the cartographer's shorthand. Short, parallel, blue lines sprouting radiate tufts signifying marsh; brief rows of horizontal dots for rough pasture; black crosses surmounting squares and circles, 'Church with Tower', 'Church with Spire', and unadorned plain crosses, 'Churches without either', without tower or spire or congregation or God, relics of the past not yet past enough to merit the reverent Gothic lettering of a 'Tumulus' (prior to A.D. 43). But the crossed swords were unequivocal, 'Site of Battle'. Why not cover the whole map with them, the total battlefield of human love and hate?

He found the intersection. He was six miles from the optimistic line of pale blue which was the North Sea. On the edge of it the legend pin-pointed the martello tower. He could risk it or make a detour of a mile and a half in the hope that at twelve-thirty a.m. he could knock up the proprietor of a pump-station in Nightshade Hill, with all its risk of question and answer discovery. He decided to grasp the hazard and drive straight ahead towards his final destination.

The other side of the iron bridge the engine faltered, picked up, coughed, back-fired, and cut out. Half a mile short. In the ensuing quietness he could hear the wind soughing round the outside of the car, in small accesses of interest, a dog sniffing at a dead bird.

Cranford sat listening to it, swearing at the difficulties and dangers this ridiculous stroke of fate had created, sifting the modifications he would now have to make. In their turn these threw up further dangers, and fuzzy unknown details, half-apprehended. To have run out of gas in another half-mile would have been a godsend, but not here. His mind wrestled with alternatives. He became aware that his head ached. He felt tired and defeated. The vast physical effort which he knew lay ahead of him commuted the feeling to one of leaden lethargy, and he began to wonder if he had the resources left to carry out his plan, which now seemed so hasty and ill-conceived. He must conserve every ounce of stamina, eliminate every uneconomic move by careful review, before attempting further action. He switched off the headlights and closed his eyes, ordering a mental calm, summoning the total ambit of his concentration. At least time was on his side. He had several hours before dawn, and the chances of anyone being about on this desolate stretch of coast was one of his least anxieties.

The tap on the window brought him up with a start, and his heart delivered a burst of systoles in his chest as though it were a machine-gun. The face on the other side of the glass, less than two inches from his own, grinned with jovial inconsequence, and a vague familiarity. Noting that his signal had been seen, the man put his hand on the door handle. Galvanized, Cranford forestalled him, swung the door open, got out, and shut it behind him.

'What do you want?' he barked.

The other seemed unperturbed by the belligerence in Cranford's question. The smile, if anything, broadened, and then Cranford recognized its owner.

'I thought it must be you,' said Bishop. 'There aren't all that many Bentleys hereabouts. What's the matter: lost your way?'

'No. Run out of petrol.'

'Good thing I stopped, then. Always keep a can in the back. Petrol pumps in this district have a habit of running dry, if you know what I mean. "Back in ten minutes", "Gone Fishing", "Closed till Monday". And at this time of night, well . . .' He laughed. 'Hang on, I'll get it for you.'

He crossed the road to where Cranford now noticed the shooting-brake had been parked on the rough grass verge. If he played it carefully and kept Bishop talking at the back of the Bentley, this could be a chance even of existence, cancelling out the former one.

'That's very good of you,' he shouted, and taking the keys out of the ignition-lock he went to the rear of the car. He had opened the filler-cap just as Bishop's headlights lit up the scene. He came shambling back with a two-gallon can.

'This isn't top quality,' he apologized, 'but it'll do for an emergency transfusion.'

Bishop laughed with satisfaction at the wit of his allusion, produced a large rusty old funnel and let the petrol hiss out of the can into the tank.

'I'm greatly obliged,' said Cranford. 'I thought I might have to spend the night in the car.'

'Seems as though your missus has decided to do that.'

'Have you been looking at her?'

The words shot out savagely, before he could stop them. Bishop flinched at the unexpected intensity of the outburst, slopping some of the petrol over the side of the funnel.

'All right, all right,' he said. 'A cat can look at a queen.' He emptied the can and screwed on the top. Cranford eyed him suspiciously.

What had he seen? What had he noticed? How long had he been peering in at Eve from the windy, salt-tanged darkness?

'What have you been doing to her?'

'Doing?'

'She looks dead-beat.'

That was O.K. Dead-beat. That was all right. That was safe. That put things within the normal terms of reference of Bishop's experience. Cranford tried to disguise the relief in his voice.

'Been to a bit of a wild party. She's sleeping it off.'

'Why do they do it?' asked Bishop. 'I mean they're no good to any man like that, are they?'

The observation rescued them both, united them both on male terra firma, foursquare against inferior female tides.

'You're bloody right,' said Cranford, and added, 'The silly bitch,' overplaying it, but the other didn't notice. He locked the filler-cap.

'How much do I owe you?'

'Oh, Christ, forget it. I'll take a couple of pints off you tomorrow at The Benbow. Glad you decided to come back. Makes a change for us yokels. Brings us a whiff of the *dolce vita* and all that.'

So his phone message had been relayed in the bar to all and sundry. That was how he wanted it to go. But not this encounter with Bishop.

'I told Bill Field, if we were coming tonight, we'd be here before midnight. I imagine they'll be in bed now.'

'That's certain. You'll have to bang hard. Those two'd sleep through an earthquake.' Bishop chuckled with obvious pleasure.

'I hate knocking people up at night. I know what it's like myself.' Cranford's voice was suitably concerned.

'Expect you do. Anyway, if you get no change out of Bill, I can give you a bed. First farm on the left, the other side of Grobblegock.'

'Wouldn't dream of it.'

'Nothing to it. Glad to help. Good night. Best of luck with Sleeping Beauty.'

Bishop laughed and lurched slightly as he made his way back to the shooting-brake.

'Thanks,' said Cranford.

He stood still until the sound of Bishop's vehicle had died away. Then he got back in the Bentley. At the third stab at the starter, the engine fired.

In less than five minutes he had stopped near the foot of the martello tower. Its mass rose up, gaunt and sheer, against the broken fluffy darkness of the racing clouds above it. He opened the rear door and gently eased his suitcase out. Eve's head lolled back, and as his hand brushed her cheek, he felt a sinking nausea grip him, but he thrust it away, making the calculated observation that the heat in the car had kept the muscles warm, that she was still not frozen in ungainly awkward rigor.

He ran up the slope to the tower and hid the suitcase out of sight, inside. He checked himself as he began to hurry back. There was no hurry. An hour for the toughest part. Then a ten mile hike. He could be on a bus-route by seven a.m. Energy must be conserved. The sound of the breakers beyond were reminder enough.

He returned to the car and, using the sidelights only, drove slowly up the road away from the tower, parallel with the bank of shingle. He estimated a mile would be enough. With the current as it had been setting yesterday, he should be able to make the beach again opposite the tower, assuming of course he could hold out that long.

A small gap in the shingle mound presented itself as if by special arrangement. He ran the Bentley off the road on to the gravel. He switched off the engine and the lights. Now the details, now the little points that would be noted, added up, made to fit the story, make the coroner wag his head in sad agreement, as they would be recounted to him within the bare walls of the small country courthouse.

He got out of the car, took a heavy spanner from the tool-kit. He found the old nail in his pocket and drove it with the spanner into one of the front tyres. Slowly the air escaped. By the time he had put back the spanner the tyre was flat.

He switched on the radio, tuning into Radio Paris. That would figure in the morning. Piano and drums. An old blues. Blue, indigo, black. The stub-end of life. Stubs. There were several of his own in the ash-trays, but Eve smoked too. No lipsticked butts? He opened her suit-case and zipped back the fitted cosmetic compartment. He smeared some lipstick on his own lips, and mouthed a couple of the stubs, and replaced them in the ashtray. He took out the lamé dress, the high-heeled sandals, and tossed them carelessly on the floor together with a pair of nylons and some underwear. Then he took his swimming trunks out of his pocket, and stripped by the side of the car, placing his own clothes and shoes neatly on the front seat. The wind plucked at his bare legs, encouraging his movements to be brisk and circumspect. His feet made no marks on the cold gravel. That was it. That was everything. Every beautiful detail. Except for the most beautiful detail of all.

He untied the rug and, leaning her forwards against him, withdrew her arms for the last time from the cossetting embrace of silk-lined fur. Then he lifted her swim-suited body up and carried her in his arms against the stiff north-easter down the bank of pebbles, his bare feet slithering amongst them, until he was at the edge of the seething bubbles flung from the first line of waves, which screamed at him their impossible challenge.

He looked along the shore. He could just make out the martello tower. It seemed too far, well over a mile from him. Miscalculation, or fear, or the sudden conviction that he was never going to reach it? He looked away, shifted his burden on to his shoulders and waded forward into the vice-like grip and ruthless turbulence ahead.

He nearly lost her at the second row of breakers, one of which felled him, but she was returned on the undertow. He pushed her in front of him like a soggy raft, until eventually, breathless and heaving, he broke into the calmer water of the troughs beyond.

He swam out for half a mile and then let her go. He paddled round a little until he was sure she was drifting further out. Just before he turned to swim back he noticed that though the bracelet was still on her wrist one of her earrings had been ripped out by a whim of the elements. She wouldn't like that. Sorry about that, Eve. Sorry, darling.

It seemed that he only had five yards to go, yet his foot couldn't touch bottom. The tower was there, and he could hear the swish of the shingle, but there was no strength in his arms or legs. Or was it his soul? Perhaps that's why he wasn't going to make it. His soul couldn't swim. Cranford began to wonder how the words would look, how the sentences would read in the obituary notice. A dignified, honourable reputation, cut off at the summit of achievement. After all that, in a way, had been the object of the exercise. A wave curled over him, forcing him down.

Part Four

THE TASSELLED FIELD

Chapter Twenty-Four

HE LAY ON his back in the shallow water near the edge of the beach. His eyes were closed against the early-morning sun. The movement of the sea gently bumped his buttocks on the sand. She lifted her feet, making plopping splashes as she came towards him.

'Johnny. Wake up, Johnny.'

He made no movement, no sign that he had heard her. She laughed at the pretence, prodding him with her toe, floating him off into deeper water.

'Johnny is not asleep. Johnny is pretending.'

She pushed him out further, with a stronger movement.

'Johnny is lazy; lazy men are no-good men. They are no good for women and no good for children. So Thalia must not let Johnny be lazy.'

This time she placed her foot on his stomach and pressed him down firmly under the water. As she expected, the action brought him to life. A hand clutched at her ankle, but she was ready for it, and, escaping, she leapt away laughing, and waded out vigorously, hearing with pleasure the commotion behind, as he scrambled to his feet, and plunged after her. She surface-dived and had swum ten strokes before he had caught her up. She squealed with excitement as he grabbed her by the arms and kissed her. He kept his mouth on hers and pulled her down under the surface, and when they came up the kiss was still there. Then he let her go, and they both paddled around, panting for air, a temporary halt being called in the ritual game.

'This is not the place. It was further out,' he said.

'No, this is it. I remember exactly. You do not remember. You are forgetting already, Johnny.'

'I'll never forget.'

'Men do. Men always forget. Women remember.'

'I remember.'

'What do you remember? Tell me, Johnny.'

'You know it by heart, Lally.'

173

'My heart wants to hear it. Tell me it all from the beginning.'

He swam towards her, and they lay on their backs, floating in the warm water, and he held her hand, as he always did, and she was happy and sad at the same time, because each time he told her was another time gone, lost for ever, a kind of ending, and yet each time was a beginning too.

'I was sitting up on that rock over there, painting.'

'It was your third day on the island.'

'No, my fourth.'

'Your third. It was your third, Johnny.' She spoke intensely, a child unwilling to allow the slightest alteration of detail in the telling of a favourite fairy-tale.

'I believe you are right. It *was* my third day.'

'You know it was.'

'I was teasing.'

'Teasing is not part of the story.'

'Well, there was this girl walking along the beach all alone, and she had on an old blue dress. . . .'

'With white buttons . . .'

'With white buttons. She seemed to be deep in thought, and very sad, because she walked slowly, looking down all the time. Occasionally she would turn over a sea-shell with her bare toe. . . .'

'Was she pretty?'

'I couldn't tell from that distance, and anyway I was concentrating on my canvas and I didn't take a great deal of notice. . . .'

'Except to see that she had a pretty body . . . ?'

'Her body was covered up in the old blue dress with the white buttons. After a time she stopped walking and stood still, looking into the water. She stayed so long without moving that I decided to put her into my picture, a little blue blob on the sand, when suddenly . . .'

'Suddenly she did something never seen by you before, but which is a very normal thing on the island.'

'But I didn't know then . . .'

'It was only your third day. Go on Johnny. Suddenly . . .'

'Suddenly this girl, this little blue blob started walking into the sea. . . .'

'In her dress . . . !'

'In her dress. And she kept on walking, paying no attention to the water wetting her dress. And I stood up and shouted at her. . . .'

'Because you thought she was going to drown herself. . . .'

'But she took no notice. . . .'

'She didn't hear you.'

174

'And so I jumped down from the rocks, and tumbled and slithered, and ran along the beach, by which time I could only see her head bobbing away out to sea. And I flung off my shoes and swam after her. . . .'

'In your trousers and shirt.'

'In my trousers and shirt, until I caught up with her. . . .'

'Just at this place.'

'A little farther out.'

'No, just here.'

'All right. Just here.'

'And then?'

'And then, instead of drowning, she turned round and smiled and spoke in English. . . .'

'What did she say?'

'"Hello. Good morning."'

'And what did you say?'

'I said, "What the hell do you think you're doing?"'

'And she said, "I'm swimming."'

'And I said, "In your clothes?"'

'And she laughed and said, "You are in *your* clothes." And you looked cross and said nothing. And then you noticed how pretty she was, so you stopped looking cross, and she told you it was a custom on the island that unmarried girls swam only in their clothes. And she said her name was Thalia, and you said your name was Johnny. Go on, Johnny. Finish the story.'

'That's all there is. That's the end.'

'That *isn't* the end. That's just the beginning.'

'Of what?'

'Of what happened next.'

'What did happen next?'

'They fell in love.'

'Who did?'

'Johnny and Lally.'

'Oh, yes.'

'And then later they got married.'

'And had a son.'

'And lived happily ever after.'

She pulled his hand down and kissed him quickly, because after the story was told it was time to enter into it, so that it might really go on for ever. But she was a woman and not a child, she did not have the total belief of a child, but only the belief of a woman, which is hope. And hope is always shot through with tiny holes of fear, and beyond

175

hope there is only faith, and that is a different thing altogether, requiring constant renewal. So when they swam back towards the shore, she found she had asked:

'Johnny, do you ever think about your wife who died?'

'Sometimes,' he said.

'You loved her?'

'At first. I told you.'

He stood up in the shallow water, and she splashed after him. His face was set, and she was sorry she had spoken, but she could not let it go.

'I am glad she is dead,' she said.

He made an irritable movement with his shoulders.

'What does it matter, if I've stopped loving her?'

She caught hold of his hand and pulled him back.

'I'm sorry, Johnny,' she said. 'It's just that, if she was alive, I would be afraid she might come and try to take you away from me.'

He looked at her seriously, and then laughed and kissed her and said:

'No one will ever do that.'

'I would kill them,' she said.

'Stop talking so much and hurry up. Paul will be crying for his breakfast.'

The sand warmed their feet as they walked up the beach to where the path began to climb between the rocks. The song of the cicadas burst out around them, and the scent of pine and saxifrage was strong, and the sun made dazzling patches of reflection where it caught tiny mirrors of quartz and silica. At the top of the path they stopped and looked down on to the beach below, where it was just possible to see the marks in the sand, made by their feet near the water's edge. Away to the left of them was the harbour, and the fishing-boats, and small indeterminate early morning sounds came up from the town behind, and surrounding it all was the overwhelming azure sparkle of the Aegean.

'It is very beautiful, my little island, isn't it, Johnny?'

'Yes. But it's mine, now, too.'

'I love it because it is where I am born.'

'I love it because it is where you are born.'

'Do you love where you are born?'

'Yes.'

'But you don't want to go back?'

'No.'

She plucked a piece of grass and put it between her small regular teeth.

'You mean you will never go away from the island?'

'Why should I?'

'Men do. Men go away. Paul will go away when he is bigger.'

'It depends what he wants to do.'

'He will be famous. I want him to be famous,' she said, and she gazed out towards the horizon, to the world where her son would be famous.

'I want him to be happy,' he said and, taking her arm they went along the path and up the steps into the house, and shut the door.

Some way out, over the gentle crinkled expanse of the sea, a white motor-yacht appeared to be setting a direct course for Kronos.

Chapter Twenty-Five

HOLDING HIS HAND, Melina Kontopoulos and her father made their way across the square. A big white boat with a funnel was coming into the harbour. Normally this would have been a most exciting happening, and she would have run and told the other children, and they would all have gone shouting along the quay to look at it before school. But this morning the boat was only a thing to notice in passing. It was not possible to think about it seriously until she began to feel better. She found that if she bent slightly forward it eased the pain which had awakened her on and off all night. She had not had the pain for two weeks, but now, suddenly, it was worse than ever before.

Every few yards the child took little running steps to match her pace with that of the man in the peak-cap. From time to time, in response to the tug at his sleeve, he slowed down and spoke to her. It was always the same thing that he said, but she pretended to listen attentively, though it had become to her a meaningless formula, like an oft-repeated prayer. With some fresh medicine the pain will go. With some fresh medicine the pain will go. Go, go. Go away, pain. Go away, pain.

To demonstrate the truth of his assertion, her father kept holding up an empty medicine bottle. She looked at it dumbly and nodded. She wanted to believe what he said. Her father was the most important man on the island, and everyone knew he was wise. If there was any quarrel people did what he told them, and she was very lucky to have such a man for a father. Her mother said so, and everyone said so, and she liked to please her father, because that is what every little girl should do. She nodded again at the empty bottle and, as if to prove that he was right, when they reached the alley between the church and the school, the pain eased off. But only for a moment, so that she was glad to sit down on the warm, stone step, while her father knocked on the door of the house.

'Doctor! Doctor!' he called. '*Xypnise. Imai ego, Kontopoulos.* Wake up. Is me, Kontopoulos.'

Nobody answered, and above them the church clock chimed. She felt sick, but said nothing, and wondered if the school bell would soon start ringing. Her father cursed, and banged on the door with his fists.

'Doctor! What is the matter? *Anixe tin porta.*'

An angry voice came from somewhere inside the house.

'What the hell is going on out there?'

'*Yatre. Anixe tin porta.*'

'Go away, you noisy bastard.'

'Doctor. Please. Open the door. Melina. She sick again.'

'Who?'

'Little Melina.'

'Is it Kontopoulos?'

'Yes. I tell you.'

'Why didn't you say so, man? No need to make such a ruddy pandemonium.'

The fat man cursed and swore, and then crossed himself, and patted his daughter consolingly on the head. The door opened and Evans appeared, red-eyed and unshaven, but fully dressed in the same crumpled suit in which he had fallen into bed, as near senseless as made no matter, the night before. He screwed up his eyes against the light, eventually bringing Kontopoulos and the child into focus.

'Christ,' he said. 'Bring her in, man. It's too ruddy bright for me out 'ere.'

They followed him into the house. The stench of drink, and stale tobacco and sweat was overpowering. Melina retched and began to cry and then stopped because crying increased the pain. Evans stumbled across to the window, and pushed open the shutters. The sun streamed in, throwing up the squalor and chaos of the room in merciless detail.

'That's better,' said Evans. 'And brighter too, isn't it? Let all things be illuminated, nothing hidden.' His voice broke into a cracked tenor. 'All things bright and beautiful . . .' and ended in a bout of coughing as he kicked a bottle under the sagging springs of the bed, shoved some books on to the floor with a clatter, and cleared a space on the table. He lifted the child up, sat her down, and grinned toothily at her.

'Don't cry now, Princess,' he said. 'Nobody's going to hurt you. Your da wouldn't stand for that, would he now? Where's the pain, Melina bach?'

He made a grimace and gestured with his hand. The child put it on her stomach and looked at him with wide eyes. Evans laughed at her reassuringly.

'Your bloody belly again, is it?'

Kontopoulos held out the empty bottle.

'Some more medicine, Doc?'

Evans waved the bottle away, and shuffled off into the other room, the room which he had tried to make into a surgery when he had first come to Kronos, when he was filled with cold anger, smarting under a sense of personal injustice. Here, on this primitive island, he vowed he would practise the skills he had painstakingly learnt; practise with no meddling interference, no bureaucratic forms to fill in, no parsimonious committees knocking pennies off his prescriptions. Here he would practise medicine as he saw it, personal, humane, in the grand tradition of the missionary spirit; medicine freely given not for gain, but for the alleviation of suffering, of making life more bearable, death less painful. Here, at least to his own satisfaction, he would demonstrate the imbecility of a narrow professional etiquette which decreed that a doctor had no right to feel and do as a man might feel and do as he pleased—to drown the sorrow of loss and grief and, because of one drunken harmless mistake, forfeit his right to work again.

For the first six months on the island he had tried; for six months he had kept off the bottle until one night, in the warm peace of a summer evening, when he was sure he had beaten the devil within, he had taken a glass lightly, confidently, just to prove his cure. In a week it was all over and all he had proved was that the bastards had been right.

The drugs and equipment he had ordered, paid for out of his savings, continued to arrive, but they were too late, for the rot had spread further than his guts. Some of the boxes still lay unopened, gathering dust, in the corner of the room. The journals still came too, even now, ironically taunting him for his life subscription, paid with burning enthusiasm the day he had qualified. Sometimes he read them, touched for an hour or so with interest and a fleeting hope of resurrection. But the spirit was broken, the fire had died out and, worse, he discovered he couldn't think as straight and clear as he used to.

But, at times such as this, when a child was sick or in pain, he stirred himself to grope back along the years, searching for a long-lost confidence as he was now searching for a lost thermometer, a simple tool any nurse could wield with precision. He found it at last, half-hidden in an ashtray among a mound of cigarette butts. He glanced round vaguely for somewhere to wash it, but there seemed to be nothing at hand, so he wiped it on his sleeve and went back into the other room.

The girl had her knees drawn up, and was moaning softly to herself. Evans smiled at her and, avoiding the glance of her father, shook the thermometer vigorously, as if indeed he were standing in some white-walled clinic beginning a day of efficiency and detached scientific certainty.

The glass tube flew out of his trembling hand on to the floor at the feet of Kontopoulos, snapping in two. Quickly the paunchy body stooped and picked up the broken halves, and offered them reverently to their owner.

Evans took them from him. What the hell did it matter? You didn't need a thermometer to see the mite had a fever. He flung the pieces into a corner of the room. It was a gesture of despair, of disgust; disgust at himself and the hopelessness of his own nature; despair at the other man for the burden of faith which he unloaded so readily on to another. He turned to the child and stroked her hair back, sensible of the sweat on her forehead. Gently he laid her down on the table, lifted her dress, and put his hand flat and light on the smooth skin of her abdomen. She held herself taut, staring up at him, still not quite trusting, still turning her head abruptly at intervals to see if her father was standing by. Evans motioned to the man, who took the small, hot hand in his. Gradually Evans felt the muscles under his fingers relax and soften. Slowly he allowed their tips to press downwards, probing deeper, first in this quadrant, then in that, watching the small face all the time for a tell-tale wince, a surer guide to an underlying site of tenderness than any question and answer.

Suddenly she cried out, and thrust his hands forcefully away.

'There now, Melina bach. That's all we have to do.'

'Is it bad, Doctor?' asked Kontopoulos.

Evans pulled down the dress again.

'No. Not too bad,' he smiled at the child.

Not too bad. Not yet. But it could be. It could be bloody bad. An acute appendix on Kronos could be a bloody tragedy. He'd seen it once before. The husband wouldn't let his wife go to Rhodes or Crete. And maybe he had been right. A ten-hour punishing trip on a rolling, pitching fishing-vessel would probably have perforated her. Then she would have died in the boat instead of amidst the love and ignorance of her own family. These simple people were born on the island and they nearly all had a terror, not so much of dying, as of not dying on the island too. But children were different, children had a different right.

'What to do, Doc?'

He regarded the swarthy features of the man in front of him; a man with pride and honour, whom in ten years he had come to know as a friend. It wouldn't do any good, but he said what he had to say.

'She should have an operation, Kostas. A tube inside is blocked. It should come out,' he said.

The response was immediate.

'O.K., Doc. You take out.'

Evans threw his head back in exasperation.

'Don't be a fool, man! It can only be done in a hospital.'

'You mean, send her away? From the island?'

'Yes.'

'Her mother would die!'

'If she doesn't, your daughter might die.'

'But also she might not?'

'No, she might not.'

Beds, fluids, antibiotics, there were packages somewhere, stable ones, probably still O.K. The whole thing could settle down. He had seen that before, too.

'And if she went, she still might die?'

'Yes. That could happen.'

The man looked at him seriously, searching his eyes for an answer. Apparently he found one, for he suddenly smiled.

'Is O.K. then, Doc. She stay here. Is better that way. You do it before. You give her more medicine make her better. You can do it, Doc. You and God.'

'Christ Almighty!' shouted Evans. 'Don't look at me like that. Put your faith in God if you must, but leave me out. I can't even shake a ruddy thermometer any more.'

Immediately he regretted his outburst, for the child sat up and clutched at her father, burying her face in his jacket.

'*Poly xala. Poly xala*,' said Evans and stroked her hair. 'We'll make you better. I'll give you some sweeties to swallow. *Glyka na sou xamoun xalo*.'

Melina's face came out of hiding and she glanced at him suspiciously. Evans smiled and nodded his head with a conviction he did not feel, and went off again into the other room.

Tearing away the cardboard savagely with his hands, in the second carton he found some terramycin. God, he hoped it was still all right. He opened a bottle and shook three of the red-brown tablets into his palm, and returned to the little girl. He put the tablets into her hand. From a cupboard he produced a flask of soda-water; opened it and poured some of the bubbling liquid into a glass. He picked up one of the tablets, put it on his own tongue, and swallowed it down with some of the soda, opening his mouth wide afterwards for her to see that the pill had gone. Then he gave her the glass.

'Now Melina do it. *Kame to esy, Melina.*'

She put a tablet in her mouth and immediately chewed it. Her face quickly registered the unpleasant taste.

'No, no. Swallow it,' said Evans.

'*Katapie to!*' ordered Kontopoulos.

But it was too late. She spat the tablet out and began to howl. Her father muttered under his breath and then turned to Evans.

'Give her the old medicine, Doc. The red one. She like that. She take that all right.'

'Listen, you great big, blithering idiot,' said Evans. 'The red medicine is no good for this. She has to take tablets, you understand? Otherwise she die. *Tha pethani.* You got that through your fat skull?'

'Yes, Doc. She die.'

'Oh God, take her home. Put her to bed. Give her two tablets every four hours. *Dio kathe tessares ores.* Got that?'

'I got it.'

'I don't care how you do it, man, but make her get the tablets down. Now take her away and I'll come and see her in about an hour. Go on, now.'

Kontopoulos put the bottle in his pocket, picked up Melina and carried her to the door. Then he grinned back at Evans.

'Don't you worry, Doc,' he said. 'Is going be all right.'

'Christ!' said Evans.

When they had gone, he opened a fresh bottle of Cypriot brandy, the one he had been saving for some ill-defined vague celebration. He sat on the bed and took a long swig.

'Oh, Christ!' he repeated, and, outside, the schoolbell started to ring.

The children took turns to ring the bell, week by week. It hung between two old wooden beams which jutted out from the side of the building. The rope passed down the wall and through an iron loop a few feet from the top of the steps. The object of the loop was to prevent little boys, and even little girls, from swinging gleefully on the end of the rope pretending to be apes.

Her twelve pupils were usually clustered round the door to greet her when she arrived each morning, but as Johnny accompanied her along the quay, as he did every day, Lally could see only the barber's son, pulling away on the bell-rope with what seemed to be excessive zeal.

'Look at Giorgio, all on his own. What can be the matter, Johnny? Where are all the others?'

'Over there on the jetty.'

He pointed to where the motor-yacht had tied up. It sported a triangular blue and white pennant at the masthead which he recognized as belonging to a number of boats which could be hired out at Piraeus, complete with crew, for private sight-seeing parties. Germans and Americans mostly, they came to the island from time to time, but as there was virtually nothing to see in the way of antiquities, they only stayed long enough to take unenthusiastic shots with their expensive cameras of the withered tree-trunk in the square, just for its Hippocratic associations. Today, the people who had hired the boat still appeared to be asleep, for there was no one on deck but a blue-jerseyed member of the crew, leaning on the rail, smoking, and shaking his head at intervals at the children, who were obviously pressing their demands to come aboard and look around.

Lally shouted towards the children and clapped her hands, but their absorption was too great for them to pay any attention.

'That won't do any good,' Wilson laughed. 'Boats are much more fun than school. You'll have to fetch them.'

'No. I do not fetch them. They come to me,' Lally replied with a flash of annoyance.

'You could stop the bell ringing. Then they will know you have arrived. Then they'll come.'

'It will be bad for them if they do not,' she said.

Amused, he put his arm round her and they walked on to the school.

'You look very fierce, Lally. If I were at school, I think I'd be frightened of you.'

She laughed then, and said:

'You would not, Johnny. I do not think you are ever frightened of anyone.'

He kissed her, as he always did, at the foot of the steps. She ran up to Giorgio and told him to stop pulling on the rope, that he was a good boy, and not naughty like the others. Giorgio scowled dubiously, Lally unlocked the schoolroom door, and bundled him inside.

Wilson walked back a little way so that he could look along the quay to see if the silencing of the bell had had the required effect. Nothing happened for a moment, and then one child looked round. Wilson beckoned to the boy. The child said something to the others; they all turned, and then, as one, they were scampering back along the jetty at full speed.

Lally appeared again at the top of the steps.

'Are they coming?' she asked.

'Yes. Hell for leather.'

'What is that?'

'It means they are frightened of what you will say,' he laughed.

Suddenly she saw his smile fade as his voice trailed off.

'You are teasing again, Johnny, aren't you?'

He did not move or answer, but continued to stare out over the harbour.

'Johnny. What is the matter?'

The children came bounding off the jetty on to the quay, and streamed past him, unheeding, up the steps.

'Johnny!' she shouted.

He looked round and she saw his face was set, and somehow different from any time that she could remember; older it seemed, and tired and sad, and she was all at once afraid because she could not understand why he looked like that, nor understand why it should make her afraid.

'I must go now,' he said.

'Why do you look so worried, Johnny?'

'Worried? Do I?'

'No. Not now. A minute ago.'

'Don't be silly,' he said. 'There's nothing I have to worry about. I'll come for you at twelve, as usual.'

The words reassured her, and the feeling was confirmed as she watched him stride briskly along the quay. He didn't look towards the harbour again, and was soon out of sight beyond the fishing-boats on his way back to the house.

She went to go up the steps, but some intuitive threat of misgiving arrested her. She turned round once more, and walked to the end of the building where she could see out across the harbour. It was a pattern of blues and whites and browns, sunlight and reflections on the water, just as she had always known it. Some fishermen were mending their nets. A sea-bird dived at a piece of refuse thrown out from one of the boats. A woman sitting on a bollard on the quay, shelling some mussels, began singing. From the motor-yacht a young man was being helped down by another on to the jetty. He was some sort of cripple because he walked with difficulty, leaning on two sticks. But there was nothing remarkable about that.

She climbed the steps again into the schoolroom. The children stopped talking, and stood up as she walked to her desk under the blackboard. Quickly she counted the heads.

'Where is Melina?' she asked.

Chapter Twenty-Six

HE OPENED THE door. The two of them stood there, the Devil and his Advocate, both wearing smiles.

Though he had worked desperately to convince himself, all the way back from the harbour, that Willy's arrival was a macabre quirk of fate, he knew it could not be so. Willy on his own might be the one-in-a-million freak coincidence, but Willy *and* Green together fixed the odds against chance beyond the range even of astronomical computation.

By the time he had reached the house other impressions, half-formed suspicions, small, remembered incidents had come leaping out at him in new guises, altered forms; the conversation with Green on the patio; Lally's mother's revelation, the day after Green's visit two weeks ago, that their guest had been photographing the paintings; Doc Evans's bucolic observations about men who asked questions like bloody policemen; yet even all these made him loth to relinquish the belief that the two men's presence on the island had some fantastic, off-beat explanation, in no way connected with himself. He was dead, and there was no one alive who could prove he wasn't.

Nevertheless, he had needed to steady himself with a brandy as soon as he had got back. Could there be a gap in the curtain somewhere, a crack in the wall? He had given his hands something to do, not exacting with a brush, but simple and purposive, with hammer and nails stretching some new canvas, so that his mind was free to test for weakness, probe for loopholes, check and recheck the stages of the escape route from the life he had left behind, voluntarily jettisoned for ever.

The wave which had seemed to submerge him past all hope of release had suddenly lifted him up and flung him, near insensible, on the wet shingle. He had lain, exhausted, with the black North Sea screaming behind, his body numb and palsied with cold, until somehow he had found the will and strength, first to kneel, then to stand, then to stumble up the crunching slope to the martello tower.

In the musty fungus-odoured darkness he had found the suitcase, and dressed himself with an agonized fumbling, compounded of cold and fatigue and rubber-covered fingers. Had he left something there, some button, some ridiculous piece of evidence, to be found by a moronic couple using the refuge of the tower for their first sexual excursion, and taken away as a sentimental reminder, later to be recalled and then produced? It wasn't even a remote possibility.

He remembered how he had walked the weary miles through the dark, wet, wind-blown landscape, past the spot where Bishop had so obligingly given him the petrol, to the main bus-route, without meeting a soul. He had attracted no looks or stares from the complacent, clay-featured, church-bound, relative-visiting, Sunday-outing passengers to Ipswich. The wash and brush-up in the public lavatory, the meal in the station buffet, the train to Liverpool Street, the purchase of a cheap pair of sunglasses, the Underground to Edgware Road, the bandaging of his face in the lavatory of the cinema, the return to a different seat, and the exit with the crowd at the end of the feature, could have left no retained impression on the impersonal, disinterested, self-centred London air.

It had not been difficult to find and rent the shabby top-floor back in the Paddington rooming-house and, once there, after a twelve-hour sleep, he had performed his own mirror-controlled, skill-challenging, final obliteration, so that there was nothing left for anyone to point out, nothing left of the man who had been drowned so tragically in the fullness of his achievement and at the height of his reputation. And through it all he had kept watch on the papers, counting the days until he was into double figures, before Eve's body had been washed up, too late to merit more than a perfunctory post-mortem. And so the one possible danger, the analysis of stomach contents not matching up to sea-water, had unobtrusively slipped by.

At the inquest all the carefully laid tricks in the car, the young constable's evidence of Eve's accident the night before bearing out Bishop's helpful testimony of her seemingly plastered state; Bill Field's confirmation of the booking at The Benbow, the Sunday tabloids, with their invented tale of a crazy, swimming dare after a sweet-life party, had sealed the verdict and set him free. There had been no cry then from her titled brother, reported to be in a state of nervous collapse in a nursing-home, a piece of news which drew its own worn allusion in the Press to the widespread depravity of life in high places. That stage had ended without a whisper of suspicion, without a ghost of uncomfortable surmise.

The passport had proved easier than he had anticipated. A couple of days, a couple of hints, and a dozen or so free drinks in a Soho strip-club bar, and not only had he disposed of the jewellery, but had walked through the control at the airport with a convincing, docu-mented, brand-new, bearded identity, to embark on a journey which had led him to the only two years of complete peace and happiness in his whole life.

Yet now, standing in front of him, was the impossibility, the night-mare carried over into reality and, with it, the dream-threat of de-struction.

'Good morning, Mr Wilson. Remember me?'

'Yes,' replied Cranford, and then, purposely, 'Brown, isn't it?'

'Green, I believe,' Fowler smiled. 'May I introduce Lord Binfield?'

'Call me Willy,' said Willy.

He made no attempt to offer his hand, but kept them both on his sticks. New ones, Cranford observed irrelevantly, stronger, with leather-covered handles in place of the old ivory.

'Hello,' he said, and decided to take the fight straight into enemy territory. 'Have we ever met before?'

Willy returned Cranford's gaze steadily. He hadn't aged at all. His over-bred porcelain-skinned prettiness, so devastating in his sister, was the type which suddenly sagged and went muddy in the early thirties.

'It's very possible, my dear fellow. I meet so many people.'

It was all as Cranford remembered it, all the old condescension. Yet there was no hint that Willy had taken up the challenge until he spoke again, and then Cranford knew it was going to be a stupid dan-gerous game.

'Though I'm pretty good at remembering faces,' said Willy.

'We're not disturbing you too early?' Fowler asked.

'It's as good a time as any.'

Cranford held open the door for them, and Willy stumped under the lintel. Fowler followed, and Cranford noticed he carried a brief-case.

'I see you haven't brought your camera this time, Green. Got all the pictures you want?'

'Sorry about that,' Fowler grinned. 'Meant to tell you, ask your permission, but we got talking and it slipped my memory, you know how it is?'

'I know how it is,' said Cranford.

'You see, the friend I told you about wanted to be sure it was worth making the journey.'

'And this is your friend?'

Willy gave Fowler a contemptuous glance.

'A business friendship, I assure you, Mr . . . er . . . ?'

'Wilson,' said Cranford. 'Johnny Wilson.' He turned to Fowler. 'I thought you were a writer?'

'He's been writing something for me,' said Willy, and sat down on one of the divans.

'Is that the book you were telling me about? Biography of someone, wasn't it?'

'That's the one,' smiled Fowler.

'Of a man called Alexander Cranford. Heard of him?' asked Willy.

'Yes, indeed. As a surgeon he was something of a legend, I believe.' Cranford offered a packet of cigarettes to Fowler. His hand was rock steady. As steady as a surgeon's hand should be, he thought ironically. 'How's the work coming on? Finished yet?'

'I'm stuck on the last chapter,' replied Fowler. 'It's often difficult to know exactly how a story will end.'

Fowler sat down, and Cranford stood with his back to the hearth, legs apart, a defensive position. He wished somehow that behind him were crackling logs instead of the profusion of fragrant mauve blossoms. He looked at Willy. Willy wasn't sure yet. Or was it that he, Cranford, wasn't sure that Willy wasn't sure? He floated out some bait.

'I should have thought that was simple enough,' he said. 'Wasn't Cranford drowned somewhere off the East Coast, a couple of years ago?'

He glanced at Willy, and his likeness to Eve brought back the sickening recollection of days of frustration and sadness which he thought he had left behind for ever.

'They never found his body,' said Willy.

'How was that?'

'He didn't drown.'

'Oh? What happened to him?'

'He got away.'

'Where?'

'With murder.'

'Of whom?'

'His wife,' said Willy. 'She was my sister.' His voice was thick with emotion.

'I'm sorry to hear that,' said Cranford. 'But I seem to remember her body was washed up, obviously drowned?'

'By Cranford. In a bath. He dumped her in the sea later.'

Cranford flicked some ash into one of the vases from Rhodes. Out on the patio, he could hear Maria singing to Paul.

'Extraordinary story. Do the police know all about this?' he asked, casually.

'The police are very unimaginative,' said Fowler.

'You mean they require evidence?'

'Proof of existence. Proof of Alexander Cranford. That's all they need. Then they could be persuaded to get going.'

They hadn't got anything, then. It was all a big guess: a carefully planned guess requiring just one slip, one piece of co-operation from him. Well, they wouldn't get it.

'I understand the difficulty you're having with your last chapter, Mr Green,' he said, and turned to Willy. 'Would you like some coffee, Lord Binfield, before you look at the pictures?'

'I haven't come to look at the pictures.'

'Oh? What have you come for?'

Cranford kept up the blank wall, the off-hand disinterested tone of someone outside the context.

'To look at you, Alex.'

Now that it had been said, now that the accusation was unsheathed and pointing unmistakably at him, he felt a release of tension, as comes after the referee's whistle or the starter's gun. He looked down at Willy, clutching his sticks, and for long seconds Willy held his stare.

'I beg your pardon?' Cranford said, coolly.

The remark fell like water on to a red-hot surface.

'You never begged anyone's pardon, least of all mine.' Willy sputtered the words out. 'But you're going to beg for mercy in the end. But you won't get it. They'll hang you, just the same.'

'What . . . ! Who the hell do you think you're talking to?'

Suddenly Willy banged his stick on the floor.

'You, Alex, you! And I've found you; me, Willy. You won't get away again. I saw you that day in the taxi, your face all bandaged up, looking like one of your own patients. It *was* you, wasn't it?'

Cranford turned to Fowler.

'Is he mad?'

'No, but you are,' shouted Willy. He tried to struggle to his feet, words gushing out in a torrent of incoherent emotion. 'Mad to do what you did. Rubber gloves, that empty instrument case in the luggage loft. That jewellery wasn't lost; Eve would never have gone swimming in that sea. She would never have gone back to that folksy little pub. It was all rotten lies you told me. Lies about her choosing you instead of me. It was me she loved, me, Willy. She hated you, and I let you stop me going up those stairs. . . . Eve, darling, wonderful Eve. . . .' His voice broke in a sob and then burst out again in a piercing rage. 'And you came up from the scum you were born in and dared to try and soil her beautiful body by bearing one of your filthy brats. . . .'

'Shut up!' shouted Cranford.

He wanted to say, 'Shut up and let me tell all the things you did; how you poisoned our life together, ruined our marriage, how you encouraged her to kill the child we could have had, how it was an accident in the bath, an accident that killed her.'

But all he could do was to shout again.

'Shut up, you raving imbecile.'

'I'll never shut up till I've got you convicted. Never, you hear? Never, never!'

At last Willy got on his feet, and almost immediately the sticks slipped on the stone floor and he fell back again on to the divan. He stayed there, breathing heavily. No more words came, but in their place he made grinding noises with his teeth. Then he began pounding a cushion with one of his sticks. Cranford walked over and removed both of them from him, without difficulty.

'Give me those, give me those back,' shrieked Willy.

'Not until I've had a satisfactory explanation of this fantastic outburst,' Cranford said, and rounded on Fowler. 'This is the second time you've intruded into my home; what the devil is it all about?'

Fowler cleared his throat.

'Lord Binfield thinks, Mr Wilson, that you are Alexander Cranford,' he said.

'Thinks? You mean he suffers from a psychopathic delusion to that effect. Why?'

'It's you, Alex, I know it's you.' Willy's tone had suddenly become plaintive. 'It's your voice, your walk, the way you move, the way you smoke a cigarette. I'd know you anywhere.'

'What raving nonsense. Do I *look* like this Cranford fellow?'

'Lord Binfield's theory,' said Fowler, 'is that you've had an operation on your face to escape identification.'

'Has he found the surgeon who did it?'

'Lord Binfield . . .'

'Let's call him "Willy", shall we? It sounds more suitable.'

Willy tried to get up again.

'There! You hear?' he croaked. 'That's how he always said it. "Willy", as though I was beneath contempt. I'm a peer and I won't have it, I won't . . .'

'Sit down,' snapped Cranford.

'Lord Bin . . . Willy . . . thinks you did it yourself.'

'Did what?'

'Operated on your own face.'

'Absurd,' laughed Cranford. 'Here, look. Can you see any scars?'

He turned his face from side to side. Fowler shook his head.

'But I wouldn't, if the job was done by Alexander Cranford. That was his great skill, wasn't it?'

'So you subscribe to this lunatic's aberration, too?'

Fowler gave a sly smile.

'I've been paid to. I've written up a report. . . .'

'The so-called biography?'

'Exactly.'

'Doc Evans was right, then. You *are* a bloody policeman?'

'Private Eye is the more fashionable term. You might like to compare these.'

He opened his briefcase, and handed Cranford a pile of photographs. Some were enlargements, copies of ones he had taken a few years back. One he recognized as having stood on Eve's dressing table. Others showed him as he was now, bearded, with re-set ears and nose, the eyes slewed up a little, and the artificial hollow he had made in the left cheek to give an asymmetrical slant to the face.

'Where the devil did you take these?' he asked Fowler.

'You very obligingly had your hair cut in the street opposite my room, the last time I was here,' was the reply.

Cranford thrust the pictures back at him.

'So what does all that add up to? Pictures of two people, with obvious differences.'

'And similarities. Measurements, three-dimensional projections, you know. They could be matched up.'

'So could a hundred others, Mr Green.'

'Fowler is actually the name. I have to use different ones now and then, for obvious reasons.'

'I don't give a damn for any of your names,' said Cranford sharply, 'but before I throw the two of you out, I might as well hear the rest of your crazy accusations. Those photographs wouldn't convince anyone.

I've not had any experience of this sort of thing but I should imagine you need concrete evidence, a recorded deformity, finger-prints, before you could begin to make out a case. Have you got anything like that?'

He watched their faces and he knew they hadn't; but he also knew there was sweat on his own.

'You see?' exclaimed Willy. 'If he weren't Alexander Cranford, he wouldn't ask. He wouldn't want to know.'

'On the contrary. Because I'm Johnny Wilson, I have every right to know what extraordinary fiction made you select me as the object of your fantasy.'

Abruptly, Willy made little bouncing movements on the divan. 'Tell him, Fowler. Tell him how I got on to him.' It was a gleeful exultation, as though he and Fowler were boys engaged in a conspiracy to pull off a daring prank.

'Very often it's the flimsiest of clues which bring home the bacon, or should I say start off the pig-hunt?' began Fowler.

'Oh, do get on,' bleated Willy.

Fowler rummaged through his papers.

'Last year, Mr Wilson, you gave a painting to a Mrs Iverson.'

'Well?'

'Well, she sold it. In London. On her way home to the States. Said it reminded her too much of her dead daughter.'

'Ye Gods, that's why she wanted it.'

'Fairly recently that picture found its way into a small Bond Street gallery. An art-critic called Manstein happened to mention it in an article. He said it was reminiscent, particularly in the treatment of the background, of the work of a painter called Maxwell Cranford.'

'So I went down to the gallery and bought it,' enthused Willy. 'Fancy that, Alex. I paid good money for it.' He cackled suddenly. 'Your money left to Eve, which came to me with everything else. Good money for one of your silly daubs, Alex. And I took it home. It was almost a replica of the picture which used to hang in your bedroom.'

Fowler spread out some more blown-up prints.

'And these rule out the possibility that it was a chance composition.'

Cranford picked up the photographs. He could see it now in every one: the same tone-values, the same feeling which, behind the figures and faces, gave the strange effect of wild animals peering out from between the trees; his father's vision, imprinted on his boyish mind, and later unconsciously repeated in all his own painting, like a signature. He cursed Mrs Iverson, and he cursed Manstein, but he cursed himself also for his own blind spot, which had prevented his noticing what had happened. He put the prints down slowly.

'So, because I paint like Maxwell Cranford, I'm his son?' he said. 'How ridiculous. I paint like him because, though I've seen little of it, I admire his work. One artist influences another. There are hundreds of examples.' His voice became incredulous. 'Is that all you had to go on? A common artistic experience? Was that enough for you to build a whole fabric of delusion, and fetch you down here?'

'It was enough for me,' cried Willy. 'And it's paid off.'

'In what way?' laughed Cranford.

'Because now I've seen you, I know. Now I'm sure. I don't care what you look like; you're Alexander Cranford, and you murdered my sister.'

'If it weren't an obvious absurdity, that could be a dangerous thing to say,' said Cranford.

'Dangerous for you, when I've said it to the Greek police.'

'Go ahead and see,' smiled Cranford. 'They'll think you're mad, of course, which you are. They won't believe you, and they won't do anything. Why should they? It isn't true. I'm Johnny Wilson. I'm a respected citizen. I've papers to prove who I am. I've married one of their own. They're glad to have me here.' His smile dropped away. 'You and I, my imbecilic lord, have nothing in common, let alone a relationship by marriage. But if you persist in your crazy assertion and try and make trouble, I warn you, I'll take you to court for everything you've got.' He turned to Fowler. 'And you too. Now get out.'

'You're Cranford,' shouted Willy. 'I know you are. Admit it. Admit it, Alex!' Willy's lips quivered. 'For Eve's sake I've got to make you admit it.'

He suddenly began to sob again. Fowler gathered up the photographs and the papers and put them in the briefcase.

'My apologies, Mr Wilson,' he said. 'I knew it was a most circumstantial theory. But then one's paid to do a job. One has to please one's clients, you understand?'

Cranford put the sticks on the divan by Willy and said to Fowler: 'Take him away. Take him to a doctor. He needs one, poor sod.'

Willy stopped his blubbering and looked from one to the other of them with hot, red-rimmed eyes.

'I'll prove it. I'll prove it, you'll see,' he whispered.

He clutched the sticks and, levering himself up, thrust off Fowler's attempts to assist him.

'You're fired,' he said.

Cranford opened the door and watched them pick their way slowly, Willy stumbling from time to time, down the difficult path. When they were out of sight, he realized he could not remember exactly when he had started to scratch his hands.

Chapter Twenty-Seven

LEAVING LITTLE MELINA, eyes dark saucers of fright, swinging from one to another of the group round the bed, as Lally returned to the school, she noticed the crippled man and his companion, making laborious progress along the quay. When she had reached the top of the steps, she paused in the shade to observe them more closely, for the path down which they had come led only up to her own house.

As they approached, she recognized the older of the two as the man who had been to see Johnny two weeks ago. And now this Mr Green —she even remembered his name—had come again, bringing, obviously, the friend he had spoken about. No wonder Johnny had looked annoyed when he had seen them across the harbour. He had been angry for a whole day after her mother had told of Mr Green's taking photographs of his paintings without permission. Yet the expression she had seen on Johnny's face a short time ago was composed of more than annoyance and, because she was still puzzled by it, she indulged an uneasy unobserved curiosity of the two visitors as they passed below her. The young man on the sticks had a beautiful face, as though he should have been a girl. It was not, however, his appearance which arrested her attention, but something he said to Green. At first she did not believe she could have heard right. She repeated it to herself several times. Then, like an explosion, all the morning's premonition burst upon her. It couldn't be true. How could anyone say that?

She opened the schoolroom door, dismissed the astonished class and, without heed of comment, ran all the way along the quay and up the path, and did not stop until, breathless, she had put her hand on the latch and lifted it.

'We can have a drink here,' said Fowler.

He pulled a chair back from a table at the Gerofinikas. Willy looked at it with distaste and, making an elaborate show, flicked the wooden slats of the seat with his handkerchief. The proprietor, mistaking this dust-removing action for a blow in the constant war against the insect world, ran into the café, and returned with a home-made fly-whisk which, with a broad grin, he presented to Willy.

'*Dia tis myiges*,' he said.

Willy regarded the man with his most exaggerated expression of disdain, the expression he kept for inferior beings such as waiters, tradesmen, members of the professions, even business men, in fact anyone who still worked for a living; unless, of course, they happened to have made enough money to buy themselves a title. Then Willy allowed them the full warmth of his nature, especially if it were reciprocated with the offer of a loan, or free hospitality. But it was an expression which was wearing thin, becoming less convincing, having less and less effect. Sometimes, as now, it had no effect at all. The man shook the fly-whisk at him, making demonstrative flicks with it, and grinned at Willy even more encouragingly. Fowler took the whisk from him.

'Thank you,' he said. 'Bring two ouzo. *Dio ouzo*.'

'O.K.,' replied the proprietor, and retired into the *taverna*.

'It's for flies,' said Fowler.

'I know that, you idiot!' snapped Willy, and sat down, laying his sticks across the next table. They remained silent, fanning themselves with table-mats in the hot shade, waiting for the drinks to come.

In the house behind the square, Doc Evans folded the bedclothes back over the child, smiled at the pinched, sweating little face, and stood up. Kontopoulos and his wife, one on each side of the bed, regarded him with patient attention. He knew the look well. A spurious calm fortitude, which hid a turmoil of fear and anguish, hope and love, a mask supplied, in such a situation, by long established custom, to parents everywhere.

With a movement of his head he motioned to the girl's father to follow him out of the oppressive room. The door to the street was open, and through it he could see the cluster of neighbours, grandmothers, mothers-to-be, the olive faces under the black hair partly hidden by head-shawls, sombre, silent, baby-clutching, waiting on disaster, waiting for the signal from him to shed tears either of relief or grief. It seemed to Evans that he knew this scene well, too, but differently lit, painted in greys and blacks, instead of reds and blues, yet showing women with fundamentally the same expressions, grouped at the pit-head, summoned there in the Welsh rain by the wailing siren of calamity.

'Listen, Kostas,' he said. 'Listen very carefully.'

195

The heavy-featured plastic Greek face set itself in a new expression of benign, almost fatuous expectation which loosed in Evans a fleeting desire to hit it.

'Do you want your daughter to live?' he asked roughly.

'Yes, Doc. Why you ask that?'

'Well, she's not going to.'

He had to do it that way, brutally. He had to lay a charge under the wall of prejudice and pig-headedness, in order to blast a hole of sanity through which the child could crawl to safety. There wasn't much time now, and success depended on so many things, not least on the girl's own strength and resistance. 'And you, Kostas, will be to blame,' he concluded.

'What you mean, Doc? Why you say that?'

'The only thing which can save her is an operation.'

'But the tablets. The teacher, she make her take the tablets. You say just now. You say if Melina do that, she be all right?'

'I said she might. It's different, now. The tablets won't do it alone. She's got to go across the water.'

'No,' said Kontopoulos, and made spreading movements with his fingers as if warding off unmentionable, unknown horrors. 'No, not that. She never come back. We never see her no more.'

'It may be too late,' said Evans, 'but it's the only chance.'

The man's face puckered like a boy's and he made clicking noises with his tongue, looking up at the rough, plastered ceiling in supplication.

'Panagia mou! Why this happen to me? Why to me?'

'It's not happening to you. It's happening to Melina.'

'But Mamma. She no let her go.'

'Tell her she must, Kostas.'

'Is no good. She love Melina so much.'

'So much she will kill her. Tell her that also.'

'Is not so easy, Doc.'

'All right. I'll tell her myself.'

'No. No, Doc. I tell her. But you got to give me time.'

'Ten minutes. I'll be at the O Byron.'

'O.K., Doc. I try. For you.'

'Christ,' said Evans.

'And if she no let her go?'

'Then go for the priest,' he said.

The waiting women folk stepped back as he brushed past them out into the street.

The proprietor of the Gerofinikas set the drinks down and held out his tray to Fowler for the money. Fowler waved it over to Willy, who scowled and threw some drachmas on to it with a clatter.

'That's the last expense you get out of me,' he said to Fowler.

The proprietor went back into the café and Fowler said:

'As I haven't had the last two weeks' expenses yet, this might be a good time to settle up the whole account.'

Willy tasted his ouzo and winced.

'What ghastly muck,' he observed.

'Two hundred and ten pounds,' said Fowler.

'Two hundred and what!' exclaimed Willy. 'You filthy little swindler.'

Fowler took a notebook out of his pocket.

'It's all down here,' he said wearily. 'King's Palace Hotel, Athens, cables to you, postage, 'phone calls, photographic materials, developing charges, hire of boat.' He glanced over towards the quay where the skipper of the vessel was sitting on a bollard contemplatively smoking his pipe. 'By the way, I told the captain you'd pay him and the crew yourself, when we got back to Piraeus.'

Willy picked up one of his sticks and began poking the end of it into a crack between two cobbles which paved the frontage of the *taverna*.

'I'm not going back to Piraeus,' he said. It was a quiet flat statement of private conviction.

'That's your affair,' Fowler shrugged. 'But as far as I'm concerned this lousy job's over.'

'I repeat again,' said Willy. 'You're fired.'

'Suits me,' replied Fowler. 'Just you write the cheque.'

'Who's that over there?'

Willy pointed with his stick across to the O Byron, where a bald-headed, elderly man had just sat down.

'His name's Evans,' said Fowler.

'The unfrocked medico?'

'Struck off. He's a lush. It's all down in my report.'

'And at one time he knew Cranford?'

'Yes. Operated on his wife years ago.'

'Which could be why he doesn't recognize him now.'

Fowler sighed.

'He doesn't recognize him now because Wilson doesn't look like Cranford; and he doesn't look like Cranford, because he isn't Cranford.'

Willy stabbed away at a crack between the cobbles.

'He is. He is,' he spoke in rhythm with the movement.

Fowler watched him. A nut-case if ever he'd seen one. When the upper classes went bonkers they did it properly. A mother-fixation on a

197

twin sister. But why should he worry? Unfounded suspicions, crazy obsessions, had proved lucrative sources of bread and butter before now. But he was sick of this one. As he listened to the repetitive jabbing of the stick, there was something about this Adonis with feet of clay which made his skin creep even in the hot bright sunlight, and against the brochure-like background of white houses, blue water, and dark-green cypress trees.

'Let it go,' said Fowler. 'You can't take it any further.'

Unheedingly, Willy continued his game with the stick for some time. Then he said:

'We should have asked to see his passport. Why didn't you do that? Why not, Fowler?'

'Because after you'd had your ball up there, he wouldn't have shown it to us. If you'd let me handle it . . .' he shrugged again and swallowed some ouzo. 'But it wouldn't make any difference. Even if you were right, do you think, after all the fantastic trouble he'd gone to, such a man would slip up on a basic detail like a passport?'

'The number and date of issue could be checked back in London.'

'The Foreign Office doesn't give that sort of information to anyone,' said Fowler, and added with acid satisfaction, 'Not even to a peer.'

'The police could get it.'

'They've got to have good reason.'

'But they have now. I've seen Cranford. What better reason than that?'

Fowler smiled pityingly, and shook his head.

'Just an idea in your skull. It isn't enough. As Wilson said, you haven't really got anything at all.'

Over at the O Byron, Fowler noticed that the fat man with the peaked cap whom he had seen on his last visit had joined the doctor at his table. There was much gesticulation, and idly he wondered what local gossip or incident was the cause of the argument and the raised voices.

'There must be something,' said Willy. He spoke with a kind of dogged desperation. 'There must be just one thing somewhere which, if I could dig it out, would make him give himself away. Then all the rest would follow.' His jaw set hard, pulling the corners of his lips down, spoiling the shape of the pretty mouth. 'Then I'd have him.' With a snap, the cobble he had been undermining popped up out of its bed. 'Like that.'

Willy's eyes shone at Fowler with an insane glint of achievement, as though he sought acknowledgement for bringing off some incredibly intricate manoeuvre.

'Look,' he said, tapping the loose stone with his stick. 'I got it out.'

'So what? Put it back,' said Fowler.

Willy glanced down at the cobble again, and seemingly it continued to give him pleasure.

'You couldn't have done that, Fowler,' he said. 'That's why you're what you are. A punk detective. You'd have given up long ago.'

Fowler laughed.

'I gave up a lot of things long ago. You don't have to. My guess is you haven't ever done them.'

Willy jammed the cobble back into the hole, and glared at him.

'Shit,' he said.

'That's right,' smiled Fowler. 'Two hundred and ten pounds worth.'

'I haven't got my cheque-book.'

Fowler felt in his pocket.

'You can use this form. I've made it out "Pay Cash". Your branch is Lloyds, Piccadilly. A piece of detection within my capabilities. Just sign here.'

Willy hesitated, then snatched the piece of paper from him and quickly scribbled his signature. Fowler blew on the ink, folded the cheque, and returned it to his pocket.

'Big deal,' he said. 'Now let me buy *you* a drink, Lord Binfield.'

Fowler was sure that if Willy had come from a different background he would have spat in his face. Indeed he would have preferred such an expressive gesture to the cold, dignified, excessively polite refusal which snatched the fleeting pleasure of a cheap victory from him.

'No, thank you, Mr Fowler,' said Willy. 'Some other time, perhaps?'

Willy picked up his sticks and clambered to his feet. He had taken a few paces from the *taverna* when there was a hail from the O Byron.

'Stop! Mister. I wish to speak!' called out Kontopoulos.

Willy halted and, with barely disguised irritation, waited until the fat anxious man had run across to the Gerofinikas.

'Is very important thing you must do,' said Kontopoulos breathlessly.

Willy leaned back a little to avoid the heavy odour of garlic.

'Are you addressing me?' he asked.

'Yes, please. My little daughter. She very sick.'

'Worrying for you, I'm sure,' said Willy.

'You got to help. You got to do what I say.'

'Oh, have I?' said Willy. 'Like hell.'

He made a movement towards the quay, but the Greek grabbed his arm with powerful fingers.

'Let go,' said Willy. 'Who the devil do you think you are?'

The man threw out his chest and said pompously:

'I am Kontopoulos. Everyone on the island do as I say.'

'Easy now, Kostas. Let me explain to the gentleman.'

Evans, who had followed his friend from the other café, pulled him back gently.

'My name is Evans. Doc Evans,' he said.

'I've heard about you,' said Willy unpleasantly. 'What is it you want?'

Evans's Celtic pride flared up at the implied insult, but he swallowed it quickly.

'This man's daughter has an acute appendix,' he said.

'Really?' was Willy's comment.

'If she can be got to a hospital, an operation could save her. Otherwise she'll die.'

'Very touching, but . . .'

'Can you take her to Rhodes? That's the nearest.'

'Why ask me, my dear fellow?' said Willy. 'There are plenty of other vessels.'

'Slow ones. Your boat could manage it in a few hours. That's all she's got.'

'You must still have some rudimentary knowledge left, Doctor Evans,' Willy sneered. 'Isn't there anything you can do?'

'I'm not a surgeon,' Evans replied patiently.

'Is that so?'

'Mister. You got to do it,' ordered Kontopoulos.

To his surprise Willy suddenly burst into laughter.

'Very well,' he said. 'I'll certainly do what I can.'

'Thank you. Thank you. *Oh theos tha se erlogisi.*'

Kontopoulos began to pump his hand up and down. Willy withdrew it with distaste.

'But it really depends on my captain,' he said. 'I'll have a word with him.'

Evans and Kontopoulos made a move to accompany him, but Willy waved them back.

'It'll save time if you leave this to me,' he said. 'He's rather a difficult character. Unlike my friend over there, who'll buy you a drink in the meantime. Like to do that, wouldn't you, Fowler?' he shouted, and hobbled off towards the man who was sitting on the bollard.

'Fowler? Mr Green, isn't it?' asked Evans.

'Yes,' said Fowler, 'but I write under the other name.'

'Who's that poor bloody cripple you got with you this time?'

'It's Lord Binfield,' said Fowler.

'Never heard of him, but if he saves this little girl, he's the Prince of Wales to me.'

200

'Must hurry. Must hurry,' said Kontopoulos anxiously. 'I fetch little Melina?'

Evans put a hand on his shoulder.

'Calm yourself, man. Another minute won't matter now. Wait and see what the captain has to say.'

The proprietor of the Gerofinikas appeared with bottle and glasses and inappropriate grin of enthusiasm at the sudden increase of business. Evans helped himself to a drink and then poured a second one. Willy finished talking to the skipper, whom they could see now hurrying away along the jetty towards the boat, and limped back towards them.

'Is all right?' shouted Kontopoulos.

'I'm afraid not,' said Willy.

'What's wrong?' asked Evans.

'Some trouble with the fuel-pipe. The crew are working on it now. The captain's gone back to chivvy them up. But it could be quite a time.'

'Bloody hell,' said Evans.

'Oh God,' said Kontopoulos. '*Sychorese me. O Theos na sosi ti Melina mou!*'

He slumped into one of the chairs and put his head on his arms.

'It isn't as desperate as it sounds, my dear fellow,' said Willy.

'It is, man,' replied Evans.

'There's something you seem to have forgotten.'

'What's that?'

'There's a highly-skilled surgeon living on the island. He might be persuaded to help you.'

'What bloody nonsense are you talking about?'

'Johnny Wilson,' said Willy. 'His real name's Cranford. I believe you used to know him, Doctor Evans?'

Willy smiled at Fowler with a look of triumph.

Chapter Twenty-Eight

'BUT PEOPLE SHOULD not say such terrible things if they are not true.'

'People often say terrible things that are not true.'

'What makes them do it, Johnny?'

'Hatred, jealousy, fear, many things.'

Cranford watched her move the baby over to her other breast. The brief journey was still long enough to bring a cry of dissatisfaction from Paul at the interruption of his, as yet, greatest happiness in life. Thalia mimicked the sound and, holding the untapped nipple between her fingers like a cigarette, guided it accurately between the pouting lips which, at the first touch, clamped on to it with the powerful adherence of a limpet, and all was quiet.

It was a scene he never grew tired of observing. The contentment in her eyes and the complementary convexities of female breast and infant cheek made a pattern of beauty which had expressed the fundamentals of love long before the word had been verbalized, let alone written down. And he, the observer, was drawn within its ambit, apart and yet part of it, because it was an event which had given his life meaning.

The breeze through the vine-leaves overhead made lanceolate shapes of dancing light along the patio, as though Monet had set the prospect for his own delight. From inside the house came age-old domestic sounds of women clearing up after a meal. High above, he could hear the steel-taut cries of swallows. The scent of the lemon-blossom filled the air with its own drowsy protective balm. This was where he had found his heaven; this he had fought for—this he would fight to keep. Yet the sound of the morning's alarums and excursions, now without the walls, kept finding echoes in her words.

'But if the man with the sticks does not know you, Johnny, why should he feel these things against you?'

'I've explained. He thinks I'm somebody else.'

'This Alexander Cranford?'

'Yes.'

'Who murdered his wife, who was the sister of the man with the sticks?'

'So he says.'

'But it is not true?'

'No. It was an accident.'

'How do you know?'

'Everyone knows. It was in all the papers.'

'But the man does not believe the papers?'

'He doesn't want to believe them.'

When she had come back, tearful, distressed, he had not wanted to tell her the story. Yet she was fired with indignation, and rained on him a barrage of questions. He quickly realized that a show of anger at such a wicked calumny, or a studied exhibition of perplexed puzzlement at what she had heard, would have stilled neither her anxiety nor her curiosity. And so, piece by piece, he had recounted the strange theory which had brought the two visitors to the island in their attempt to shackle him with their absurd accusations. As he had gradually convinced her of the impossibility of what had been suggested, she had become calmer. During the meal, though, she had been quieter than usual, and Maria had to drag the answers out of her as to why she was home early, how Melina was sick again, how she had been able to get the child to take the tablets given her by Doc Evans. And now that they were settled in the regular afternoon routine, Cranford saw that illogical intuitive fears still vaguely beset her, and she could not leave them alone.

'It would be a terrible thing, if what he believes was true,' she said, and held the baby over her shoulder and patted his back.

'Who?'

'The man with the sticks.'

'I suppose so.'

Cranford tried to give the impression that for him the matter had now receded, had taken on a trivial colouring, soon to be forgotten altogether. He held out his hands for his son and, passing her hand under the baby's nappy as a safeguard, Thalia carried the now sleepy satisfied bundle over to its father.

'And he just made everything up?'

She kept worrying at it, like a dog with a bone.

'It is in his mind. His mind is sick,' he said.

She began to prepare the cradle, shaking out the blanket and kneading in her hands the little straw palliasse.

'And the other man, the husband. He is a doctor?'

'He is dead. He died in the same accident.'

'But before he died, he was a doctor?'

'A surgeon.'

'Like Doc Evans?'

'No. He is a physician. A surgeon does operations.'

'It must be a wonderful thing to be that.'

'Perhaps.'

'I am sure of it.'

She took the baby from his arms and laid him down in the cradle.

'I think Paul will be a surgeon.'

'Why?'

She kissed the baby and tucked the blanket loosely round him.

'He is very gentle. But strong too. Strong and gentle, like you, Johnny.'

She came and sat on the bench by Cranford and took hold of his hands, which thankfully had lost once more the itching sensation which, like a fell reminder of an almost forgotten curse, had briefly attacked him just before Willy and his hired companion had retreated. Lally looked up at him, searching his face, as though she were trying to reassess it, see it anew for the first time. He smiled and kissed her on the nose. The playful gesture did not dispel her earnest gaze.

'It is terrible that this man should say such things about you, Johnny.'

She was turning the bone over again, gnawing at it, unable to release it. He took his hands from hers and said brusquely,

'It doesn't matter. It doesn't matter what he says.'

'Not if he says these things to other people?'

'They won't believe him. You didn't, Lally, did you?' It sounded like an accusation, a threat.

'No,' she answered. 'But then I love you.'

'Would you still love me, if it were true?'

'A woman cannot stop loving. A man yes, but not a woman.'

This quiet simple statement moved him with such affection, such sadness, such happiness that he took her in his arms and kissed her with all the passionate dominance of his body, which was at the same time a submission of his whole spirit. Only when Maria had run on to the patio and called to them excitedly, did they break from the embrace; only then did they remember dimly the knocking, and only now did they give attention to the noise of voices, many voices, gabbling and clamouring, sounding through the house from the other side.

'*Grigora, ela, theloun tou, Johnny!*' cried Maria.

'*Pois ton theli?*' Lally got up from the bench.

'*O Kathenas.*'

'What is it?' asked Cranford.

'I do not understand. Something must have happened in the village. I will go and find out.' She turned to her sister. '*Na Kytazis ton Parlo, Maria.*'

A voice called unmistakably above the others.

'Johnny? Are you there, Johnny?'

Cranford stood up.

'Sounds like Doc Evans,' he said. 'You stay here.'

'No,' she replied. 'I come too.'

She followed him down the steps and across the room to the open door.

As soon as they appeared, the voices died down. There were about twenty of them, mostly men, but some women, to Cranford familiar faces all. Most of the names he knew too, and what they did with their lives.

'*Kalimera*,' he said.

Though, in the two years he had lived among them, helped with their meagre harvest, lent a hand from time to time with a lucky catch of fish, his efforts to master a rudimentary knowledge of modern Greek had been barely successful. He had only managed to learn enough to exchange a greeting, make an observation about the seasons, ask after relatives, accept and give a drink or a cigarette. Yet there was a warmth of heart, a dogged loyalty, a natural courtesy in the island character, which broke through the restrictions of any language barrier. So quickly, it seemed, had he been accepted, become part of their life, and he theirs, that he had grown to feel an unspoken depth of communication with these unlettered people which he had rarely felt in the glossy social world he had chosen to leave behind. But now, though nothing had yet been spoken, he sensed a mood of doubt in the dusky features which failed to respond to his smile of welcome. His friend in the peaked cap and Evans were standing in front of the others. Kontopoulos stepped forward.

'Mister Wilson,' he said. 'Is very important we speak.'

'Go ahead,' replied Cranford.

'Little Melina. She very sick.'

'Lally told me. I'm very sorry to hear it, Kostas.'

'Is no time now to go across the water.'

'What is it, Doc?' he asked Evans.

'Pain before vomiting. Fever. Pulse a hundred and twelve. Tender over McBurney's point. Guarding in the right iliac fossa. Does that mean anything to you? If it does, for Christ's sake man, say so.'

The words came at Cranford like an accusation flung by a prosecuting counsel towards the witness box. But here was no impartial judicial gathering, deliberating in the sombre greyness of a city courtroom. Here were the sharp colours of feeling, the passionate sounds of emotion, rushing up to involve him in the answer which, if he gave the true one, would set off the first rumblings of an earthquake which would grow and reverberate until the whole edifice of his happiness crumbled about him, taking with it Lally and Paul and all the serene future he had tried to shore-up against the whiplash of time past. It was clear what Willy had told them, and as he looked round at his jury, at the waiting pairs of dark eyes, he could see they were prepared to believe, that they wanted to believe, what they had been told.

He marvelled at the incredible kink of circumstance which had led to this confrontation. But for the chance multiplication of a million bacteria in a small useless blind tube of bowel inside a child of eight, they might have shrugged or laughed at such a suggestion. Johnny a surgeon? Johnny was their friend. Johnny was married to Lally. Johnny was one of them. But nevertheless a question had been asked, and they wanted an answer.

He glanced at Lally and saw that she too was waiting with growing incredulity at his hesitation. He looked away again. Why should he be involved, why should he? This was a sacrifice he should not be asked to make. He had sacrificed enough. He had the right to disengage, and he had exercised that right and by it he must stand. He had only to shake his head at Evans and they would go away. Yet as the seconds crept by and still he did not answer, he knew that he had passed already the point whence he could retreat, that there was never any retreat, that his dream was a selfish arrogant dream which, like a dream, had suddenly no substance. And all at once he saw what had gone wrong, what had been missing, what he had lacked in the years he had pretended so successfully to heal the sick. It was there in the face of Doc Evans, the lined, broken-down face of a broken-down discredited colleague. It was compassion; and as he spoke at last, he wondered why he had never felt it before.

'Yes,' he said. 'Those words mean a great deal to me.'

'Then you *are* Alexander Cranford?' asked Evans.

There was a moment before he nodded, and in it Lally had pushed past him.

'No! It is not true! It can't be true! It is a lie, a terrible lie!'

She shouted at them, repeating her condemnation with a rage of vehemence, again and again. They stood dumbly, absorbing the tirade with shocked impassivity, until her voice began to crack and the tears came and she turned to Cranford.

'It is not true, Johnny. Tell them it is not true. You're Johnny. Johnny. Not the other one,' she cried.

He put his arms round her, and held her quivering body against him. 'I'm Johnny, too,' he whispered.

At length her weeping ceased. Quietly she pushed him from her. Her eyes struck him with the shock of uncovered deceit, and all the bitterness of broken faith.

'Why? Why, Johnny? Why did you have to tell them?'

He put his hand out to her, but she drew away.

'Why?' she repeated.

'Because we have Paul,' he said. 'And one day he will be as old as Melina.'

He kissed her quickly then, and since he could bear no longer the look of despair on her troubled face, he turned back to the crowd of silent watching people. He nodded to Evans and forced a smile.

'All right, Doctor,' he said. 'Let's go and look at your patient.'

He grasped Kontopoulos by the elbow, and the rest, tongues loosed again in excited speculation, followed them down the rocky path towards the harbour, where the white hull of the motor-vessel shone in the sunlight.

Chapter Twenty-Nine

FOWLER WAS CONSCIOUS of a familiar sensation, which only when Willy said, 'They'll be bringing the child over soon,' could he pin down precisely. It was the same suppressed excitement which occurred before the starter flicked the tapes away, or the players ran on to the field, the same anticipation which spread like an infection before the curtain went up, or the bulls came nosing and bucking into the arena. It was most like the last, because from the table at the Gerofinikas where he sat, the dazzling sunlight of the square and the eddies of dust thrown up by the comings and goings of many feet had, in its atmosphere, the smell of danger, and the primitive appeal of death in the afternoon. Yet the feeling had a sour undercurrent which spoilt the excitement and added disappointment to the anticipation, since one of the protagonists of the battle, the slender young man who sat beside him, seemed already to have won. Like many people, Fowler was usually on the losing side of things, and secretly he wanted the favourite to stumble.

Willy sat upright in his chair, eyes alive and observant, breathing deeply, hands clasped with fingers interlocked, his whole demeanour one of restrained triumph. It occurred to Fowler that this was the portrait of vengeance, no longer pent up, but exulting in the supreme pleasure of its enactment.

Triumph had escaped from Willy with a delighted cry of, 'What did I tell you, Fowler? Just one thing to make him give himself away,' when the group headed by the man who must be Cranford after all,

Doc Evans and Kontopoulos, had come back along the quay and disappeared up the street behind the square. A few minutes later Cranford had reappeared with Evans, who had made off to his own house down the alley between the church and the school. Thalia also had come along the quay then and, some distance behind her, Fowler recognized the younger sister carrying the baby. The bustling pageant had for a brief moment been suspended as Cranford and his wife met at the foot of the steps. They had stood without speaking, a few feet apart, and then she had run forward and kissed him, and together they had gone up into the school.

'Very touching,' Willy had said. 'But she won't have him for very long. Nor will he ever know the pleasure of seeing that disgusting brat grow up.'

Fowler had nearly left then, for he had begun to wish he had not been a link in the chain which, with doomlike clanking, seemed to disturb the quiet siesta of the little town. Immediately he had been annoyed by the sentiment, knowing that his capacity for such lapses was why he had so often, and so rightly, been judged a punk at his job.

The next performer to make a re-entry was Evans, carrying some boxes. Two women were with him, humping baskets and sheets and blankets and what looked like cooking utensils. There were some younger youths and girls with full buckets of water. A man and a boy came out of a house next to the O Byron lifting a sack of wood and a can of oil. All converged on the school.

The church bell began to ring and the priest appeared at the church door. The summons brought out more of the small community who, from all directions, walked towards the sound of the bell and, bobbing devoutly to their pastor, entered the church behind him. The expectant gathering near the school was now talking with much gesture and breath-sucking exclamation. Curious stares were addressed to Fowler and Willy where they sat like a political candidate and his agent, awaiting the result of an election. Smoke came belching out of the school chimney and an acrid whiff of it reminded Fowler of some November childhood bonfire, and yet as the grim satisfaction on Willy's face seemed to grow more intense, into Fowler's mind leapt unpleasant fleeting thoughts of gas-chambers and the ineradicable sin of total human degradation.

'Here they come,' said Willy.

Across the square Fowler saw Kontopoulos bearing Melina in his arms. Her mother, in weeping attendance, shawl over head, kept up with the large fat man. The crowd turned and, in hushed immobility, waited for the stricken family to reach them.

'You know something?' whispered Willy gleefully. 'They'll tear Cranford apart if he makes a mistake in there.'

Suddenly Fowler felt sick. He got up.

'Where are you going?' asked Willy.

'I don't know,' he replied.

Willy shrugged.

'You *are* a fool,' he drawled. 'You'll miss all the fun.'

Fowler walked away quickly, the crowd parting to let him pass.

Cranford had decided to use the school as his improvised operating-theatre as much for the large windows on three sides, which flooded the airy room with all-important light, as for the tiled floor which was scrubbed daily, and the generous stove large enough to take several saucepans and tureens at the same time. The island's midwife and her apprentice stood by Thalia, watching the vessels as they came up to the boil over the roaring woodfire fed by the village chandler and his son. The atmosphere incongruously reminded Cranford of preparations more for a church jumble-sale than the hazardous surgical adventure which he had set in motion. At the same time the sound of the flames, and the intentness of the silent waiting women, added a sinister under-tone suggesting the preliminaries to a human sacrifice. He cast the thought away and invoked the success of the enterprise, which he knew depended largely on the contents of Evans's neglected boxes and cartons.

He pushed two long bench-desks together and covered them with blankets to make a trough-like operating-table. The concavity would allow easier control of any struggling, and act as a safeguard against a chance fall or other injurious mishap. So far, so good. But how far, really? Was he not, for the appeasement of some deep guilt of his own, attempting an audacious, spectacular escapade which, if he brought it off, would in some way wipe his personal slate clean? He looked his conscience in the face. Two years ago it would have been true, but not now. Now, in personal terms, he had nothing to gain, perhaps now he had lost everything anyway. Now there was only one motivation, one which he had paid lipservice to since he had qualified, but which only now, and for the first time, fired him with a passionate aching want: to save life.

He weighed the odds critically. Appendices had been removed in worse conditions, in worse places. The job had been done in the jungle with the aid of a penknife, a roughly fashioned bamboo needle, strips of creeper for ligatures, under the deadening umbrella of a bottle of scotch. But such heroic deeds had been carried out by tough, trained men on tougher companions, men attuned to pain, and with screw-tight courage. Here the victim was a little child, filled with a child's terror of strange, unknown things, unable to understand, let alone respond with stoicism, to what had to be done, or appreciate the fatal alternative.

Cursing intermittently, Evans unpacked the goods he had ordered so many years ago. Most of the stuff was useless, irrelevant: placebos and simple remedies for simple conditions, wildly inappropriate for the task in hand, aspirin, codeine, alkalis, tonics, carminatives, aperients, ointments, splints of all sizes, the trappings of first-aid. The sight filled Cranford with a nightmare panic, demanding the abandonment of the whole project. He countered it with an implacable refusal to accept defeat.

'Let's take it in sequence,' he said to Evans. 'Premedication. Anything?'

'Morphine. A sixth of a grain tablets. A tube of twelve.'

'No atropine, no scopolamine?'

'What the hell would I have wanted with those?' asked Evans indignantly.

'I'm not criticizing,' said Cranford.

It was essential to protect the older man's feelings, in order to guarantee his co-operation for what lay ahead.

'The morphine'll do fine. Age eight plus. Half a tablet, would you say?'

'How do we give it? Both these syringes are smashed. What bloody use are hypo-needles on their own?'

'Rubber tubing will do,' said Cranford. 'Lally,' he called to her. 'Your fountain-pen. The one I gave you. Where is it?'

'In my desk, Johnny.'

'Get it, will you?' He turned back to Evans. 'Anaesthetic. Have we got anything?'

'Three ethylchloride sprays.'

'Perfect.'

'But they're for local, man, not general.'

'It'll be all right. Strap four layers of bandage over this.'

From the table where the jumble of cooking instruments brought by one of the women had been put, he picked up a small sieve and handed it to Evans. Lally brought him the pen. While he unscrewed the end and broke the pen open, he said:

'Right. Show me what instruments you've got.'

Evans opened the small metal surgical box. There were two Spencer-Wells forceps, three curved cutting needles, a pair of scissors, an eye-spud, a probe, a scalpel handle and two unbroken tubes, one of catgut and one of nylon suture material.

'Thank God we're O.K. for the needlework,' said Cranford. He removed the piece of rubber tube from the pen. 'In fact, Evans, we're going to be O.K. all round.'

'With no scalpel blades? Even you can't dissect with a handle.'

'Tell that boy to run up to Nico's and bring back his cut-throat razor,' Cranford said to Lally.

'Yes, Johnny.'

She went to the boy and spoke rapidly in Greek.

'What about retractors?' Evans persisted.

Cranford picked up four large spoons from the table, and after a little struggle bent the handles at right-angles over the edge of the desk.

'Retractors,' he grinned at Evans, and gathered them up with the scissors, forceps, needles and tube, and took them over to the stove. Selecting one of the smaller saucepans, he dropped them all into the boiling water and came back to Evans, who was making a passable porous mask out of the sieve and bandages.

'I know you were a famous surgeon, Mister Cranford,' said Evans, 'but so was Lister and, without asepsis, even he had a fantastic mortality rate.'

'I'd say we're a little in front of Lister,' smiled Cranford, 'but a good way behind Fleming. We've one bottle of Dettol, which is way ahead of the old man's carbolic; unfortunately this penicillin is long past its usable date, but we've got bags of sulphonamide, which puts us somewhere in the late thirties. Tear this sheet up, Lally, and make me some pieces about a foot square.'

While she obeyed, Cranford put two bowls on the teacher's desk and, with gestures, persuaded the midwife to half-fill them with boiling water from the tureen. He added some cold from a bucket to one of them and placed by it a chunk of crude soap and the scrubbing brush. He poured half the bottle of Dettol into each bowl. Lally brought him the pieces of sheet and he put them to soak in one of them. He smiled at her.

'When it is time to start,' he said, 'you will do everything I tell you?'

She looked at him, her eyes dark and serious. He could see the faint dried stains on her cheeks, left by the tears.

'It is going to be all right, Johnny?'

'Yes. Melina will be all right.'

'And afterwards? You. What will happen to you?'

'We mustn't worry about that, now,' he said, and, taking the soap, began washing his hands.

The door opened and the murmuring voices of the people outside came into the room briefly with Kontopoulos as, followed by the still weeping mother, he carried the child inside.

'Evans, get that morphine dissolved in a spoon, will you?' he said, but saw that the old doctor had anticipated him and was preparing the pain-killing shot. Shaking the water off his hands, Cranford went over to Kontopoulos.

'Melina is here, Johnny,' said the man simply.

'Good,' said Cranford and smiled encouragingly at Melina. 'Put her down on the blankets. You and your wife can stay with her for a time. I am going to give her something first to make the pain less, and to make her sleepy. Will you tell her there will just be a prick in her arm?'

Kontopoulos nodded and, muttering softly to her, he laid his daughter in the padded trough made by the desks. Cranford poured the water out of the saucepan. He placed one of the Dettol-soaked pieces of sheet on the table and picked out a hypodermic needle and the short length of rubber tubing. For one moment he thought the diameter of the tube would be too great to make a tight connexion with the base of the needle, but to his relief he even had some difficulty in fitting it over the nozzle. The improvised syringe having been assembled, he squeezed the rubber tube between his finger and thumb, expelling all the air, and put the point of the needle under the solution in the spoon held out by Evans. He partially released the pressure and the fluid level dropped as the morphine was sucked up the hollow bore of the needle.

'A twelfth of a grain?'

'I shouldn't wonder,' replied Evans.

'Right. Hold her arm. And Lally, you keep talking to the mother.'

The child gave a brief squeal as the needle pierced the skin, but the tube held, and with a sharp pinch of his fingers, Cranford felt the slight resistance as the morphine was shot firmly into the soft fibres of the triceps. He pulled the needle out and then, patting Melina's cheek, laughed and, to her surprised incomprehension, said, 'What a good girl. I wish I had a little girl like you.'

Lally translated, and the remark was taken up by Kontopoulos, and his wife and the two women and the man by the stove, like an incantation.

'Ti Kalo Koristi! Ti Kalo Koristi!'

Gradually the fear on the child's face began to diminish and she offered no resistance as Cranford exposed her abdomen.

'Now we are going to wash your tummy, and make it very, very clean,' he said.

Evans brought the bowl and soap and washed the skin thoroughly. Then Cranford covered the whole area with a Dettol-soaked piece of sheet and told Lally to see that it was not touched. The boy came back with the razor and Evans was quick enough to prevent Kontopoulos or the others seeing it before he put it in the saucepan with the other instruments and covered them again with boiling water.

'We'll start in about twenty minutes,' said Cranford. 'All right with you, Mister Anaesthetist?'

'I suppose you realize, man, that if she should stop breathing, I've no coramine, no stimulants?' said Evans.

'You've got me,' said Cranford.

Evans looked at him and abruptly the toothy grin appeared.

'You're a bloody, conceited, lovely boy, Johnny,' he said.

Cranford turned away and looked out of the windows across the harbour. The peace of the afternoon had settled on it, with that subtle change of light which he had grown to know and love. The snaking reflections in the water had deepened a few shades, and the sky had taken on an alabaster quality near the horizon which gave the impression that beyond it lay not the racing turmoil of the life he had tried to leave behind, but the edge of the world itself, where only the classic gods of the Ancients were permitted to live and have their being.

A lone figure, walking along the jetty towards the white yacht, he recognized as Fowler. The sight made him realize that in the burning concentration and planning of the last hour he had forgotten about Willy and the threat which remained. He had so far not considered what he was going to do. He could stay put and let the ponderous machinery of investigation take its course. Then at a certain stage he would have to go across the water to plead his innocence, with only faint hope of success. What jury would believe that his actions had been motivated by self-disgust and the desire to preserve his reputation; to tie off neatly part of his life which had come to an end, in order to start a fresh one with honour? He could take Lally and Paul, and perhaps for years keep up a running retreat across the world, always looking over his shoulder. The prospect filled him with despair. He was in a corner and no further retreat was possible. And all because of one damning piece of identification—the attempt to save this one child's life.

But he did not regret his decision. Wasn't it all a just penalty? A penalty for his arrogance, for his deliberate withdrawal from all the obligations which his oath as a doctor could never release him? He looked at his hands. The skin was firm. All irritation had gone, gone for ever. Manstein had been right. When he had walked down the path with Evans and briefly told him the story, he had not cared whether he had been believed, because the telling of it had released a sudden insight which itself resolved his old conflicts. He was not a painter; he was a surgeon after all, and the irony, which was now his sentence too, was that he could not return to a recognized surgeon's life. It was gone, sunk, like Eve, and the heaven he had exchanged her for was ripped open too, leaving nothing.

He glanced back from the window at Evans. He, too, was an outcast from the same exacting profession; he too had been caught up in the same inescapable situation. The mantle of Hippocrates might become stained and tattered, or even torn off whole, but here and there threads of it clung forever to those who had once worn it.

'I'm going to scrub up now,' said Cranford. 'Get everyone out except Lally. It'll be better that way.'

The older man nodded and, while Cranford felt the familiar harsh touch of the brush and saw the white lather of soap encase his arms up to the elbows, his mind came down on to the problems of the next twenty minutes, like an old but well-oiled and cared-for piece of machinery. When the room was empty save for the three of them and the child, now quietly somnolent, he said to Lally:

'Tell her she's going to smell the funny medicine, and that she must sniff as hard as she can.' He turned to Evans. 'O.K. You can start, professor.'

Lally translated to the child as Evans began spraying the ethylchloride on to the home-made mask. It was a scented pleasant smell and the child sniffed as bidden, and said something to Lally.

'What does she say?' asked Cranford.

'She says it is like flowers.'

'Let's hope there won't be any other bloody flowers,' muttered Evans, and started to lower the mask until it was about two inches from Melina's face. She moved her head suddenly and tried to sit up, but Lally held her firmly. A flash of sheer panic shot across the little features. She opened her mouth to shout, but the intake of breath drew down the heavy fumes, filling her lungs, and with the next breath the mask had descended completely. Above it her eyelids fluttered. Then her jaw sagged and Evans held it forward with his hand, turning the head sideways, and continued to spray the mask.

'I wish we'd got a bloody airway,' he said.

'Never mind,' said Cranford. 'Lally, pour away the water from the saucepan and bring it to me quickly.'

While she did this, he removed from the other bowl the pieces of Dettol-soaked sheet. He took the one which covered the child's stomach and folded it back over her chest. With two others he reduced the operating area of the skin to a manageable size. He pressed his fingers into the gentle curve of the abdomen.

'Good work: she's nearly relaxed,' he said to Evans. 'Lally, go and scrub your hands and arms just like I did.'

She nodded and obeyed with serious application. Cranford prodded the abdomen again.

'O.K., Evans?'

'O.K. She's breathing nicely now.'

Cranford picked up the razor from the saucepan. For a moment he held the blue-glinting blade in his hand. This was going to atone for all the years of wrinkles and bags and sagging breasts. This was the truth, which lay somewhere between Munro and himself, somewhere in the territory where Manstein and Khouri and Dinsley walked each day.

Lally returned and stood on the other side of the desk.

'I thought we wear things over our faces?' she said.

Cranford smiled at Evans.

'Not in unqualified circles, like ours,' he said, and drew the blade firmly across the skin.

The two-inch wound gaped, the yellow subcutaneous fat growing tiny red dots where the small vessels began to bleed. Cranford clipped two with the Spencer-Wells forceps and tied them off with catgut. He removed the forceps and fitted the bent ends of the spoon-handles into each side of the wound and pulled them apart.

'Hold these like that,' he said to Lally.

She did so and he looked at her, watching her reaction.

'It is all right, Johnny,' she said. 'I am not going to faint.'

He smiled and with the blunt side of the razor split the pink muscle fibres of the external oblique. He placed the spoon-handles in the split and pulled them apart once again for Lally to hold. He made the second split in the muscle beneath in the opposite direction and put in the two other spoons to keep this apart.

'You have four to hold now,' he said.

She gripped the spoons firmly and, after a little adjustment, he split the third layer of the transversalis, pushing aside the white filament of the iliohypogastric nerve. He tied off another vessel and then, using a Spencer-Wells, lifted the bluish, shiny peritoneum. Taking up the

215

scissors he snapped the membrane. A little clear fluid escaped. He enlarged the opening and re-set the retractors.

'There it is,' he said.

Lally looked at the swollen reddish-blue structure, which reminded her of a small grape on a stalk.

'Is that all it is?' she asked.

'That's all. But in a couple of hours that would burst, and then peritonitis, and then almost certainly goodbye to little Melina. All right up there?' he called to Evans.

'Yes, but get on with it, man.'

It was difficult with only two pairs of forceps to mobilize the curtain of tissue which suspended the appendix from the bowel, but he managed to free the mesentery at about half his normal working-speed, until the inflamed tube was freed up to the base of the caecum. He lifted it aside, and with one of the curved needles threaded a purse-string length of catgut round its base in the caecal wall.

'Now it comes out,' he said.

He put a ligature of gut round the base of the appendix, secured it tightly and, with the razor, cut the organ above the knot. He pushed the stump down with a pair of forceps.

'Can you hold this as well?' he asked Lally. 'Let go of one of the retractors . . . I mean one of the spoons.'

Quite steadily and circumspectly she did as she was asked and as he pulled the purse-string suture tight and fastened it off, he felt a great wave of affection, of pride in her, which was quite separate from the love and longing which was the normal counterpart of his response to her existence.

'Thank you, Sister,' he smiled. 'Now all we have to do is put everything back as we found it.'

He poured sulphanomide powder liberally into the wound. Twice the spoon-handles slipped on the way out, twice he had to retrace his steps to tie off a bleeding point, but the amount of catgut was just enough, and at length he had put six nylon stitches neatly across the skin incision, and covered it with a bandage.

'Well, that's it,' he said. 'With more of your terramycin, Doctor, little Melina's going to live.'

'She's not breathing,' said Evans.

The mask, now removed, exposed, all too clearly, the blue-grey features.

'How long?' he shouted at Evans.

'Ten seconds, fifteen. . . .'

'Why didn't you tell me?'

'I'm telling you now, man.'

Cranford put his ear to the chest which no longer moved up and down. Faintly he heard the irregular beats of the heart.

'Out of the way,' he said and brushed Evans roughly aside.

He put a finger in the child's mouth and hooked her tongue to the side. Then taking a deep breath, he placed his mouth over the dark cyanosed lips and expelled the air from his own lungs into the smaller ones below. He went on for five minutes. Standing back, he waited for the response he prayed for with all his mind and soul.

The child suddenly gave a gasp, and a second one, and then her chest slowly settled down to a regular rhythm. The colour came into her skin like the dawn flooding the sea with pink light.

'Christ,' said Evans. 'Thank Christ.'

Cranford turned to Lally. Silently the tears were streaming down her face. He put his arm round her and pressed her head gently against him.

Chapter Thirty

THE CROWD ROUND the school had a patient air, which contrasted with Willy's edgy anticipation. Both waited on the outcome of the exceptional goings-on inside. To both the afternoon had taken on the significance of life and death. But life and death to the islanders were a product of God's will, and for them a certain detachment was possible. This did not apply to passions such as hatred and revenge which had nothing to do with God at all. But they had to do with Willy, and consequently he watched for the door at the top of the steps to open with a more personal intensity than the simple people standing in the sun.

The quietness of the gathering jangled at his nerves. Willy despised these unwashed peasants, not so much for their fatalistic acceptance of events as for the fact that to him, a patrician, they were, like most of the human race, inferior beings, part of the great ocean of lower orders.

Yet, he supposed, he should be grateful to them. They were his witnesses. They would provide almost an embarrassment of evidence that

217

this man, who had masqueraded as a painter, had lived a lie amongst them for two years.

The operation was an event which could not be explained away. It was also a fact which required investigating. He, Willy, had the explanation, and he, Willy, could now initiate an official investigation. Wilson was Cranford. Cranford was a murderer. He would wriggle, of course, and it would be interesting to watch him, but the verdict was certain.

It was amusing, he reflected, that such a simple trick had brought his quarry to bay. In spite of the discomfort of the wooden chair outside the Gerofinikas, Willy decided that this was the most exciting and satisfying afternoon of his life. Whatever had been achieved inside the stone building opposite, when he stepped outside it was only a question of time before dear Alex would be forced to appeal in vain against sentence of death.

A murmur from the crowd sharpened his attention. The school door opened and Doc Evans appeared. He beckoned to the fat man in the peaked cap, and he and his wife pushed up the steps and went inside. A moment later the couple emerged. The man held the child in his arms, and with a beaming face shouted something in Greek which Willy could not understand, but whose meaning was clear. Voices took up the words and added others until the square was filled with excited chatter. Kontopoulos handed Melina to her mother, and a way was made for her to come down the steps. The women crowded round, and some of them accompanied her across the square like a guard of honour, as she carried home her precious living burden.

Meanwhile, in an unsuppressed access of relief and by way of celebration, Kontopoulos began ringing the school bell. The sound fetched the priest, and those who had been at prayer, out of the church.

Suddenly the bell stopped, and a cheer went up which merged into sustained applause as Cranford, Lally and Doc Evans came out of the building. Then the handshaking began and the three of them, accompanied by Kontopoulos, descended into the sunlight. Lally spoke to Maria, kissed the baby, and her sister took the child back along the quay.

Willy's throat tightened. He gripped his sticks and got to his feet. It was time to show these stupid bumpkins that the man they were acclaiming as some sort of saviour was a cheat, a liar, an evil man, whose true destiny was the gallows. Willy banged with one of his sticks on the table as if he were calling a meeting to order.

'Mr Wilson,' he shouted.

The sound from behind them turned the heads of the crowd, and the voices dropped away. Cranford looked over at Willy across the silence for some seconds. Then he made his way unhurriedly through the press of people until the two of them were standing face to face in front of the *taverna.*

'What can I do for you, Willy?' he said.

Willy's eyes shone at him triumphantly and malevolently.

'Now that you've demonstrated so ably who you are, Alex,' Willy replied, 'this would seem to be the time to tell your plebeian friends exactly what you are. Or shall I tell them for you?'

'And what might it be that you're wanting to tell them?' asked Evans.

He and Kontopoulos had come up behind Cranford. Willy regarded them with undisguised contempt.

'That your precious Johnny Wilson is a common murderer,' he said.

'I see,' replied Evans. 'Well now, that's a bloody serious accusation you're making, isn't it?'

Evans turned to Kontopoulos and whispered something in his ear. Kontopoulos nodded and, putting his cap straight, stepped forward in front of the other two.

'I am police here,' he announced gravely. 'What is it you say?'

'This man killed my sister,' said Willy irritably, and gestured with a stick towards Cranford. 'As I told you before, his name is Alexander Cranford. . . .'

'This man?' The round Greek face became a study in total incredulity. 'This man is Johnny Wilson. He is old friend.'

'No doubt,' snapped Willy. 'But he still murdered my sister.'

'Is true, Johnny?' asked Kontopoulos.

Cranford felt a hand come into his, and he was aware that Lally was standing beside him as he shook his head at Kontopoulos.

'No. It is not true,' he replied quietly.

Kontopoulos shrugged expressively at Willy.

'You see?'

'My dear fellow,' Willy's voice began to shake with anger. 'What do you expect him to say? You can't just take his word for it.'

'Why not? If Johnny say "No", is O.K. by me.'

'But this is ridiculous. . . .'

Kontopoulos laughed and clasped Cranford's arm.

'What you want? For me to arrest my friend?'

'Now look here,' said Willy. 'I don't want to report you to your superiors in Athens. . . .'

Kontopoulos's laugh became uproarious before it cut off abruptly.

'Athens!' He spat on the ground and thrust his face towards Willy.

'Now *you* look here. Is not Athens. Is Kronos. And no one tell me, Kontopoulos, what to do on Kronos. I tell *them*. You got that?'

Willy gripped the handles of his sticks, and made prodding movements with the ferrules in the dusty ground while he tried to keep his temper in some sort of control. It was outrageous. They'd had the proof exposed almost before their eyes. What was the matter with them? He glared at Kontopoulos. This fool of a peasant had got to be made to understand. He moistened his lips with his tongue and tried a different approach.

'I'm sure you're very efficient, officer,' he said. 'But do you mind if I ask you a question?'

Kontopoulos gave a stiff little bow.

'O.K.'

'If Johnny Wilson is in fact Johnny Wilson,' said Willy, 'and he is an engineer who decided to become a painter and settle down here, how could such a man carry out a surgical operation on your little girl?'

'What the bloody hell are you talking about?' said Evans. 'I did the operation. Johnny helped me. So did his wife.'

'Liar!' Willy shouted at Evans. 'You said you weren't a surgeon. That's why you wanted me to take the child on the boat.' He rounded on the others. 'You're lying. Lying to shield him. You're, all of you, lying!'

'So were *you* lying about the boat, my lord.'

Fowler's voice came from the edge of the crowd. The others turned as he broke from them and walked over to Willy.

'I've just found out you promised that wretched captain twenty quid to pretend to immobilize the engine. . . .'

'Keep out of this, Fowler . . .' said Willy.

'You didn't give a damn that that child might have died. . . .'

'Shut up!' Willy screamed.

'All you cared about was your own crazy obsession for revenge. Well, revenge isn't evidence, and my lousy report wouldn't convince a baby. So you can count that out. And you can count me out with it.' He threw something on the ground in front of Willy. 'And you can take your lousy cheque back.'

Fowler turned on his heel and walked away to the O Byron.

In the silence which followed his footsteps, Willy looked wildly from one to the other of the four people who still stood in front of him. He opened his mouth to speak, but his jaws quivered and the words jerked out disjointedly, his voice thick with rage and indignation and the undercurrent of fear.

'He's lying . . . I didn't . . . don't believe him. . . .'

'You tell me the boat is no good?' Kontopoulos bellowed. 'And all the time, my little Melina . . .'

He raised his arm to strike Willy, but Cranford caught it before it could descend.

'No Kostas,' he said. 'It was a good thing. She would have died before she got to Rhodes.' Firmly he pulled Kontopoulos away from Willy, who was cringing back, white-faced, against the table. 'Come on. As the boat's all right, there's nothing to keep Lord Binfield here any longer.'

Kontopoulos continued to glare at Willy, and then his tensed body relaxed and he responded to Cranford's suggestion.

'You're right, Johnny,' he said. 'In ten minutes he will be gone from the island. Like Melina, he does not wish to die yet.'

Kontopoulos turned to the crowd and gestured to them as if they were beasts of the field being turned loose to graze. They chattered a few words of puzzled comment to one another, but after a few seconds they obeyed the implied order, and began to disperse.

'My little patient'll be awake now, I shouldn't wonder,' Evans said to Kontopoulos. 'She'll want to see you, Kostas.'

'O.K., Doc,' said Kontopoulos, and they moved away towards the street behind the square.

'Come on home, Johnny,' Lally pulled at Cranford's arm. 'Paul will be waiting for us, too.'

Cranford looked at Willy. He was still leaning against the table, his face a blank, pale mask, his hands clutching his sticks. And so, suddenly, it was all over, and there was nothing left to be done. The simple loyalty of the people Cranford had put into his dream had risen up and protected him. Now he could go back to sleep again and dream some more.

'Goodbye, Willy,' he said and, putting his arm round Lally, turned and began to walk away.

From across the square Fowler saw the bright steel glint in the sun, but before he could stand up and shout a warning, Willy had made the two stumbling paces towards Cranford and lunged at his back. The blade of the swordstick sank in just below the shoulder. Cranford flung up his arms and cried out. As Willy pulled back the weapon, Cranford spun round, his face screwed up with pain and surprise. He tried to say something and tottered forwards a few paces, clutching on to Lally, before he fell to the ground, by the tree-trunk in the centre of the square.

There was a fraction of a moment when the whole scene seemed

221

to freeze like a flash-photograph. Then Lally screamed and Fowler and Kontopoulos and Evans were running towards the stricken man. Willy stood still a second longer as if he too could not believe the signal splash of red in the dust, before panic gripped him.

Willy started off towards the jetty. It was a crab-like festinating gait, punctuated by half-stumbles and curses. Although he had only one stick as an aid, the other being at the ready in case of attack, he covered the ground with surprising speed. Kontopoulos shouted at him, but Willy, head down, kept desperately on his way. Three men ran towards the harbour, blocking his escape. Two more dashed towards the school on his other flank. Kontopoulos walked steadily after him from behind, completing the semi-circle, which began to reduce its radius inexorably.

Willy stopped and swung round to face them. He made aggressive jabs with the swordstick.

'I'll use it. I'll kill any of you, if you come near me,' he shouted.

There was a brief hesitation, and then silently, almost leisurely, they came on towards him. He backed away in the only direction he could go, which was towards the quay.

'Keep back, keep back,' cried Willy. 'He's a murderer, you fools . . . I had to do it . . . He killed my sister . . . don't you understand?'

He was a few feet from the edge of the quay now and suddenly he realized he could retreat no further.

'Stop! Stop! I'll kill you, I don't care now . . . Stop,' he shouted; but the men came on, closing the space between them. Willy backed away, glancing over his shoulder. Suddenly his face puckered and he threw down the swordstick.

'All right: I won't hurt you. I promise you. Just stay where you are. Please, I can't swim . . . I'm a cripple . . . you can see that. Please!'

His voice ended in a wail as one thick-soled shoe caught the edge of a rounded cobble. No one touched him, but the steady movement forward of his adversaries was as effective as if he had been picked up bodily and hurled into the water. Screaming, Willy toppled over into the harbour. He came up once, clutching hopelessly at the air. He saw the dark faces peering down at him, without expression from the top of the wall. 'Evie,' he said, and then disappeared beneath the surface.

They waited without speaking for a few minutes, watching the fragmented reflections join, part, and join again, until they fused into continuous, gently undulating lengths of colour. Kontopoulos kicked the swordstick over the edge of the quay. It sank immediately. The other stick made slow pivoting movements as it floated a few feet from the harbour wall.

Cranford remembered their binding his chest, and vaguely he had the impression of another lesser pain in his arm. He couldn't for a time think of a reason for this, until with a sense of intense satisfaction, he realized that Evans had used the home-made syringe they had manufactured for Melina. He wondered if Evans had given him a quarter or half a grain of morphine. He wanted to say that he was a big man and that he could take half a grain with complete safety, but Lally's sweet face came into view and she whispered something to him. He puzzled over it because the words were indistinct, but it didn't seem to matter. He was aware that he was being carried along the jetty, and that from time to time she was touching his forehead with her lips.

By the time they reached the boat, the searing compression in his chest seemed to lift and he wanted to sit up so that he could look at her properly, but hands quietly restrained him, and Evans said:

'No, Johnny. Stay still. You'll increase the haemorrhage. If you keep quiet, man, we'll get you to Rhodes in good time.'

Cranford lay back on the improvised stretcher. Lally bent down and kissed him.

'Goodbye, Johnny,' she said. 'You will come back? Promise, Johnny?'

He nodded and smiled at her.

'You know, Evans,' he said, 'we've got to set up an emergency service. For the islands. You and I. We could do it.'

'Don't talk now, Johnny.'

'We'd need a helicopter, of course, and . . . money from somewhere. . . .' His voice broke off as the pain tore upwards into his throat. 'But it could be done . . . it could be done.'

He lost consciousness then, and they carried him on to the ship. Lally waited until they had cast off, and the engines were moving the boat out towards the harbour entrance. Then she turned away and ran along the jetty and up the path to the house. She picked up Paul from his cradle and took him to the door, and held him close to her.

The yacht with its trailing wash reminded her of a shooting star she had once seen crossing the blue of the heavens. The boat moved more slowly, of course, but it carried with it, as it grew smaller, the same feeling of hope and wonder and sadness.